'Greg Rucka is one of the best writers in the world. The fact that he is so good in so many different media is a testament to that fact. No one media can hold him. Any new project of his is a call for pop culture celebration.' Brian Michael Bendis, writer of *Ultimate Spider-Man*, *Ultimate X-Men* and *Ultimate Fantastic Four*

'Greg Rucka is a refreshingly bold talent.' Dennis Lehane

'An interesting setting, a likeable hero, an appropriately clever villain, and a gripping story. A real corker.' *Booklist*

'Rucka gets his new series featuring ex-Delta Force Master Sergeant Jad Bell off to a smashing start with this pitch-perfect thriller. This lean, mean thriller with just the right amount of character development and unexpected complications will appeal to all who enjoy this genre but particularly to readers who like a strong hero along the lines of Lee Child's Jack Reacher. Highly recommended' *Library Journal*

'Read Greg Rucka. It's that simple. Open one of his books and what you've got is a fistful of dynamite.' *Cincinnati Enquirer*

'Rucka is the real deal. If this one doesn't make you stay up late rooting for the _____ n't have a heartbe_____ r Reich, *New Yo_____ eception*

ALSO BY GREG RUCKA

GREG RUCKA

ALPHA

MULHOLLAND
BOOKS
_____
HODDER

First published in Great Britain in 2012 by Mulholland Books
An imprint of Hodder & Stoughton
An Hachette UK company

First published in paperback in 2014

1

A CIP catalogue record for this title is available from the British Library

Paperback ISBN 978 1 444 73394 5
eBook ISBN 978 1 444 73393 8

Printed and bound by CPI Group (UK) Ltd, Croydon, CR0 4YY

Hodder & Stoughton policy is to use papers that are natural, renewable
and recyclable products and made from wood grown in sustainable
forests. The logging and manufacturing processes are expected to
conform to the environmental regulations of the country of origin.

Hodder & Stoughton Ltd
338 Euston Road
London NW1 3BH

www.hodder.co.uk

This is for Jennifer.
Thank you.
Always.

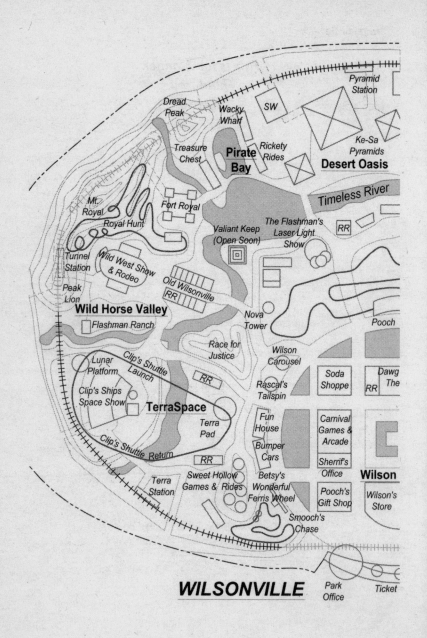

Pyramid Station

SW

Dread Peak

Wacky Wharf

Rickety Rides

Ke-Sa Pyramids

Desert Oasis

Treasure Chest

Pirate Bay

Timeless River

Mt. Royal

Fort Royal

Valiant Keep (Open Soon)

The Flashman's Laser Light Show

RR

Royal Hunt

Tunnel Station

Wild West Show & Rodeo

Old Wilsonville

RR

Peak Lion

Wild Horse Valley

Nova Tower

Pooch

Flashman Ranch

Race for Justice

Wilson Carousel

Lunar Platform

Clip's Shuttle Launch

RR

Rascal's Tailspin

Soda Shoppe

Dawg The

RR

Clip's Ships Space Show

TerraSpace

Terra Pad

Fun House

Carnival Games & Arcade

Bumper Cars

Clip's Shuttle Return

RR

Sherrif's Office

Wilson

Terra Station

Sweet Hollow Games & Rides

Betsy's Wonderful Ferris Wheel

Pooch's Gift Shop

Wilson's Store

Smooch's Chase

WILSONVILLE

Park Office

Ticket

Employee Services

Lion's Safari

Lilac's Secret Garden

Gazebo

Forest Station

Service Tunnel Access and Staging

Speakeasy

Collectibles

Euro Strasse

Boutique

Agent Rose's Safehouse

RR

Forest Path

Gordo's Flying Ball

Hendar's Lair

Soaring Thyme

Forest Path

Pursuit

Gordo's Yesteryear Ballpark

Prince Stripe's Slide

SW

Wilson Hotel

Days atre

RR

Wilson Rstrnt.

Wild World

RR

Statues

Candy Store

Musical Fun

Wilson Travel

Information

Cannonball Plunge

The Flower Sisters Mystical Show

Wilson Hotel Station

RR

Town

Wilson History Museum

Flower Sisters Boutique

Wild World LIVE!

Town Station

Booths

1st Aid & Cust. Service

ALPHA

Prologue

MARIO VESQUES was sure he was going to make it, right up until he saw the knife in the dog's hand.

He had no idea where the blade came from; what he did have was just enough time to realize he was in trouble, and then the cartoon animal was lunging at him in a way that Vesques recognized, had seen before, but yet couldn't immediately place. Only as he got his left forearm up for a cross-block, felt the tip of the knife nicking skin as it split his sleeve, did it click.

Modern Army, as taught at Fort Benning, Georgia, courtesy of the United States Army; and through the adrenaline rush he saw the irony that he and whoever was wearing the Pooch suit shared the same pedigree. The absurdity of it all—Vesques in his maintenance coveralls and this man in his dog suit, right paw missing to reveal a Caucasian hand and the blade it held—that they had shared, at some point, the same masters, perhaps the same history, perhaps even the same instructors. That they might've, somewhere, sometime, stood together as brothers in arms.

But the blade was stabbing at him again and again, and Vesques was backpedaling now, stumbling once more through the door he'd just exited, the compressor room off the Flashman West maintenance tunnel, the one running east-west the length of the park. Dimmer light within, after-hours power management, and Vesques knew the room was a death trap, that there was no way out of it other than the one the dog now blocked.

The whole thing had been a fluke, what had seemed to be, finally, a stroke of good luck that had turned inexplicably, absurdly bad. Six weeks almost Vesques had been working the park, placed there just to make sure things stayed safe, that no one got bold, got any bright ideas. Six weeks working on a whisper that nobody believed would pan out—and he didn't, either, to tell the truth, thought it another wild-goose assignment. But he did his job, the job he was trained to do, and tonight—*tonight*—he had thought about maybe checking the compressors, just to be sure. He hadn't known what he was looking for, but intuition had said, hey, air-conditioning, put something into circulation, and he had listened, because in training they had told him that intuition was more often what would save his life than take it.

Except this time.

After-hours staffing, maintenance and custodial working one to six, nobody supposed to be around except other men and women wearing the same coveralls Mario Vesques now wore. Which was why, when he saw Pooch heading into compressor 4, off Flashman West, well, that was definitely worth checking out. Which was why he'd waited until Pooch had emerged again after two minutes, had headed down the tunnel and disappeared, before going to take a look himself.

Shining his flashlight over and around the ductwork,

the pipes and compressors, even getting down on his belly until the beam revealed a shape just poking out from behind the compressor itself. Reaching, straining for it, and his fingers had closed on the tail of a nylon duffel bag. Pulled the bag free, looked inside. A folded, paper-thin jumpsuit. A gas mask. A disassembled pistol, and Vesques guessed that was how it had entered the park, one piece at a time. A cell phone, but that wasn't the jackpot, as far as he was concerned. The jackpot was the radio, military-grade hardware with not one but two extra batteries, and that meant there was a plan in place, one that required communication and coordination, and this was only one part of it.

So he zipped the duffel shut and he put it back where it belonged, and on a whim swept his light around the room one more time, into the dark corners. Reflected light jumped back at him.

He'd gone in for a closer look, seen that his flashlight had bounced from the screen of a disposable cell phone, and that the phone wasn't alone. Wired up, and good, a proper IED, but a small one, so small he could barely find the charge on it. The phone itself taped to a small plastic baggie, and powder in the baggie, and his throat had gone dry at that. Not the explosive, oh, no, that wasn't what made his stomach cramp; but that powder, whatever that powder might be, he was sure that was trouble.

Trouble enough that it was time to go, time to make the call and report what he'd found. Time to maybe get the operators in here, people who knew what they were doing with biological agents and IEDs and the like.

Left it where he found it, and he'd backed out of the

room, turned, and seen Pooch ten feet away.

Holding a knife.

Tools on his belt jangling, flashlight still in hand, Vesques brought it up, across, trying to club at the hand holding the knife. Hitting high, what should've been a bone-crushing blow lost in the padding on the costumed arm, and now Pooch was slamming into him, full-body, the same costume cushioning the impact but doing nothing to diminish the weight. They fell back together, Vesques dropping the flashlight, both hands seeking the knife, and then the white heat bursting through his vision.

Tasting copper in his mouth.

The vibration of his head hitting concrete again, the blurred flash of Pooch looming over him, human hand and dog's paw, the knife gone. His hair tearing. Kicking back, struggling, and then the world losing sound, vision splintering, as his skull was bashed into the floor.

And his last thought, bitter and angry, as he saw Pooch's insipid, eternal grin.

Mission failed.

Chapter One

"JUST HOW old are you?" Bell asks.

She stops, her back to him, arms raised, T-shirt exposing bare back to bra. It's ten at night in Skagway, Alaska, the start of July, and sunlight still hints the sky, slants through the blinds at the window, touching pale skin and painting it bronze. Then she finishes the movement, draws the shirt over her head, discards it with a toss as her black hair falls down her back. She half turns, grins at him, pure mirth.

"Old enough," she says.

This is probably true, Bell thinks, at least in the abstract. Most of the summer population up here are college kids, working forest-service internships or manning the cafés and storefront industries that cater to the regularly scheduled cruise ship arrivals. Tourists come like clockwork, swarm through the town like worker ants in a managed rush for souvenirs and photographs, retreat before dinner for their all-you-can-eat floating buffets. This girl, she's at *least* twenty, Bell figures, though he could be wrong; gauging ages has never been his strongest suit. Height, weight, distinguishing details, those he can record and repeat at the drop of a hat, nearly twenty years of training having turned the act into one of instinct. But ages? He's never gotten the hang of that, and it's been nagging him for the last two weeks of flirtation with this young woman who's been pouring his morning coffee at the Black Bean. Now she's unlacing her hiking boots, and not unintentionally giving him a view of her cleavage, and Bell has to admit that her cleavage, like the rest of her, is more than a little alluring.

Boots, kicked off, land in the corner, and she straightens to face him while reaching around to unfasten her bra. She's grinning like before, white teeth visible in her growing smile, an amusement that again has Bell wondering at her age. Young enough that sex is a game, something only ever played for fun. It's been a long time since he stood in front of someone like this, to do this, and instead of feeling older than she, now he's feeling suddenly younger, adolescent and hormonal, and he resists the urge to mock himself.

"Why?" she asks. "How old are you?"

"Old enough to know better."

That gets a laugh, and she begins unbuttoning her Levi's.

"You going to watch or get undressed?"

Bell thinks that getting undressed is probably the best idea.

There are two sniper teams positioned around the market square, two men to each, and Bell has command. They came in at night unseen, buried themselves amid wreckage and refuse, two rifles, two cones of fire, and a long wait for a killing that may not come to pass. CIA intel fed through JSOC and into the field, and four operators are now in a place they technically shouldn't be, waiting to kill a very, very bad man. It is a dawn that calls for precision work.

"Spell me," Bell says, taking his eye from the scope, lowering his head, blinking fatigue away. Despite six hours of motionless waiting, his body feels fine, relaxed and steady. It's the eye that needs the regularly scheduled maintenance. Beside him, Chaindragger shifts from behind the spotting scope, settles behind the rifle. Somewhere across the square, Cardboard and Bonebreaker are doing the same thing, alternating watch to stay razor-ready.

Sun rises, bleaching the world with heat, the square coming alive. Old men with white beards and ageless women swathed in black, children beginning to spill from homes and hovels, raising dust as they play. Bell watches as six of them begin kicking a soccer ball they've made from plastic bags and all the tape they could scrounge up. It's a good ball. When the smallest of the players pounds a kick into it, it flies true.

Bone's voice comes into his ear. "Warlock? Vehicle, White."

Bell swings the spotting scope to the north side of the square, picks up the vehicle instantly. It's a battered Benz thirty-plus years past warranty, rusted panels and peeling paint. The car coasts to a stop, squeezes between a Transit van and a donkey cart, idles. A Toyota pickup slides past. The Benz rolls forward another twenty meters or so. Stops again, now alongside the largest of the fruit-and-grain stalls on the square. Door opens.

"That him?" Chaindragger murmurs.

Bell stays on the man, the weathered skin and scraggly beard. Boy's eyes in a man's face.

"Red," Bell says, and he keys his mike. "Red. Negative target."

Confirmations come back. Bell watches the man vanish into the crowd, disappear forever.

There's silence, but Bell knows they're all thinking the same thing.

"Warlock?" Bone says, finally. "This is some fucked-up shit."

Bell says nothing for several seconds before rolling to his side and reaching for the sat phone that leads back to Brickyard. "Fuck it," he says. "Sending it uphill."

"Roger that," Chaindragger says with quiet emphasis.

The square continues filling up, full of life. The Benz isn't the only car in the square, not by a long shot.

But all four shooters know it's the only one that's going to explode.

The last sunlight goes, replaced by a low moonrise, and she comes back from the bathroom carrying a glass of water, stops at the side of the bed. Bell, on his back, looks up at her, watches as she drinks, then brings the water to his lips as if aiding an invalid. He swallows, feeling thick and drowsy, out of practice in too many ways. The last time he had sex was with Amy, four months ago now, just after the divorce went final. A final fuck hurrah, making love with a passion that took them both by surprise. After, they'd lain together for half an hour in silence before she'd left his side for the last time, moving to dress.

"Why are we doing this again?" Bell asked.

"Because you're a good lay," Amy said. "And so am I."

"Not my reference."

"I know your reference, soldier." She turned from his gaze to pull on her panties, an awkward modesty that transformed eighteen years of marriage, of intimacy, into wasted days. "We don't love each other anymore."

This girl, who's not Amy, sets the glass aside, then slips back into the bed, rolling onto her belly, breasts pressing against Bell's chest. He feels where her body has turned cool from the night air beyond the blankets, feels her stealing his own body heat to replace hers. She props herself up on an elbow, rests a cheek in her palm. With her other hand, she begins to tour his body. An index finger traces the puckered line along Bell's left shoulder.

"How'd you get this?"

Bell turns his head to look at the scar, turns his head back to stare at the ceiling. "I got shot."

"You were in Iraq?"

"Sometimes."

"Afghanistan?"

"Sometimes."

"Army?"

"Sometimes."

She laughs, concluding that nothing he says can be trusted. Drags a finger across Bell's chest, then down, stopping at the right lower abdominal. "This one?"

"Shrapnel."

Her hand moves lower, takes a slight detour, and

she offers a naughty grin before continuing to his right thigh.

"Knife?"

"Something sharp, yeah."

"Roll over."

Bell obliges. She examines his arms, takes his right hand in hers. He feels the slight brush of her fingertip between his thumb and forefinger, distant, as if from far away.

"This a callus?"

"That is a callus."

"How do you get a callus like that? There?"

It's a gun callus, earned by putting thousands of rounds through a pistol seven days a week, from morning to night to morning again. It's earned on the range and in the Shooting House, live-fire exercises on endless repeat until shooting is like breathing, until missing is Not An Option, and it's kept by taking that honed skill and applying it to the enemy. It is a killer's callus, a warrior's mark, an operator's badge of honor.

He doesn't say any of that.

"Yard work," Bell tells her.

She looks at him, eyebrow arched, then bends her head so her hair brushes over him in a wave. He feels her tongue light between his fingers, her lips as she kisses her way along his arm, onto his back, where she stops again.

"This one?"

"Shot."

"It's ugly."

"Wasn't too bad."

"Does it hurt?" she asks. "Getting shot?"

He doesn't answer at first. Thinking of Amy again, how she never once asked. How her face would fall and her eyes would turn dark, how her lips would draw thin and tight. But she would never make a sound. She never would ask.

"Like you wouldn't believe," Bell says.

Bell switches the sat phone off. Chaindragger's heard just one half of the conversation, but he knows what's coming, and still he hasn't moved.

"Pack it up," Bell says, and then says it again for the benefit of the radios.

"We got a VBIED parked down there—," Bone starts to say.

"We are ordered to pull out." Bell cuts him off. "Brickyard says mission abort, return to LZ Venus."

There is another heartbeat's pause, then the confirmations come back to Bell's ear. Chaindragger is already at his knees, breaking down the rifle. A shout carries through the hot, still air, and Bell looks out at the square once more. Without optics, more than one hundred meters away, figures look like animation tests, waggling, hopping, running back and forth. He sees the makeshift soccer ball sailing through the air, bounce to a stop in front of the parked Benz.

"Sons of bitches," he mutters.

Chaindragger looks up at him. Like Bell and the rest of the squad, he's let his hair grow out, now to his shoulders, his beard a scraggly mass of black hanging from his coffee-dark face. Wearing the local color, the way all of them are, baggy trousers and a long shirt-coat to the thighs.

"It's wrong, Top," Chaindragger says. "We're better than this."

Bell blinks at him. Looks back to the square, the sun now high enough to give glare to the air itself, it seems. He sighs, knowing he'll catch hell for this from every echelon between here and Florida.

"LZ Venus." Bell pulls his pistol from where it's been riding at the small of his back, moves it to the front of his pants, then heads for the stairs. "I'll catch up."

He's sitting on the edge of the bed, smoking one of the American Spirits from her pack, when daylight begins to return. Dawn peeking through the blinds, as if hoping to catch them in flagrante delicto. She's sleeping still, her lips parted slightly, as if, even in dreams, she remains mildly amused by Jad Bell.

Bell finishes the smoke, walks to the window, pulls the tilt cord, and the slats part and more light flows. He feels it on his naked body, stares out at the trees, wondering how much longer he'll have to do this, wondering when it'll end. He's made his way from Baja to here in the last four months, left the day after the papers were signed. Hugging the coast north, sleeping in his car or in a tent or just under the stars, taking the odd job now and again. Video chats via laptop with Amy every week, mostly so he could talk to Athena. They didn't have much to say; she was pissed as hell at him, and he couldn't blame her. She was six when the war started, Bell remembers. Ten years is a long time.

Guilt flashes, and he turns to look at the girl in the bed, sees that she's opened her eyes, is watching him. The smile is gone.

"You want to talk about it?" she asks.

"No," Bell tells her, and turns back to the window.

Bell runs a circuit of the square, keeping eyes on the Benz, and he's thinking the whole time that there's a whole slew of reasons Brickyard told them to abort, and that getting atomized by a vehicle-borne improvised explosive device is probably at the top of that list.

This is a fucking fool's errand, Bell thinks. VBIED, and too many variables. Is it on a timer? Is it call-in activated? Radio detonated? And if one of the last two, then some son of a bitch is on overwatch with a phone or transmitter in his hand, waiting to press the button, and he will—he absofuckinglutely will—do just that thing if he sees Bell getting curious about the Benz.

Which means approaching that car is out of the question, at least for the moment.

"Black, clear," Cardboard says in his ear.

"The fuck are you doing?" Bell has to turn to a building face, keeping his voice low.

"Black is clear," Cardboard repeats, the hint of his Alabama drawl stronger on the last word. "South of the square is clear. And as we were positioned Red and Green, then your overwatch on that vehicle, Warlock, we must deduce, is on White."

Bell looks to the south side of the square, then the west, then the east. Colors are direction: White north, Black south, Red and Green for east and west respectively. Nowhere does he see Bone, Chaindragger, or Cardboard, but that's not a surprise; no more of a surprise than the fact that none of the squad has done as ordered. Bell shakes his head slightly, then realizes the building he's sheltering in front of is on the White side, the north side, of the square. If there's overwatch on the VBIED, it's going to be in here.

"Guess I better take a look inside," he says.

"I guess you'd better," Bonebreaker says, and Bell can swear to God the man's trying not to laugh at him. "Unless you want someone to come hold your hand, Top?"

"Think I've got this—"

"Target, target, target," Chaindragger hisses, cutting in. "Approaching Green, say again, I have eyes on target."

He showers after her. She lives light, the bathroom uncluttered, only essentials, and apparently makeup consists of an eyeliner and a lipstick, both courtesy of Burt's Bees. When he's dressed, she takes his hand, and they walk together to the Bean along streets that are just beginning to stir. Her hand is warm and slight, and his feels big around it, and when they turn the corner onto Broadway she leans her head against his shoulder, squeezes his upper arm through the overshirt he's wearing. Fourth of July bunting and American flags still hang from houses. Bell looks back, can see the stacks of two cruise ships in the port. It's early enough that the onslaught has yet to begin.

They separate entering the Bean, she disappearing behind the counter into the back to emerge half a minute later tying a barista's apron around her middle. There's a scattering of local color present, and Bell earns a nod from one or two, recognition. He's been around just long enough that the outsider edge is beginning to dull, but still, he's viewed as transient. She pulls him a double espresso, puts a blueberry muffin on a chipped plate for him, brushes the back of his hand with hers as he takes them. Bell moves to a table with a view of the window. There's a copy of the *Skagway News* on a chair, and he takes it up, reads while listening to the growing murmur of conversation around him. Outside, the first tourists have penetrated this far, peering into windows as if visiting a zoo.

He finishes his breakfast and she slips out from behind the counter, bringing him a new cup, fresh coffee this time, and takes the empty espresso away. Fingertips brush the back of his neck as he turns, and when he swings his head to follow her, she's looking back at him, the mirthful grin, full of promise for tonight. He can't help grinning in response, then turns back to the paper, catches sight of a man he knows too well through the window, on the opposite side of the street, moving among the clots of tourists.

He folds his newspaper, sips his coffee, watches this man he knows step inside. Watches him stop at the counter, talk to her. A coffee to go. He exits again with paper cup in hand, turning right, past the window once more, then out of sight.

For a moment, Bell seriously considers not moving, and the thought surprises him. He likes Skagway, he likes this girl, this place, mucking through the woods and fly fishing, the thought of the solitary, silent winters, and, he realizes, there would be worse places to live and die. But he no sooner thinks it than he knows it's not home, though he's damned if he knows what or where home is anymore.

He takes his coffee with him as he steps outside.

She watches him go, wonders why he didn't say good-bye.

"Board, Bone," Bell says. "Clear White."

Both men come back, roger that. Bell can hear each of them moving even in the brief instant they radio their confirmations.

"Chain, where?"

"On Green, crossing Red. I'm parallel, ten meters."

"Give him room to breathe."

"On it."

Bell steps out of the way of two burka-clad women walking hand in hand with their children. The noise in the square is constant—voices, livestock, vehicles, conversation and shouts, haggling and haranguing. Bone and Board pass him on either side, no one exchanging looks, and Bell picks up Chaindragger first, opposite him on the Black side, and then, a half second later, spots the target coming up to his left. The man is walking alone, indistinguishable from any other man in the market, indistinguishable from the squad, in fact. Just another tanned face in dusty clothes with a beard and ragged hair sticking out from beneath his hat. And like just about every other god-damn male over the age of ten in the region, packing an AK slung over his shoulder.

There is nothing good about this situation, Bell thinks. They move on target and it goes wrong, the overwatch on the Benz panics. It's all about the timing now; if Board and Bone can locate and neutralize the overwatch, if they can secure the bomb, then he'll have a free run on the target. But if they can't, if the target doesn't have the common decency to remove himself to a location where he can be quietly put down, the whole thing's a scratch.

Bell times his approach, passes behind his target without a glance, and the man continues threading his way through the crowds. The plastic soccer ball suddenly rises, arcing through the air, and from the corner of his eye, Bell sees the target head it down, back to the cluster of kids. Laughter and approval, and for a second Bell wonders if those children would be so delighted if they knew the man who just joined their game for an instant has lost count of the men, women, and children he's murdered.

"White Alpha, clear," Bone says. "Moving to Bravo."

First floor clear, moving to the second, and the building only offers three floors, which would make things so much easier, except it's not the only building on that side of the square. Bell turns, following after the target, maybe eight meters between them. Chain is on his left, falling back; he'll cut north, try to get ahead of their man.

They're getting closer to that Benz.

"Bravo clear, moving to Charlie."

Bell is about to confirm when there's the rip of AK fire to his right, to the White, the north, side. The crisp crack of 7.62 on full auto, then a second assault rifle joining the first, and all at once the market square bursts into an entirely different frenzy, weapons slipping from shoulders, women and children starting to scatter as voices rise from warning to hysteria. The target stops and pivots, his weapon coming up in his hands, and Bell can read his calm amid the sudden chaos, knows that in half a second, the man in front of him will read the same thing, and see him as the enemy.

With no pause, still walking forward, Bell draws his pistol from its place at his waist and places two shots in the target, head and neck, a double-tap released without conscious thought. The target drops, deadweight, and Bell keeps moving, pistol now against his thigh. People surge on all sides, and for an instant Bell believes no one has noticed, is about to call for Bone and Board, for the Sitrep, when he finds himself staring at one of the soccer players, a boy no more than twelve, that absurd jury-rigged ball in his hands. For just that instant, they're looking into one another's eyes, and then Board is in his ear.

"Clear," he's saying. "Had it on dial-in, we're clear."

"Venus," Bell says. "Now."

They all roger that, and Bell and the boy stare at each other for a half second longer, and then the boy is backing away, turning, running. Chaindragger is coming toward Bell now, and they fall in together, picking up speed, starting to hustle with the crowd, blending in. Cardboard and Bonebreaker appear, making toward the Green side, but hold up for half a second, waiting so they can group up again. Bone takes the opportunity to look past them into the emptying square, spots the body on the ground.

"Paid in full," he says.

Bell keeps moving. The flow of traffic has changed

with the lack of gunfire, and now a woman screams, one of their freshly laid corpses revealed. People rush back into the square, voices rising again, confusion, consternation. They skirt the corner of the mosque, and they're just about to turn when the pressure wave hits them, leading the blast from the Benz.

Bell feels himself lifted from the ground, feels his legs fly out from beneath him. He lands hard, somehow on his back, head ringing and bile in his throat. He attempts to roll, can't manage it on the first try, curses himself, and pushes again, this time making it onto his stomach. He's been turned around, he realizes, facing the square again.

The blessing of the blast is that it steals his hearing, and so he can't hear the pain, only see it, but that, in its own way, makes it worse. Through dust and smoke, he can see that where the car was there is now nothing, a crater ringed in black, and all around, on every side, there is blood and meat and the dumb show of those miraculously spared blinking in their concussion-stupor. He hears a thread of someone's keening, sees the dead. Old men and young, women and boys and girls, and there are the wounded, clutching at themselves where holes that shouldn't be are, where limbs that once were have gone absent. Bell's gaze falls on the boy, the plastic ball in his hand, its bottom half sheared by the blast.

Just like the boy.

Board is pulling Bell to his feet, shouting at him, words dim. Bell nods, knows what he's asking. Bone is supporting Chain, blood rushing down the side of his face in a sheet. They push off, heading for their vehi-

cle, then for Venus and Brickyard, trying to put this all behind them.

Knowing they never will.

Bell finds him two blocks down, standing at the corner, and it'd be a believable tourist act if it weren't for the military-issue haircut and the ramrod posture. Civvies notwithstanding, you can take the man out of uniform, but some men—you will never take the uniform from the man.

"Jad," the man says, apparently admiring the trees.

"Colonel," Bell says.

The man turns to look at him, the slight curl of a smile as he takes Bell in, then shakes his head. "You look like a pilgrim who's lost his way, Master Sergeant."

Bell considers that, then finishes his coffee. There's a garbage can at the edge of the abused lawn beside him, and he sets the empty cup atop it. "You're here to help me find it?"

"I'm here to offer you a job," Colonel Daniel Ruiz tells him.

Chapter Two

THE EMPIRE was born from a boy, a girl, and a dog.

This was post–Second World War, the start of the baby boom generation, and there was a market for all three, though the truth is that it was the dog who made things happen, it was Pooch who was the real hit, and Gordo and Betsy were really only along for the ride, at least at the start. But Willis Wilson, twenty-six years old and recently returned from the Western front, had just enough genius in him to market the dog with the brother-sister pair, and since you couldn't get the one without the others, he succeeded in marketing all three at once. And market them he did, slipping between newly made Madison Avenue satin sheets with an eagerness that, to abuse the metaphor, would have made a whore blush.

The second part of Wilson's genius was an understanding of the incipient collector's nature of a child's mind. Kids collect things; they always have. From interesting pebbles to pressed flowers to bits of string to baseball cards to comics to model horses to books about dinosaurs or trains or heavy earth-moving construction machines, collecting is, perhaps, one of the means by which children come to terms with their world, one of the means by which they learn.

And, certainly, one of the means by which they play.

With Gordo, Betsy, and Pooch, Wilson made damn certain that there was always something else to collect. The trio were recast over and over again, thrown into new environments with new accessories, new costumes, and new narratives to support them. All but the most basic sets were marketed in limited runs, available for only a limited time. Beginning with the Cowboys and Indians Set in 1948 (with Gordo the Cowboy, Betsy the Squaw, and Pooch the Texas Ranger Dog), followed closely by the Space Explorer Set (Gordo the Space Explorer, Betsy the Space Homemaker, and Pooch the Space Dog) the same year, and then by the All Grown Up Set (Gordo the Executive, Betsy the Homemaker, and Pooch the House Dog), Wilson Toys succeeded in making, marketing, and, most important, selling toys that children wanted.

With a vengeance.

Gordo and Betsy's roster of friends grew. More accessories, more toys, more play sets, and, from there, books, radio, and, inevitably, television, and the metamorphosis of Wilson Toys into Wilson Entertainment. *Lovable Pooch* debuted on NBC in 1958, much in the mold of other children's television programs of the time. Gordo and Betsy presented fun and games and displayed their commitment to self-promotion before a live studio audience, with each show culminating in the debut of an all-new Pooch cartoon. The show was staggering in its mediocrity, but it exploded the popularity of the characters. A second offering followed in 1961, the hour-long variety show *Gordo and Betsy's*

Showcase, which introduced and furthered the adventures of Wilson Entertainment's ever-growing cast of characters.

By the time *Gordo and Betsy's Showcase* went off the air in 1977, it had served as the gateway drug to Wilson Entertainment for three successive generations.

In 1955, Wilson purchased the rights to Clip Flashman, a second-tier pulp-comics character who had enjoyed brief popularity in the late thirties and early forties as a Buck Rogers/Flash Gordon knockoff. Flashman, like his more successful counterparts, traveled interstellar space with his best girl, Penny, at his side, and between repeated battles to save the universe managed to seduce just about every alien queen he came across (and there were a lot of alien queens out there who needed seducing). Promoting "American values" even as he defended the Star System Alliance, the character was seen—even at the time—as laughably simplistic and painfully derivative.

Wilson saw the same in Clip Flashman, but he saw far greater potential, and set about revising the character in a manner that, much as he had with Gordo, Betsy, and Pooch, would enable Wilson Entertainment to exploit the franchise to its fullest. No longer was there Clip Flashman, Defender of the Star System Alliance. Now there was a comprehensive—and painfully complicated—Flashman mythology, which included a timeline that "discovered" other heroes of the same name and that recast Clip as a future iteration of a continuing and unbroken legacy of heroism. Clip was joined by Skip Flashman, Cowboy Extraordinaire;

Royal Flashman, Backwoodsman and Revolutionary War Hero; Lion Flashman, Two-Fisted Adventurer; Justice Flashman, Secret Agent; Valiant Flashman, Knight of the Round Table; and, ultimately, the Flashman, Superhero.

The combination of complex mythology and endless collectibility made the Flashman franchise an enormous and immediate success among preteen and teenage boys. It certainly didn't hurt that in every incarnation, Flashman had at least one sexy, mysterious femme fatale to tangle with time and again. By 1960, the year before Wilson's passing, the Flashman franchise had expanded to novels and comic books, and the first of what would be many feature films was in development.

Upon his death, Wilson's estate was inherited by his wife, Grace, and their two daughters. Like her husband, Grace had long since identified Disney as Wilson Entertainment's main competitor, and while she lacked her husband's creative spark, she more than made up for it with an almost savage business acumen. Despite the success of Pooch and his ilk, despite the continuing loyalty of the Flashman fan base, Wilson Entertainment had yet to break out of the American market, something that Grace understood as crucial to the company's future. She wanted what she saw in Anaheim; she wanted a piece of the Disney pie, and to obtain that, she needed Disney's universal appeal.

The problem was that Gordo and Betsy were unmistakably American, and, worse, rapidly becoming dated. Of all the Wilson Entertainment characters, including the Flashman franchise, Pooch was the only one to have made any substantial gains in the international market, primarily through animation. It didn't take a market research team for Grace Wilson to see why: Pooch didn't walk, didn't talk, didn't wear clothes. For all his lovable hijinks and overly affectionate lunacy, Pooch was, through and through, just a dog. And there are few animals as universally accepted and loved as a dog, as a quick peek over at Uncle Walt's camp only served to emphasize.

It took six years of development, until 1967, before Grace Wilson introduced the Flower Sisters to the world in a debut as carefully orchestrated as any Wilson Entertainment had done before or has done since. Unveiled in Wilson Entertainment's first full-length animated film, the Flower Sisters were targeted at the audience the Flashman franchise had left behind, namely, girls. Moreover, there wasn't a human to be found anywhere in their domain. The Flower Sisters existed in the Wild World, where anthropomorphized animals walked and talked and wore wonderful clothes. A world where Lilac, a meerkat, and Lily, a gazelle, and Lavender, a lioness, could be the best of friends, and all share the same shy devotion to the noble Prince Stripe, Tiger of the Realm.

The movie became an instant classic. The dolls became instant bestsellers. And Grace Wilson got what she wanted.

The Flower Sisters were big in Japan.

Ground was broken for the Wilson Entertainment Park and Resort—commonly called WilsonVille—in April of 1978, near Irvine, California, with construction completed in January of 1980. Previews and VIP tours ran throughout the late spring, ending with the park's grand opening on June 4. Like everything else Wilson Entertainment had done up to that point, it was an expertly executed affair, the culmination of nearly a decade's marketing and sales work. The park had been rated by the Orange County fire marshal for a maximum capacity of one hundred thousand people, and all passes for the grand opening had been sold two years in advance of the day.

WilsonVille advertising took aim at Disney and the Magic Kingdom directly, painting the park in Anaheim as "tired" and "old." WilsonVille, the advertising promised, was the newest, and the best, and had something for everyone. Guests could raid ancient pyramids with Lion Flashman in a desperate race to stop Agent Rose from escaping with the Mystic Eye of Ke-Sa. Parents and children were invited to float along the Timeless River with Lilac, Lily, and Lavender acting as their personal guides while they searched for the missing Prince Stripe. Children of all ages could experience screams and thrills as they rode the fastest, tallest wooden roller coaster in the world—Pooch Pursuit—based, marginally, on the Oscar-winning short cartoon of the same name.

And that was just what was featured in the brochure.

On average, WilsonVille sees more than thirty thousand visitors a day, more than twice that number during the peak summer season and on holidays— Christmas, New Year's, and the Fourth of July all being exceptionally busy. A minimum of three thousand "Friends" staff the park, but the number can rise to just shy of six thousand during the aforementioned peak periods. "Friends" is the WilsonVille catch-all word to describe park staff, from the mostly unseen custodial crew to the performers working in costume on stage and at large in the park to the catering personnel and clerks. If you're wearing a WilsonVille name tag, you're everyone's friend, whether you like it or not.

The park went nonsmoking in 1998, and alcohol is not permitted or served anywhere within its confines, save for the members-only club, the Speakeasy. The unmarked door to the club is concealed amid the apparent stonework walls adjacent to Agent Rose's Safe House, beside a jewelry shop, and requires a password for entry. Membership is available solely to season-pass holders for an additional fee, and to select VIPs in the company of senior Wilson Entertainment officials.

WilsonVille is open from 8:00 a.m. until 1:00 a.m. seven days a week, 365 days a year, although on Fridays and Saturdays there is a "Secret Sunrise," when individuals who have purchased the privilege can enter the park as early as 7:00 a.m.

Since its opening, the park has ceased operations on only one occasion, September 11, 2001. Rides were brought to a halt and all attractions were closed. Park guests were then escorted by Friends from the premises via preestablished evacuation routes. Outside the park, they were refunded their entry fees and given free day passes by way of apology. The WilsonVille gates were then barred, and a security sweep of the entire 156-acre park, as well as its surrounding support buildings and parking structures, was performed.

Nothing was found.

The park resumed normal operations the following morning.

Almost.

Chapter Three

"YOU COME recommended." The man, Matthew Marcelin, smiles, shaking Bell's hand. "Highly recommended."

"All lies," Bell says.

Marcelin laughs politely, raises the buff-colored folder in his free hand. The W-E of Wilson Entertainment is embossed, surprisingly subtly, on its face. "If so, you've got a lot of impressive people willing to lie on your behalf. Take a seat."

Bell does, and Marcelin follows suit, dropping into a warship-gray Aeron chair behind a chrome-bordered desk. Bell puts him in his early forties, but he can't be certain—that age thing again. The man is balding, bespectacled, and wearing a suit that puts the one Bell is wearing to shame, and Bell's suit isn't poorly made by any stretch. Marcelin sits with his back to the floor-to-ceiling tinted window, and through it Bell can see glimpses of Irvine and the profile of WilsonVille itself, the park visibly active even from this distance. The crests of two separate roller coasters, their trains of cars whipping in and out of view. There's the point of a pyramid, and something that looks suspiciously like the summit of Mount Everest. A stretch of green, the canopy of some faraway and make-believe forest.

Heat haze distorts it all, a sliver of the Pacific in the far distance, shimmering in the July Southern California sunshine.

Marcelin flips the folder open with one hand, uses the other to slide his mouse along a Gordo, Betsy, and Pooch mouse pad, clicks without looking at what he's doing. Glances up at Bell with the briefly pained expression of a man who's forgotten his manners.

"I didn't ask: Would you like something to drink, Jon? Is Jon all right? Or do you prefer Jonathan?"

"Friends call me Jad."

"Then I'll take the invitation. Water? Soda? Coffee? We can do you a latte, if you like. There's a barista in the lobby; I'm sure you passed the stand on the way in—no trouble to send someone down for something."

Bell did indeed see the barista, a woman who in no way looked to him like the one at the Black Bean, the girl in Skagway, and yet by her presence brought her immediately back to mind. Steaming milk in a metal pitcher beneath a lobby-wide mural of the Flower Sisters and their friends, serving a line of Bluetooth-wearing executives, and Bell could swear they were all half his age.

"I'm good, thanks, Mr. Marcelin."

"It's Matt, please."

"I'm good, thanks, Matt."

Marcelin nods, drops his eyes to the folder again. His eyeglasses slide down his nose, and he uses his thumb to push them back into place, not his index finger. Bell notes it, hates himself for doing so, for thinking the gesture odd, for wondering what it might mean when it doesn't have to mean anything. Marcelin is still reading, so Bell goes back to looking over the office.

It's a big office, a corner office, but pretty much what Bell had been led to expect. Park memorabilia, statues of Pooch in various poses, some of Gordo and Betsy, too. A movie poster of the latest Flashman feature film, this one featuring Dread Flashman, pirate-rogue and Scourge of the Mirror Sea. A powered-down television set, and a remarkably modest glory wall of only three photographs. Bell takes that as a sign of Matthew Marcelin's restraint, because Matthew Marcelin is chief of park operations and at a guess is pulling down seven figures annually, easy. A man like that is going to have more than just a photograph of himself with the current First Family; another with the assembled Friends of WilsonVille, taken—Bell assumes—outside the park gates; and another with the archbishop of the Archdiocese of Los Angeles.

"You talk to David Gonzalez recently?" Marcelin sits back in his chair as he asks the question, conversational. He's got a good manner, and though they've only spoken once prior, by phone, he's relaxed with Bell, as if he's known him for years.

"You know David?"

"He does some consulting for us now that he's left the Bureau."

"Haven't talked to him in two, maybe three years."

"I gave him a call about you, you know. He tells me I can't do better."

"He's being generous. I didn't know he'd gone private."

"About eighteen months ago."

"He consults for you?"

"We brought him in to do a walk-through of the offices. You noticed the security, I'm sure." For emphasis, Marcelin lifts the Wilson Entertainment IFF chip–enabled ID badge that's clipped to his lapel.

"That's not in the job purview, is it?"

"No, no, it's a park position. If you're still interested, of course."

Bell raises his hands slightly, shrugs at the same time. "Why I'm here."

"Have you ever been to WilsonVille before, Jad?"

"No." He pauses, thinking about all the times he and Amy had talked about making the trip, taking Athena to see the Flower Sisters in person. But it had never reached operational planning, had stayed a theoretical family vacation. "No. Never managed to make it happen."

Marcelin rises. "I think I can fix that for you."

It takes just under twenty minutes to drive the five miles from Wilson Entertainment's corporate HQ to the park, a Friday in summer's traffic, and Bell thinks it would've been faster to walk. Marcelin drives a new Audi sedan, air-conditioned comfort, and they wind through acres of packed parking lot before reaching the VIP spaces. The park, even from outside, is visibly crowded, and for the first time Bell has a true sense of its scale. One thing to study the maps of 156 acres of WilsonVille; another thing entirely to meet it in person for the first time.

Marcelin parks, waits for Bell to join him, then turns and gestures toward the redbrick promenade that leads to the main gates. Ticket booths line the approach on both sides, roped walkways to guide the guests to each window, and there's an audible buzz of excitement, children's voices mixing with teen laughter and adult grumbling. A thin seam of music threads through the air, piped from hidden speakers, what sounds like a movie sound track to Bell's ears. The ticket booths themselves are designed to look like oversize doghouses, Plexiglas windows at the front and back, access doors on the side.

"Normally, I'd take you through the main entrance, give you the full experience," Marcelin is saying. "But the crowd's a little thick today. The alternate entrance is this way; we tend to use it for VIPs or special events."

"Those aren't the only two accesses to the park?"

"Oh, God, no. There's facility maintenance along the northern side, chain-link and ugly as sin, then the inner park wall, twelve feet high, concrete. We do everything in our power to hide that stuff from the guests. Normally, that'd be the way I'd have brought you in, but seeing as it's your first time, well…" Marcelin trails off, heading toward a side gate done in what appears to be weathered wrought iron but on closer inspection Bell thinks it's stainless steel with a very good paint job.

Before they even reach the gate, a young black woman has appeared, wearing a blue blazer with a small W-E embroidered in gold thread above the left breast, an elegant and matching name tag pinned in position right below it.

"Mr. Marcelin, always nice to see you, sir!"

Marcelin takes a fraction of a second, just long enough to note the woman's name on her tag, responds to her cheer in kind. "Nice to see you, too, Marjorie. This is Mr. Bell."

"Welcome to WilsonVille, Mr. Bell." Marjorie's smile is luminescent, almost unbelievable in its sincerity. She holds a radio in her left hand, against her thigh, so discreetly it's easy to miss. She's turning back to Marcelin. "Is there anything you need today, sir?"

"Can you give me the number?"

"Just a moment." She takes a step back from the two men, still smiling, turns as she raises her radio.

Marcelin leans in. "Security staff."

"Is that the uniform?"

"No, she's dressed as a greeter. There's no security uniform per se, though most support staff wear the blue blazer so they can be recognized. Outside that, as long as it's park-approved wear, it's fine. Most of your people will be working plainclothes, so to speak. Some in costume."

Bell removes his sunglasses, looks back toward the main gate. A discreet redbrick path slopes from where they're standing toward the entrance, and a quick count gives him eighteen men and women in what looks to him like "park-approved wear" circulating in the immediate vicinity of the turnstiles, and some of them are clearly cheerfully answering questions and offering directions. But not all of them—perhaps half that number, sharing the same cheerful smiles, is doing nothing but keeping a careful watch on the entering crowds.

"It's all eyeball on entry?" he asks Marcelin.

"You mean of the guests? Yeah, we considered

metal detectors post–nine eleven, but it was deemed unviable. Just too many people coming in and out. Bags are screened after ticket purchase but before reaching the entry. We've got a battery of sensors and the like running as well; you'll see those when we go up to the command post."

Marjorie is back. "They're expecting to hit sixty-four thousand visitors today, Mr. Marcelin."

Marcelin makes a face, then quickly hides the expression with a smile. "Thank you."

"Have a lovely time, sir. Mr. Bell." She moves off again, takes up a position in the shade provided by the canopy that overhangs the gate.

It's a whirlwind tour.

Matthew Marcelin leads the way along grand walkways and semihidden paths, around kiosks and attractions, speaking all the while about the park, its history, and the history of Wilson Entertainment. They pass the Flower Sisters Theater, moving with a sudden surge of the crowd as the show lets out along the banks of the Timeless River, then through the edge of the Wild World Woods, where Lilac, Lily, and Lavender are seated in a pavilion, signing autographs and posing for pictures. Bell is surprised to see that the Flower Sisters do not wear masks but instead sport elaborate makeup with their costumes.

"Character portrayals have very stiff requirements," Marcelin tells him quietly as they watch the three women cheerfully engage their admirers. "Lilac, for instance, must be five feet two exactly, with weight between one hundred and one ten, tops. Lily has a little more play—five seven to five eight—but cannot weigh more than one twenty-five, and she's got to be strong enough to wear the harness for her horns. Hard to find someone tall enough who's also strong enough *and* who can convey the necessary grace of a gazelle. Lavender is five five to five six, but weight is less of an issue. The part is very active, a lot of jumping and tumbling, so they tend to carry more muscle. We normally cast athletes—gymnasts are best, cheerleaders almost as good—for the part."

"You said security officers dress as characters?"

"We actually call them safety officers, and yes, on any given day maybe ten percent of the performers are also working security."

"Also?"

"They're required to fulfill the needs of their role if called upon."

Bell nods, listening as he watches the three women banter and laugh with each other as much as with their crowd of young fans. Lavender does a handstand suddenly, much to everyone's delight, then proceeds to walk about like that to cheers and laughter. Lily scolds her for showing off, and just as quickly, Lilac reminds the other two that they're all friends, and that they all love one another.

A sudden hush comes over the Flower Sisters. Lilac points in Bell's and Marcelin's direction, emitting what is, even to Bell's ears, an alarmingly cute squeak before hiding behind Lily. Lily draws herself up to her full height, something that makes her seem even taller due to the gazelle's horns she's sporting, and then Lavender is taking up a protective stance in front of the other two.

For a moment, Bell wonders if they're reacting to Marcelin when he hears a growl from behind him.

"Hendar!" Lavender says. "You're not welcome here!"

All heads turn, small voices gasp, and several children actually recoil, hiding behind parents in much the same fashion that Lilac is now hiding behind Lily. Bell turns with the rest of them, finds that he's looking at a man, five ten, dressed in black and moving toward them with a predator's purpose. His makeup is as black as his clothing—a jungle cat, a jaguar.

Hendar the jaguar growls, "But we could have so much fun together, Lavender."

There's a tittering from some of the parents, more quavering from the fans, and Marcelin is motioning to Bell that they should move on. His last glimpse of the impromptu show is of Hendar circling the pavilion as he and Lavender snarl at one another while Lily and Lilac apparently use the opportunity to concoct some cunning plan.

They visit the Pyramids of Ke-Sa, watch what appears to be an endless throng of college-age men and women queuing up to ride the attraction. From within the largest pyramid, Bell can hear unearthly laughter, gunshots, and screams of glee as passengers on the ride are assaulted and assailed by the evil that Agent Rose has unwittingly unleashed. Further along, they're suddenly in the Old West, where Skip Flashman is having a roping contest with some tough hombres in the shadow of Dead Man's Mine. From the side of Mount Royal, mine cars loaded with shrieking passengers appear, then vanish again into the tunnels. They stop outside the enclosure to the Clip Flashman show in Terra Space, where it's paired with a tower ride done up as a 1950s rocket ship, the Star System Alliance Defense. The Friends working the attraction all wear retro-future period garb, the line tended by men and women in one-piece mechanic's coveralls, caps, and belts heavy with space-age tools. One of the Friends, a man in his late twenties with an Afro-Caribbean complexion and the name Isaiah embroidered on his breast pocket, offers Bell a Clip Flashman comic from a pouch on his belt.

"No, thank you," Bell says.

"Never too old for adventure, man!" Isaiah counters, pushing the comic into his hands. "The adventure never ends!"

He returns to working the line, and Bell keeps a straight face, watching him go, and wondering how long Chaindragger has been in place here.

"Let's take a break, get a drink," Marcelin says as they leave the bright red rocket ship behind them. "I'm sure you've got questions."

"A drink would be good."

Thus far, they've been describing the park counterclockwise, but now Marcelin reverses direction and they're heading northeast once more, this time along different pathways. If anything, the park has gotten more crowded since they started the tour, and the sign at the entrance to Pooch Pursuit warns that the wait is seventy-five minutes from this point, and still there are people lining up in the shadow of the enormous wooden roller coaster.

Marcelin cuts directly north, suddenly, along a narrow alleyway with shops tucked away on either side. The architecture has abruptly shifted from middle America to early-twentieth-century Europe, right down to the cobblestones beneath Bell's feet. A jeweler's on one side, high-end WilsonVille Clothing beside it, and opposite them, an art gallery. A bronze one-to-two scale statue of Pooch is on display in the window: asking price, six thousand dollars.

Bell can understand waiting seventy-five minutes to ride a roller coaster. He would never do it himself, but it is, at least, explicable. But six large for a glorified paperweight?

Marcelin has stopped beneath an archway, the words GATEWAY TO ADVENTURE chiseled into the stone above. He knocks on an almost concealed door, and immediately a wooden slat slides back, a gruff voice asking, "Password."

"It's a dog's life," Marcelin says.

Bell does his damnedest not to laugh out loud.

The door opens, and down a flight of stairs Bell finds himself in a small and rather cozy bar. The descent into cool and quiet is so sudden, in fact, that it's only as he takes a seat in one of the booths that he realizes just how intensely noisy the park is. Some two dozen more guests are in here, all of them adults, most of them in groups, nobody drinking alone. A cocktail waitress comes to the table immediately, hands each of them a drinks menu. Marcelin orders a beer, and Bell does the same, and Marcelin upgrades to a pitcher for the two of them.

"Only place in the park to get alcohol," Marcelin

says. "Members only—you get the password when you get your membership. I find it particularly ironic that the club's called the Speakeasy."

"Not by accident."

"Very little that happens in the Wilson Entertainment empire happens by accident, Jad." Marcelin grins, straightens up in the booth as the waitress returns with the pitcher of beer, two glasses, and a bowl of pretzels. The pretzels are in the shape of Gordo, Betsy, and Pooch. "Give you an example. You saw Hendar?"

"Hendar?"

"The jaguar, when we were walking through the Wild World. The thing with the Flower Sisters."

"Sure."

"Hendar is a perfect example of what I'm talking about. He debuted DTV almost a decade ago."

"DTV?"

"Direct to video. Flower Sisters—like the Flashman franchise—is on a very strict schedule. With the Flowers, it's three DTVs a year, one feature every third year. But DTV, variable income stream. Lot of times the releases, they just fly right under the mainstream radar, it's only the diehards who notice them. Parents buying them for their kids as presents and substitute babysitters. This one, this DTV, was called *Flowers in the Fall.*"

"Cute."

"Hell, yes. Cute pays for my daughter at Stanford and two alimonies." Marcelin pours beer for each of them, still speaking. "Anyway, movie came out, and we got hit from all sides. Parents groups went nuts. Accused us of trying to corrupt their pwecious wittle childwen."

Bell grins, tastes his beer. He's expecting something that's been through a horse first, and is surprised by the hoppiness, the pleasantly bitter and clean taste that immediately washes away the coating of park that has caked the inside of his mouth. Marcelin nods in approval.

"Penny's Pale Ale. We put our name on something— or the name of one of our characters on something, more precisely—we damn well make it quality. You can only get it one place. Right here."

Bell tops off each of their glasses. "*Flowers in the Fall.*"

"Right. The primary accusation was that Wilson Entertainment was racist."

"Racist."

"Hendar. Jaguar. Villain. Black." Marcelin shrugs. "I can see where it came from, but it's a bullshit accusation. They're *animals,* for fuck's sake. If you're going to call us racist for having a jaguar as a bad guy, you better accuse us of miscegenation at the same time. I mean, Jesus Christ, we've got a meerkat, a gazelle, and a lioness all dewy-eyed over a tiger. But nobody ever talks about *that.* Let alone the fact that Lavender should've quite literally had Lilac and Lily for lunch ages ago.

"But that's not really why they got up in arms, see? It wasn't because he was black. It's because he was sexy."

"Ah."

"You see the crowd around the pavilion? You see how they changed when Hendar arrived?"

"The kids went for cover."

"And the moms started paying attention, especially the under-thirties. See what I'm saying? I mean, in the course of the film, Hendar stalks each of the sisters separately, and he's effectively trying to seduce them. Lilac, Lily, Lavender, they're all supposed to be fourteen, fifteen, if we were to provide equivalent ages, right? And Prince Stripe, he's fifteen, and very much the nonthreatening male, even if he is supposed to be a fucking tiger. That's by design here, you get it? It's all supposed to be presexual, just on the cusp.

"Hendar's design breaks that mold. He's supposed to be older, more mature. He's supposed to be a Bad Boy. And let me tell you, Jad, Hendar was a fucking windfall. He's been in every Flowers feature since he debuted, and he's in at least one DTV every cycle. And all those girls we were losing when they hit their midteens, they're back, they're staying with us through college now."

"Don't see how this was an accident."

"It wasn't; that's my point. No matter what we might have said at the time, no matter how many times we swore up and down that people were reading too much into it, that it was only a cartoon. It was as deliberate as sharpening a pencil."

"Sharpening a pencil?"

"Something very deliberate, at any rate. I was going to say 'pulling a trigger,' but didn't want to risk being rude."

Bell drinks more of his beer. "Long as you're not shooting at me, we're good. I've had enough of that."

Marcelin nods, looking at Bell, and the question is in his eyes, but he doesn't ask. Bell appreciates that.

"Not something you'll have to worry about here."

"Security doesn't go armed?"

"No one goes armed. There's a no-weapons policy in the park and the resort. Not even nonlethal. Can't risk using pepper spray or mace or whatnot for fear of dispersal, hitting people beside whoever you're trying to subdue. You imagine that lawsuit?" Marcelin drains what's left in his glass, sets it down. "Shall we wrap this up?"

"By all means."

"Then let me show you what I hope will be your new office."

Wilson Town, the entry to and the heart of the park, is built to look like a town square, an idealized replica of a time and place that Bell is certain never truly existed outside of dreams. Perhaps one hundred yards from the main entrance and smack in the middle of the flow of traffic sits a small, perfectly green park. In the center, a fountain surrounding a joyful statue of Gordo, Betsy, and Pooch. Cafés and ice cream parlors, boutiques full of memorabilia, everything is available on the square. The concentration of characters here is denser, too, positioned to meet guests as they enter, and it's as Marcelin is leading the way to the park's police station that Bell sees his first Gordo, Betsy, and Pooch.

Unlike the other characters he's encountered so far, these are complete suits, making all three appear as if they had been plucked from their cartoon world and cruelly invested with a third dimension. All are signing autographs, no small challenge with their oversize hands. Except for Pooch. Bell sees that even with a human performer inside the costume, Pooch remains a dog, albeit a giant one. Running around on all fours, hopping up on his hind legs to dance in front of guests. When he signs an autograph, he does so with the pen in his mouth.

Marcelin stops, letting Bell take in the sight. The crowd bustles in every direction, those entering the park and those who've had enough of this scorching summer day. Lemonade flows into novelty cups sold from carts, sweets and treats from every side, ice cream, pretzels, cotton candy, candied apples, and sugar-dusted churros with fudge-swirl dipping sauce.

Bell thinks WilsonVille is a rough place to be a diabetic.

He tilts his head, looking at the buildings around the square. All are two to three stories. He spots camera emplacements, more of the same ones he's been noting all around the park, despite their concealment. He's about to ask Marcelin how they manage the video when a red-haired woman is suddenly trying to pin a badge to his lapel. She is stunning, a light Mediterranean complexion, wearing a leather flight suit and knee-high boots, one arm slung through the face of a silver space helmet, its mirrored visor raised. The flight suit looks black at first, but when the sunlight hits it full-on, a purple is revealed, and Bell thinks he sees glitter or some other sparkling material coating it as well. He's guessing she's midtwenties, and her beauty isn't simply exotic, and it's not just the costume making him think that.

"You've been deputized!" she tells him, straightening his coat. "Report to Commander Flashman at once!"

She motions over her shoulder, to where Clip Flashman is standing some ten feet away, his own silver space helmet hanging from his belt, handing out badges and signing autographs for a gaggle of excited children. At her voice, Clip raises his head, checking her back, then returns his attention to his eager fans. Bell hears the artificial click of shutters, digital cameras rattling off photo after photo. A lot of the lenses seem to be focused on the redhead.

"And you are?" Bell asks.

She takes a step back in surprise, reappraises him critically. "Lieutenant Penny Starr, citizen!"

"I see."

"Earthlings." Penny Starr tosses her blood-red hair, rolls her eyes. "You're *so* provincial."

"No doubt."

She studies him, head to toe, as if evaluating his status as a recruit. A couple voices are calling out to her, asking for photographs, but she doesn't break focus. Finally, she straightens, snapping off a crisp salute.

"As you were," Penny Starr says, then pivots smartly on her toe and moves quickly back to Clip's side. Bell can't help watching as she goes, as she is immediately surrounded by a second throng of admirers, these almost entirely male, almost all of them of the young-adult-and-up variety. He absolutely understands the attraction.

"A hit with the boys," Bell says.

"And some of the ladies, too," Marcelin says. "We're an equal-opportunity provider, so to speak. This way."

Bell follows as they enter the police station, sneaking one last glance back at Penny Starr and Clip Flashman before stepping out of the sunlight and heat. The interior is like the exterior, some remembered ideal of a police precinct. A boy of perhaps eight or nine is seated on a bench to their left as they enter, raining tears in silence, a silver-haired man in a blue blazer resting on one knee in front of him. Don't you worry, the man is saying. My parents used to get lost all the time. We'll find them.

Marcelin moves to an unobtrusive side door, painted to blend in with the wood-paneled decor, passes his ID badge over some unseen sensor hidden in the wall. There's the nearly subsonic *thunk* of a magnetic bolt releasing, and Bell steps through after him.

The illusion of WilsonVille shatters, and shatters utterly. The hallway they're standing in now is concrete, the flight of stairs Bell ascends galvanized steel, and, as they reach the second floor, the room they enter is, in every way, modern. Banks of video monitors line either side, more than twenty people staffing them, headsets on and entirely focused on their screens. Voices overlapping, all speaking softly, recording and reporting, and a quick check tells Bell that at least one-quarter of this surveillance is dedicated to the park's entrance—the exterior promenade, ticket booths, and approach. The steady thrum and whir of electronics fills the background, unseen fans working to circulate air for people and machines.

Marcelin stands, silent, while Bell takes in the command post. Bell walks the room slowly, peering over one shoulder, then another, to monitor after monitor. They're using video primarily, images in color, high-res, though Bell is certain the cameras must have some low-light or even night-vision capacity for after the sun goes down, for those dark corners. A full bank of sixteen separate screens monitors the park's perimeter, effectively covering every possible angle and approach. One terminal monitors air quality at multiple locations, both within attractions and facilities as well as out in the open. Another station is devoted to thermal imaging, recording results from six cameras placed along the promenade and just inside the main gate. One after another, people pass the lenses, oblivious, and one by one, their body temperatures are recorded.

"What's the trigger?" Bell asks the woman working the station.

"One-oh-one. That's for summer. One hundred in winter."

"And then?"

She steals a glance away from her monitors, one eye narrowing in suspicion. "I'm sorry, who are you again?"

Marcelin glides forward. "This is Mr. Bell. He's with me."

"If they trigger, protocol is to radio one of the units on the gate. We pull the guest out of line and escort him to the doctor's office on the square." She looks from her monitor to Marcelin, seeking some sort of permission, which he grants with a slight nod. "We screen for SARS or swine flu or whatever bug the CDC may be warning us about at the time. If you'll excuse me, I need to be concentrating on this."

Bell thanks her, turns back to the air quality station. "Chem-bio?" he asks.

Marcelin nods. "And radiation. It's the Spartan II system, I think it's called. There are sensors placed throughout the park."

"It's that comprehensive?"

"You name it, it's searching for it. Ricin, tabun, sarin, mustard, cyanogen, phosgene, ethylene oxide, even botulinum. The list goes on and on."

The hint of a frown on Bell's face. Most of these agents, he knows their vectors, has studied them, has studied their effects. He's had to, can think of at least two dozen times in the past decade that he and his team had to deal with one or another of them. Botulinum, too, but to his knowledge no one has ever been able to weaponize it yet, and thank the gods and goddesses of warriors everywhere, because botulinum is the True Nightmare Scenario, beyond even anthrax or sarin or any of their cousins. Aerosolized, weaponized botulinum makes its biotoxin cousins look like they're still playing in the sandbox.

Marcelin can read his expression. "You don't like it?"

Bell chooses his words carefully. "I don't know the system. But you're describing a wide search, and it makes me wonder if your Spartan, in trying to do it all, may not be doing any of it well."

Marcelin shakes his head slightly. "I'd love a better system, but as far as we know, it's not being manufactured, not even at the military level. Agent- and vector-specific monitoring systems were considered post–nine eleven, but the cost was prohibitive, both in equipment and manpower."

"I can imagine." Bell can, too, but he suspects another factor at work as well. WilsonVille has gone to great lengths to keep its visitors from knowing they're being watched. More monitors, more sensors, more cameras would be that much more difficult to hide. They would shatter the illusion, and in WilsonVille, Bell already understands, the illusion is everything.

At another station, a video is reversing, showing a young man surreptitiously yanking what looks to be a Lilac doll down the front of his pants. The screen flickers, shows real time, and the young man is now tête-à-tête with a much larger, but just as young, gentleman in a WilsonVille blazer and khakis. They leave the camera's view together, and Bell notes that at no time did the WilsonVille employee put a hand on the shoplifter.

"He'll bring him here," Marcelin says in Bell's ear. "We'll have someone from the Irvine police department meet them."

"You press charges?"

"We always press charges. Let's go into the conference room."

"So here's the job," Marcelin says. He's sitting in almost the same posture, the same manner that he had earlier in the day, in his office. The chairs in the conference room are Aerons as well. "Deputy director of WilsonVille park safety. Salaried position, starts at five hundred and fifty K, and of course that gives you free year-round passes to all Wilson Entertainment venues for yourself and your family. Medical, stock, etc., we can discuss later. The job is six days a week, you get six weeks' paid vacation annually, and paid sick leave. You would report to and work under the director of park and resort safety, Eric Porter."

"And for all this I'm expected to do what?"

Marcelin gestures in the direction of the room full of monitors. "Primary duties are to ensure the safety and security of our employees and guests. Secondary responsibilities are to minimize breakage, vandalism, and theft, most normally in the form of shoplifting."

"Sounds my speed," Bell says.

"Bullshit," Marcelin says. "You're overqualified for the position, and we both know it."

Bell doesn't say anything, and this time he thinks Marcelin is going to try to wait him out. The silence stretches, brushing up against becoming awkward. He wonders idly if Chaindragger's cover contained any mention of military service, if he had any awkward questions to avoid during his job interview. He suspects not.

"You heard about the murder?" Marcelin asks, finally.

"I did not," Bell lies.

"One of our employees was found dead out by the northwest parking lot, the staff lot. He'd been beaten and stabbed."

"They made an arrest?"

Marcelin shakes his head. "Investigation is ongoing."

"I hadn't heard."

Marcelin studies him further, scratches the back of

his neck, seems on the verge of saying something more, asking something more. Bell can see the wheels turning. He'd suspected Marcelin was smart; now he's certain of it.

"What were you? Special Forces? Green Beret?"

"Like that."

"But not that. And you just drop out of the sky to fill this position, and all the right people are saying that you're my man for the job. I'm no more paranoid than the next guy, but this doesn't seem like a coincidence to me."

"Coincidences do happen."

Marcelin shakes his head. "Job vacates and here you are. I have to ask. Is something going to happen to my park, Jad?"

"Not as far as I know, Matt."

It takes a couple of seconds, then Marcelin sighs.

"You're either legit or you're not," he says. "But like I said, all the right people are telling me you're a gift, and I'm not going to look that horse in the mouth. Most people in your position, they leave the military, they go either corporate or private."

"This doesn't count as corporate?"

"We're not exactly KBR, Jad."

"Not my thing."

"No, apparently not. So what do you say?"

Bell thinks, wonders just how hard to get he should play this. Not hard at all, he decides, offering Marcelin his hand.

"When can I start?" he asks.

Chapter Four

GABRIEL FULLER hates Pooch.

He hates his boundless enthusiasm and his good-natured idiocy and his desire to chase every ball that's thrown his way. He hates his lack of pedigree, his complete renunciation of anything that might've, once, harked back to his wolf ancestry. He hates the simplicity that dictates that Pooch loves Gordo and Betsy and All Kids; hates that he goes crazy when offered a bone but is nowhere allowed to piss, shit, or fuck. He hates the fact that, even after all this time, he cannot be certain if Pooch is a boy or a girl.

Every Friend who portrays a character in WilsonVille has "allowed behavior," which is another way of saying "things you must and must not do." Some are general rules, applicable to every employee in the park: for instance, under no circumstances are they allowed to strike a park visitor. Self-explanatory, but good to remember on days when the fifth little tyke in a row has vomited on your paws or climbed onto your back and then taken a tinkle. Some are specific to character: for instance, Lily is forbidden to remove her antlers in public view. Doing so can result in immediate dismissal for "violation of character."

Pooch's rules are very simple. One, Pooch is a dog.

Two, as a dog, he walks on all fours. Three, as a well-trained dog, he does tricks, and he does them on command: Pooch can fetch; Pooch can hop up on his hind legs for hugs and to dance about; Pooch can walk on his forepaws for short distances, to indicate excitement or approval; and, in the ultimate hypocrisy, Pooch can sign his name.

But he has to sign with his mouth.

This means that Gabriel Fuller, wearing eighteen pounds of Pooch costume, including a headpiece that stinks of sweat and shed skin cells, spends most of his days in the park walking on all fours. And when he's not doing that, he's pretty much guaranteed to be walking on his hands as often as his legs, because that's what the masses have come to see. Sometimes, Gordo gives a kid a ball, and he gets to fetch it.

Signing autographs is actually the easiest task, though it requires some balance to execute properly. The headpiece is such that control of the mouth and tongue are accomplished by a wire system in the forepaws. When signing, Gabriel Fuller takes the offered pen into his mouth, closing it, then frees one of his hands—being right-handed, his right—from the paw and moves it up his front, to the inside of the mask. In this way, he can sign his name using his hand. But this also means that, while on all fours, he has to support most of his upper body on his left hand. His upper body plus the weight of the costume. Sometimes he'll sit on his haunches to do it, but it's a hard posture to hold for more than thirty seconds or so at a time.

At least management understands that the costumes are physically taxing, and for every thirty minutes he spends in the park Gabriel Fuller gets to spend sixty on break. By the time he's made it to one of the employee areas and gotten out of his headpiece and freed enough of his upper body to effectively use his hands, he has forty minutes left. He's drenched with sweat and dying of thirst, especially if it's been a hot day (and almost every day seems to be a hot day). He sits on a bench in one of the common areas that anchor the theme park's tunnel system, and sometimes he gets to chat with other Friends, but most of the time he's given a wide berth, because he reeks. The female performers, in particular, avoid him, especially the Flower Sisters.

There's prestige in whom you're wearing. Right now, Gordo, Pooch, and Betsy are at the bottom of the ladder, though it's anybody's guess who's in last place of the three. Probably Gordo, who has steadfastly refused to grow with the times, it seems; Betsy, at least, got to move "tomboy" in the last few decades, out of her floral print dresses and into cutoffs and sneakers. For the men, though, *the* character to be right now is Hendar. Hendar gets marriage proposals, and sometimes Mom has been known to whisper an indecent proposal in his ear, or even slip him a hotel key card. It works in private, too, with the Friends cast as Hendar renowned for "picking up a Penny" with impressive frequency. For the women, the prestige part is a toss-up, either Agent Rose or Nova. Penny Starr's jumpsuit is tight, of course, but Nova's superhero outfit actually gets to show a little skin, and her costume has some cool accoutrements. Agent Rose gets the trench coat and the hat and a comedy-tragedy porcelain mask with the lips painted blood-red, and who doesn't love a Bad Girl?

All this means that, more often than not, Gabriel Fuller is left alone when he's not out in public, not chasing Gordo's goddamn oversize soft foam baseball or dancing in circles around Betsy or having someone pee on his back. He's left alone, and even if he's wearing half a giant mutt costume, he's often unnoticed. This suits him fine. It's time he's used well in the last couple weeks, mapping the service tunnels and marking the generator locations and the pump rooms and generally getting the lay of the parts of WilsonVille that sixty-plus thousand people a day don't even pause to consider. The apparatus within the apparatus; the world that allows the park to exist.

Gabriel Fuller has been doing prep, and it's almost complete. Gabriel Fuller has set eight charges, loaded a cache with the equipment he'll need when it all goes down. He's done this because it's what the Uzbek told him to do. He's done this because, when it all goes down, he'll be on the inside, he'll be running the show on the ground.

Gabriel Fuller is ready in mind, if not in heart.

Gabriel Fuller is not Gabriel Fuller's real name.

He still doesn't know who he works for, even after all this time, even after nearly seven years.

That was a different life ago, and a far different world from one where places like WilsonVille could even be imagined. At that time, his world was what he had been able to make of it, mostly through cunning and to a lesser extent through strength, and it had been those two traits that had brought him, before he was Gabriel Fuller and still called Matias, to the Uzbek's attention.

They'd met at a party Matias was throwing for his crew, back in Odessa. He and his boys had brought over half a ton of raw heroin from Afghanistan the previous week, and already most of it had made its way to Moscow. Even after the bribes, the cuts, all the hands that had reached out for their share, it had been a dynamic haul, and there was reason to celebrate. Normally, Matias ran a tight ship, but this time he'd let loose the reins for one night, thrown the party himself. There was booze and cigarettes, some pot, and a lot of girls, all of them pretty and most of them young.

The Uzbek's appearance came as a surprise; he was uninvited but not unknown. Matias had seen him a handful of times before, had heard some stories, had asked some discreet questions. The stories were broad-stroke myth, about how the Uzbek had done this thing or that thing, like how he'd cut the balls off some UN guy and fed them to him, or how he'd taken the ringleader of a gang moving black market gasoline and made him drink a gallon of the stuff, then cut him open and thrown a match. The stories backed the answers to Matias's questions, even if the stories weren't true; in no uncertain terms, the Uzbek was Not to Be Fucked With. Connected, he'd been told, and Matias had said something about the big players in Russia, gotten a head shake in return. Not just Moscow, no, bigger than that. *Connected,* you understand?

Matias didn't, couldn't conceive of something bigger than the power in Moscow, but he got the message, and he passed the word: his boys, they stayed the fuck out of the Uzbek's way, out of the Uzbek's business. Twice already, Matias had killed jobs that could've been lucrative, just to stay on the safe side.

So Matias's first thought on seeing the Uzbek walk through the door in his tailored suit and his long hair and those wire-rim round-frame glasses with the tinted lenses was pretty much, Oh, fuck me running, we cut into his score. And his second thought was to wonder how quickly he could get out of the country, and how much of his money he might be able to take with him. If the Uzbek was as connected as all that, then killing him wasn't going to help; killing him would only make things worse, and would mean Matias would be that much longer for the dying. Although he had done some dark things in his short life already, he didn't fancy being turned into a flambé.

It was Vladimir, the biggest of his boys and not the nicest by a long shot, who came to him.

"This guy, he says he wants to talk to you."

Matias hadn't taken his eyes from the Uzbek since the man had arrived, watching where he stood perfectly still just inside the door to the condo, letting the pretty girls and tough boys party around him. The Uzbek watching Matias the same way Matias was watching him.

"He say what about?"

"No. He's that guy, the one you told us—"

"I fucking know who he is." Matias ran fingers through his hair, shot the vodka he'd been drinking down his throat, made his way over. The Uzbek didn't move, didn't seem to blink, and for all there was to read in his expression, Matias might as well have been illiterate. Fleetingly, Matias wondered if the Uzbek would just shoot him then and there.

But the Uzbek smiled. "Matias. We haven't met."

"No."

"We should talk. There a place we can talk, without all this noise?"

"You mean alone?"

"I'm not chasing your ass cherry, Matias, you can relax."

Maybe not literally, Matias thought, but he shrugged and led the way out of the room, through the master bedroom, where two of his boys and three of the girls were contorting themselves without clothes. Matias didn't care, and from what he caught of the Uzbek's reflection in the glass doors, neither did the other man. Slid the doors back, stepped out onto the balcony, into the nighttime view of Odessa, down to the Black Sea. You could see lights of the ships moving about the port, life on the waterfront. It was late spring, not cold, but not quite warm enough.

"You a trusting man, Matias?" The Uzbek indicated the drop.

"You want me dead, I'm dead." Matias shrugged, much as he had before, but he liked the fact that the Uzbek had called him a man. That was something he normally had to fight for.

But the Uzbek undercut it immediately. "How old are you?"

Matias felt the tension race up his back, felt the fleeting satisfaction vanishing. "Twenty."

The Uzbek shook his head, leaned forward on the

railing, and knocked a cigarette from its pack into his hand. He made fire from a lighter, paused before touching it to the tobacco. "You don't have to lie."

"I'm not lying."

"Then that's a pity."

"Why?"

A plume of smoke. "We thought you were younger. You look younger. We thought maybe sixteen, seventeen."

"You like boys."

The Uzbek exhaled, watched his smoke disappear into the night air. If Matias's implication had offended or annoyed or even registered, he couldn't tell.

"We like potential," the Uzbek said. "But twenty, Matias...that's too old, I'm afraid."

"So maybe I'm not twenty."

"Ah."

"Maybe sixteen, that's true."

"Sure. And you've been running your crew, what, four years?"

Matias nodded, thinking that the Uzbek already knew the answers to the questions he was asking; thinking that the Uzbek maybe wasn't here to kill him, and if not, now wondering just what the fuck this player wanted. He was sensitive about his age with good reason, had needed to fight, even kill people who thought his youth meant he was unworthy of their respect. It was how he'd started, smuggling cigarettes, and Old Grigori had come to him and told him to cut him in or he'd get cut, cut and left to bleed out. Grigori, fifty years old, who hadn't caught up to the times, and the next day Matias had gone to him under the pretense of bringing tribute, and instead used a tire iron to modify their arrangement. When that was done, Grigori had more gray matter outside than in, and what had been his now belonged to Matias, including his crew, including his customers.

He'd been twelve then.

So now, sixteen—or maybe seventeen, he really wasn't sure—and he didn't know what he was feeling. Felt his brow furrowing as he searched out the emotion, and all the while the Uzbek kept his silence, smoking his cigarette and apparently in no hurry to explain himself. It took some digging before Matias found the name to what he was feeling, realized he was curious. He couldn't remember the last time he'd felt *that*.

"So sixteen is good?"

The Uzbek nodded.

"What is sixteen good for?"

Flicking the cigarette away, watching the ember spark orange in the sky until it vanished. "Because we can make something out of you."

Then the Uzbek explained what that meant.

Still no names, no explanations beyond the most basic. Yes, this meant Matias was part of the same organization, the same machine, that the Uzbek served. Yes, that meant the same protections, the same benefits. Money, sure; comfort, absolutely; respect, that would be earned, but already Matias had respect, enough respect that they would come to him with this offer.

There is a man, the Uzbek told Matias, a man who lives in shadow, a man whose name you will never know. But this man has noticed you, Matias. He likes what he's seen of you, what he's heard. He likes that you're not some brat who thinks a pistol makes him a king, who thinks God is a bullet. Too many fucking kids, they work their muscle, not their mind, and thugs, hell, thugs are cheap, thugs are easy. Thugs are a dime a dozen, right? But this man, Matias, he likes that you can move a half ton of heroin a thousand miles and do it right, without fucking it up, without getting greedy or turning stupid. He likes that you've been smart enough to stay out of our way, and he likes that you're not some broken psycho fuck. You're not a broken psycho fuck, are you, Matias? We're not going to find some dog bones under your bed and DVDs of you fucking their entrails, nothing like that?

"Nothing like that."

What he likes, Matias, is that you have that rarest of combinations found in youth; ambition and restraint. That means you're a thinker, and that maybe even you're smart. He calls this potential. Awesome potential.

This man whose name you will never know, he has reach, the Uzbek said, and his reach is increasing. He has a vision and a plan, and someone like you would be welcome within it. Follow instructions, do as you're told, keep being smart, and it will pay dividends, big dividends. It will make Odessa a memory, and will pave your future with gold.

"What do I have to do?" Matias asked.

"You have to go to school," the Uzbek said.

*   *   *

It was almost a year later that he arrived in Los Angeles. He traveled under a false name, he couldn't even remember it now if he tried, because as soon as he arrived, it was done, literally burned. The Uzbek had arranged a condo for him, and a car, and he was enrolled in the community college, and his name was Gabriel Fuller, and he was an American, though his mother had been from Ukraine. He had a bank account and a stipend and papers for everything, and the instructions were simple enough, as they were with Pooch.

One, he was to stay clean. No drugs, no guns, nothing that would make the law look at him twice. Be clean and stay clean, no record, and this was vital, the Uzbek said. No speeding tickets, nothing.

Second, get that language, and get rid of that accent. Know your American, so you can be American.

Third, take the courses at the college, meet the people, blend in. Take whatever you want, but if maybe some sciences are in there, that wouldn't be bad, you know? Maybe some math and some physics, too, because the more you know, the more useful to us you become, and the more useful, the more respect, the more the reward.

The day his papers said he'd turned eighteen, he received an e-mail from the Uzbek. In truth, Matias had celebrated—a poor word for letting the day pass without note—what he suspected was the date almost six months prior. But on Gabriel Fuller's eighteenth birthday, at least, there came this e-mail, sent through the anonymous account Matias checked every day, which, for almost a year, had remained empty. So it took him by surprise when he saw the letter, read it, and it was so simple, and he began to truly understand what they were after.

> Happy Birthday, Gabriel.
> Time to serve your country. Army or marines.
> One term of service will be fine.

He went with the army, signed on for the 4YO, four-year obligation, took the training and the pay, regular infantry, learned the weapons and the tactics and found himself in Afghanistan once again, and there were times during that deployment that he wondered if this had been a good idea or not. Moments when his unit was taking fire, when his friends died. They were his friends, truly, because he was Gabriel Fuller, and even if he had only been pretending, those bastards trying to kill them sure as hell were using real bullets and rockets and grenades.

He was Gabriel Fuller, and he was a soldier in the army of the United States of America, and he didn't need the Uzbek to tell him why he was doing this. Free training from the most advanced, best fighting force anywhere in the world.

He could see how that might be useful.

He was out after his second tour, had made himself a specialist before departing, and the army wanted him to stay. But the Uzbek, who had been silent since wishing him happy birthday so long ago, reached out again, and said that was enough. Perhaps he might want to explore what the GI Bill had to offer?

Perhaps he might like to pursue a degree in engineering, in fact? Or economics? Or chemistry?

His fifth semester at UCLA, he and some friends had gone to the movies in Westwood, seen a film about this chick who was wrongly accused of being a spy. He hadn't been paying much attention to the movie, because among the friends was this girl, Dana, and he thought maybe she liked him the way he liked her, and about minute forty he discovered that she did. So he missed most of the film, instead tasting her mouth and letting her taste his, and it wasn't really until the next morning, when they parted and he was heading to class, that he found himself thinking at all about what he'd seen, what he'd heard while lost in the taste and touch and feel of Dana.

A sleeper agent, someone on the screen had said. A long-term sleeper agent, placed and forgotten, known to no one. Until the day comes, the call arrives, and the sleeper is activated. Until the sleeper awakens.

It stopped him, standing just outside of Royce Hall, and he felt like a fucking idiot.

That's me, he thought. *I'm a sleeper, and I don't know who for, or why, or what, or when I'm going to wake up.*

And it occurred to him then that if this was his dream, if he was asleep, as sweet as this dream had become, it would end. He would wake. When the time came, he would wake, and he wouldn't have a choice in the matter.

He would wake, whether he wanted to or not.

The Uzbek contacted him in late winter, the same way he had every time before.

I am coming for a visit in the spring, to talk about your summer job.

Dana was studying special education, working with the developmentally and physically disabled, and she was making summer plans along those lines. But she wanted them to spend the summer together, and so she asked what he was going to do, and even though Gabriel knew he shouldn't, he told her the truth.

"I'm working at WilsonVille," he said. He had applied immediately after the Uzbek's visit, as instructed, had already received word that his security screening had been approved. He was due to attend his first orientation and training seminar that weekend.

She laughed, then, thought he was joking. Saw from his look that he wasn't. "Seriously?"

"Already applied and was accepted."

"To do what?"

"Whatever they'll let me." He shrugged. "Probably picking up garbage. What about you?"

"I was thinking about going home. There's this camp for the deaf I used to volunteer at, I was going to work there." Her family was from Illinois, outside of Chicago someplace. They were talking in her dorm room, and she looked at him thoughtfully for a couple of seconds after saying that. Then reached over to the foot of her bed. A small collection of stuffed animals resided there, would inevitably end up on the floor whenever they made love. She picked up one of them, a sweet-looking gazelle.

"But now I'm thinking maybe not," Dana said. She was still holding the animal, one index finger slowly stroking its breast up and down as she looked at him. The curl of her lip formed a slight smile as she met his eyes, and the gesture had nothing to do with the little gazelle in her hands. The thrill it gave Gabriel took him by surprise, made him want her right then and right there.

"We could get our own place," she said. "Just for the summer, you and me."

And despite everything the Uzbek had said, despite everything he already knew and everything he was beginning to suspect, Gabriel Fuller nodded. The Uzbek would give him hell when he found out, of course. The Uzbek wouldn't like it.

But the Uzbek, Gabriel Fuller thought, had never been in love.

"I'd like that," he said.

Chapter Five

EACH DAY starts much the same for Bell. He pulls himself out of his rack at five to five in the morning, coasting on autopilot, at least until he's outside and stretching. Then he starts his run. He's living in a condo now, a barely furnished open-plan space with a great view of the ocean, and it's less than half a mile from his front door to the beach. He runs alongside the surf, early morning mist eager to burn away to a fresh summer day. It takes him roughly forty-five minutes to hit his seven miles, and then it's a shower, dressing, drinking a hell of a lot of water and a little orange juice.

Then he takes his weapon, checks and loads it, then settles it in the holster just behind his right hip. No-weapons policy in the park be damned; he's carried a Colt M1911 .45 since one was put into his hands after he'd cleared selection. He can still remember Sergeant Mordino, call sign Icestorm, handing it to him.

"Go big or go home," he'd said.

Mordino had been one of the first on the ground when they went into Afghanistan, had died on a ridge-line in Tora Bora. Their guides had fed them bullshit, left them high and dry in a mortar storm, and Mordino had been out in the open. One of many warriors who lived on in Bell's memory.

He pauses before heading out the door to stuff two pieces of fruit into his pockets. He's been enjoying apples lately, but the summer stone fruits are a treat, and the last week, he's been going with plums, eating them in the car on the way to work, licking spilled juice from the side of his hand as he drives.

It's six fifteen when he's pulling out in a leased BMW coupe and his phone starts to ring. Every morning, same time, on the nose. This is the morning briefing, a quick call organized by his superior, the director of park and resort safety, Eric Porter. Bell and Porter are joined by two others, a man named Wallford, who serves as Porter's assistant, and by Matthew Marcelin. Marcelin normally keeps his silence on these calls, his presence simply there so that he can stay informed, and sometimes Bell wonders if he's even awake. It's Wallford who does most of the talking, and the calls are pretty much all the same, a quick rundown on any intelligence they've received from sources within government or law enforcement, any warnings, advisories, and so on. If there's a big group coming to the park, or VIPs visiting, and if so, what manner of VIP they might be. WilsonVille is a favorite stop for foreign dignitaries and their families, and they come to the park so regularly that there is a Secret Service liaison whose job it is to coordinate with park security.

So they go over all these things, and anything else that might matter, and the call normally doesn't last longer than fifteen minutes. Fifteen minutes, five days a week, for almost three weeks now, and that's been more than enough time for Bell to decide that he doesn't much like Eric Porter and that the jury is still out on his man Jerome Wallford. More than enough time for Bell to be certain that they don't much like him, either. Maybe it's a vestigial interservice cock-swinging contest, maybe it's just bad chemistry among all involved. But Bell wonders if maybe it's not something else, something more.

It started early, too, started the moment he met them, the day after Marcelin had hired him. Wallford escorting Bell into Porter's office, then remaining in the room with them, standing just behind and off to the left, the position deliberate, in the periphery. You are watched, Mr. Bell, you are being evaluated. To prove the point, he wasn't offered a seat, and Porter remained behind his desk, absorbed in whatever was on his monitor for fully half a minute before bothering to acknowledge Bell's presence.

"Marcelin should've consulted with me before hiring you," was the first thing Porter said.

"I guess I made a good impression."

"He says you were army."

It wasn't a question, but Bell decided to treat it as one. "Little under twenty years."

"Doing what?"

"Little of this, little of that."

"You being coy with me, Mr. Bell?"

"Not my intent, Mr. Porter."

Wallford, just outside his periphery, said, "You know we can find out."

Again, it hadn't been a question, but this time Bell didn't feel the need to answer.

"Your job is to keep the park safe," Porter said. "That's all it is. Keep the park safe, keep the kids under control, keep the breakage to a minimum. You're not pounding ground here. We have the whole, you have a piece, understand? If the matter goes outside the gates, it's outside your purview. You understand? If it's outside the gates, you refer it to Wallford, he brings it to me."

"Sure."

"We clear on this? Do you understand, Mr. Bell?"

"Sure."

The look Bell got told him that his answer lacked something, perhaps enthusiasm, perhaps the requisite sincerity or obsequiousness that Porter felt was his due. The look Bell got told him that Porter didn't have much faith in the ability of soldiers to follow orders, and if Porter thought *that,* he probably didn't think much of soldiers in the first place.

Bell had held hands with the CIA enough in the past to recognize it for what it was: typical Company bull-shit.

Less than a week later, during the morning call, things got worse. The Secret Service liaison, a woman named Linda Jovanovic, was on the line with them, going over details for a dignitary visit, and Bell had been holding his tongue, letting Wallford take the lead on Porter's behalf. They'd proceeded to the issue of coverage while in the park, the close detail work, and Bell finally offered that he'd had some experience in that department, and that Jovanovic's people could rely on his discretion and aid.

"Jad?" Linda Jovanovic said. "Jad Bell, is that you?"

"How you doing, Linda?"

"I think my blood pressure just dropped ten points, that's how I am. Fucking relieved is how I am. Give me your number; I'll have my detail leader contact you directly."

They'd wrapped the call, and Bell had been parking the BMW, making his way into the park, when his phone rang again. Porter on the line, all indignation and insult.

"You do not overstep, you do not make us look bad," Porter said. "You fucking do not do that ever again, understand?"

"We're all on the same side," Bell said. "Aren't we, Eric?"

Three weeks, then, Bell feels he's got his legs under him. It's not an easy job, not by any stretch, but mostly it's managing details, and that's something he's learned to do very well indeed in the last twenty years. And like the army, WilsonVille has trained its people, and Bell is surrounded by men and women who know their jobs.

One of them, a woman named Shoshana Nuri, has proven very helpful. He met her the start of his second week, found her waiting outside his office with a list of the various group tours that would be hitting the park that day. There were some two dozen, including a couple of graduating high school classes making late celebratory trips, and another smattering of special-needs and developmentally disabled groups. WilsonVille maintains a database of its employees, marks those with supplementary or secondary skills of use, those who can work as translators or interpreters and the like, and Nuri had already prepared a short list of Friends to call upon should extra assistance be required for any of the guests. One family reunion; three church outings; a kid from the Make-A-Wish Foundation, dying from terminal lymphoma.

Nuri handed him the sheet, and Bell wasn't sure what to do with it at first, mostly because he was staring at her. Shockingly pretty, short coal-black hair and hazel eyes, vaguely Persian features, but that wasn't why he stared. He'd seen her before, and for the life of him he couldn't remember where or when.

"The high school kids don't tend to be a problem," Shoshana Nuri told him. "They get noisy, rambunctious, sometimes they try to sneak booze into the park, but we tend to catch that during the bag check."

"You changed your hair," Bell said abruptly.

She reappraised him. "It was a wig."

"So I'd guessed."

"I'm impressed. Most people can't recognize me outside of costume."

"It took a while for the penny to drop."

She kept the same expression, the pun either ignored or disregarded. "Like I said, I think it's the wig. Throws people off."

"That must be it," said Bell, certain that her form-fitting Penny Starr flight suit was a factor as well.

He's working six days a week. Fridays, during his routine walkabout of the park, he completes the drop from Chaindragger at Terra Space. Isaiah offers him the latest Clip Flashman comic, and Bell takes it, and back in his office he opens it and reads the note that's been enclosed, always the same. NSTR. Nothing significant to report. He tucks the note away to be burned later, sends an e-mail to Brickyard via an anonymous account, passing it along.

Mondays he takes off, the quietest day in the park. Those days, Bell tries to sleep late and fails, spends a chunk of it reading, catching up on the news. His languages are getting a little rusty from disuse, and chasing newspapers online is a good way to refresh his Arabic, his Russian, his Pashto. There's a shooting club as well, and he spends an hour on the range, pounding out rounds. Does his laundry, does his shopping, and by the time that's done, he's thinking about cooking himself dinner and maybe going to see a movie, which he never does. Doesn't matter how much he wants to see something in the theater, he can't bring himself to sit in the dark alone.

His third Monday in, his third official day off, late in the afternoon, he heads to a brew pub he's been hearing about, place called the Yard House, on one edge of an outdoor mall in Irvine. He finds Colonel Ruiz there, as expected; out of uniform, blue jeans, a black T-shirt, waiting in a booth off to the side when Bell arrives. The colonel is apparently watching three different ball games play out on three different televisions at the same time, and Bell has a sense memory, triggered in the way Ruiz's eyes flick from one screen to the next, remembering the TOC. For a fraction of a second, he can hear the voices, see the satellite imagery, smell the electronics, the recycled air, the stale coffee of the Tactical Operations Center.

It's gone as quickly as it comes. Bell takes a seat.

The selection of beers available can only be described as overwhelming. He finally settles for an IPA out of San Francisco. The noise in the space is consistent, just shy of loud, with so many people alcohol-lubricated that the volume steals attention. It's a good place to talk.

"How's the job?" Ruiz sips from his own glass, eyes flicking from one game to another. This is their first face-to-face since Bell's placement within WilsonVille. Ruiz speaks casually, conversational volume. Whispering draws suspicion, after all.

"Like any other." Bell pulls the latest comic book acquired from Chaindragger from his jacket pocket, sends it across the table. Same message as every time before. "Always an adventure."

Ruiz takes the comic, cracks a grin, flips through it until he finds Chain's report. He closes the comic again, moves it to rest beside him on his seat. "Tell me."

"I'm light." Bell goes silent as the waiter sets his drink on the table, saunters off. "I'm tasked for four. You promised me four. Rest of my team."

"You may have heard, there's a war on."

"Old news. I've got Chain."

"You've got Chain plus one."

"I don't know my plus one, my plus one wasn't picked by me, my plus one is a variable and untested and therefore I do not include my plus one."

"Your plus one checks out."

"I didn't do the check. She's Company. I'm still light."

"There are a lot of parks to cover, Master Sergeant. I had to put Board and Bone in play elsewhere."

"Am I getting any more?"

Ruiz shakes his head so slightly it'd be easy to miss, except Bell knew it was coming.

"No change?" Bell asks. "Nothing new?"

"NSTR. Action as before." Ruiz takes another drink, glances over at him. "Anything you want to share?"

"Vesques."

"What about him?"

"He was moved before he was murdered."

"That was our conclusion as well."

"Moved out of the park."

"What I'd do."

"What I'd do, too, if it came to that. But if you had to move him out of the park, that means you initially neutralized him *in* the park. Which means you had a reason to do it. Which means it's an internal threat, not an external one."

"Find the reason he was moved."

Bell uses his chin to indicate where Ruiz has set the comic. "Chain's been looking, been looking six weeks now, almost. Negative result so far. If there's something hidden inside the park, neither of us can find it."

"Find the reason."

"I'm light."

"Yes, you are."

"But you're moving people elsewhere. This is the lead. Vesques is the lead. But you're moving people elsewhere. Unless you're telling me there's something hard that's come up elsewhere."

"There is not. What there is, Jad, is over five hundred theme parks in this country. Did you know that? Over five hundred theme parks in the United States alone. Add the politics and the interservice bullshit and you're lucky you're not working this alone with your dick in your hands."

"This is the lead. If this goes down, it'll be on a big park, not on fucking Happy Oaks in Peoria or wherever. Everyone thinks you hit these places from outside, it makes sense, I know that. Wear a vest, take a walk, ruin everybody's day who's buying a ticket. I know that. But Vesques was killed *inside*. This is something else, this is not looking like the playbook scenario. This is the lead."

Ruiz empties his glass, sets it on the table, rocks it back and forth between his palms. He's stopped watching the game, brown eyes on Bell. His age is starting to show, the hard living beginning to present its bill. Mostly, it shows around his eyes, crow's-feet that never go away, a slight sagging of flesh at his cheeks.

"I'll see what I can do."

"Soon."

"Soon." The glass stops dancing between his hands. "Anything else?"

"Wallford and Porter."

"See also: politics. Porter was high in the Company."

"Wallford?"

"Don't worry about him. Porter, he's an asshole, not an enemy."

"Enemies have assholes."

"Then don't stand behind him."

Bell grins at that, enjoys the joke for a second before letting it fade. "Anything for me?"

"If it rolls, it'll roll before the end of the summer. Makes the most sense."

"Only whispers?"

"We had concrete, we'd shut them down. You're not the only one who's seeing the scenario as you describe it. But 'better safe than sorry' is not a phrase that parses well when billions of dollars are at stake. You can't just shut these places down on a rumor. Too much money could be lost, and money, always, talks loudest."

"They'll lose billions more."

"They'll lose more than that," Ruiz says. He digs his wallet from his pocket, throws a twenty on the table. Grabs his jacket and the comic book. "Keep your powder dry."

Bell watches him go. Finishes his beer as his phone chimes, a text message incoming. It's from Athena; it's from his daughter.

Can u talk?

He smiles, the conversation with Ruiz forgotten for the moment, types his response.

Give me half an hour.

Asshole, Athena tells him.

Do not talk to your father like that, Bell answers. Where is your mother does your mother know you talk to me like that?

She's grinning at him on the monitor, shakes her head. Bell thinks she's the most beautiful girl in the world, his daughter, that somehow she got the right genes, all from Amy, no question.

So guess what? Athena asks.

I cannot begin to guess what Gray Eyes.

I am going to see you.

Her smile is self-satisfied, filled with the pleasure of knowing she's brought joy to someone she loves.

Do not tease me, Bell tells her. You should not tease your father.

Athena mocks a pout, then shakes her head. Her hands fly. No really no teasing!

When?

Next weekend Saturday Mr. Howe and Mom on a class trip.

Bell shakes his head at the same time as Athena reads his expression, her own falling, confusion turning into hurt.

You do not want to see me?

"That's not—," Bell starts, stops, then starts again, this time with his hands. No you know better than that I always want to see you.

You could have fooled me the way you look!

Bad timing Athena the timing not great.

She glares at him, hands out of sight. Then they're up again, and she's signing so quickly he's in danger of losing her words. The hurt has turned into anger, but Bell can see the edges of its desperation, see his daughter reaching for it to hide the pain he's just inadvertently caused her.

You know what? Athena says. Fuck you and fuck timing you never have time always bad time or something or you go someplace or something I thought you would be happy excited to see me but always the same and you left you are the one who left—

They're signing over one another, now, Bell trying to make himself understood.

I did not leave you your mother and I—

—always did you go and came back and—

Bell gives up. Watches his daughter yelling at him through her hands, waits until she runs out of steam, until the tears are welling in her eyes. She blinks angrily, and then they stare at one another, and Bell is again caught by the power of his daughter's gaze. Absolute attention, a focus that would make a sniper jealous, and he's getting it full force now, even across the Internet.

Can I say something now? he finally asks her.

She blinks, cocks her head. Flashes an angry smile, reaching out toward the monitor, toward him.

The screen goes dark. She's gone, and Bell is thinking that technology has made the whole act of hanging up on someone a much more painful process than ever before.

"What's this about Howe taking the class to WilsonVille?"

"What the hell did you say to her?" Amy says.

"Are you coming to the park? Athena said you're coming Saturday."

"We fly in next Friday, leaving late on Sunday. What did you say to her, Jad?"

Bell stares past his reflection in the window. The sun is setting on the Pacific, golden glare off the water burning his eyes. He turns away, adjusts the phone against his ear.

"I need you to talk to Howe. I need you to postpone this trip."

"You need? Jad, they've been planning this all year. You have any idea how many bake sales your daughter and I made brownies for? How many quilt squares we sewed? This is a class trip; I can't just tell him it's suddenly off."

"Postpone it."

"We've already bought the tickets, Jad!"

"I am asking you to postpone the trip, Amy."

She knows him well enough to know the tone. There's a moment's hesitation. "Can you give me a reason?"

"I cannot."

"I need to tell him something, Jad. Jesus, I need you to give me something I can tell him."

"It's bad timing. You know I wouldn't ask this if the reason wasn't good."

"I thought you were out." The accusation is sharp and unmistakable, and when the pause has stretched long enough that she knows he's not going to answer it, she sighs. Resignation. "I'll talk to him."

"Let me know."

"Sir, yes, sir," Amy says, and hangs up.

Bell stands at his window. The apartment is very still and very silent.

When he was a younger man, he thinks, being alone was not a problem. When he had a wife and a daughter and a home to return to, he could, perhaps, afford to be alone.

When it was a choice.

Amy's text comes the next morning.

> Howe says no way to cancel.
> See you Saturday.

Chapter Six

DANA'S WORKING float in the Wild World, either assigned to the lines at Gordo's Yesteryear Ballpark,
Soaring Thyme, Cannonball Plunge, or working as an
usher during the Flower Sisters Mystical Show. She's
on call as an interpreter, too, so Gabriel sees her, if
he's lucky, maybe once or twice during the day, and
only for a few minutes. Most of the time they spend
together, it's after hours. They rented an apartment at
the beginning of summer, here in town so they don't
have to commute to and from Los Angeles every day.
Nights, they're both so tired they have dinner, curl up
to maybe watch a video, find the strength to make love,
and then pretty much pass out.

Thursday morning, though, Gabriel has an e-mail
waiting from the Uzbek, and Thursday night, he has to
make an excuse.

"I'm going to be late getting back tonight," he tells
her. "Couple army buddies are in town; I'm going to
meet them for drinks."

Dana smirks. "No girls allowed?"

"Beer and bragging," Gabriel agrees, answering
with a grin. "I love you too much to ask you to sit
through that."

"I think maybe you do, too." She leans in, runs her fingers through his hair, then kisses his mouth gently. "You do what you have to do. Have some fun."

When they talk about such things, Dana makes no secret of what she thinks of the U.S. fighting so many wars in so many places for, in her opinion, oil and nothing but. But she's never let her opposition to the conflicts become an opposition to soldiers, and there are times Gabriel thinks she is, perhaps, proud of him for his service. Times like that, he thinks that he is, perhaps, proud of his service as well.

So it's Thursday night and Gabriel is going to meet the Uzbek at the DoubleTree near the business park, the place called the Irvine Spectrum. There's a lot of tech located there, including some major computer game company that, apparently, has more money than God. Gabriel wonders if the Uzbek's already trying to find a way to get a slice of that pie, too, if he hasn't already, and thinking that he realizes he's nervous, that he's not looking forward to this.

He parks his Prius, moves from the fading day's heat into the air-conditioning of the lobby, then straight to the elevators. Nobody gives him a glance, asks to see his key, asks if they can help him. It's ten minutes of eight, exactly, when he knocks on the Uzbek's door.

He hears a bolt turn, the door unlocking. A moment, then it's opening. The Uzbek backs up, allows Gabriel inside, and then he's got the door locked again, slipping past him, moving to the desk. There's a laptop open, and the Uzbek shuts it.

"It will be this weekend," the Uzbek says, turning to

face him. His English is accented, but only just. "It will be Saturday."

"What do I need to know?" Gabriel asks.

It's almost one in the morning when he gets back to their apartment. Quiet and dark, Gabriel stands in the main room, just stands there. His thoughts tumble, chase each other about in conflict, and he thinks these are the last days of his dream, can feel it fragmenting and tearing, dandelion fluff whipped away in a storm. He can remember a boy with a tire iron, and he does not know who that boy is, where he came from, or where he went.

He's still standing just like that when he realizes that Dana has come out of their little bedroom, is watching him. He didn't hear her and he didn't see her, but he knew she was there, holding herself in the doorway. She's wearing a tank top and panties, what she wears to sleep in most times before they both end up wearing nothing at all. Lavender is on the tank top, the irony of the words FRIENDSHIP IS TRUST printed in faded lettering beneath the character. She brushes hair back from her face, tucks it behind her ear.

"Are you okay, baby?" she asks.

Gabriel nods, moves to her. Sets his hands on her hips, and she's warm and solid and tangible, not a dream at all, and when he kisses her she wraps her arms around him.

"You're sure?"

"Let me show you," he says, and he lifts her up, and she wraps her legs about his hips, and he takes her back to their bed.

* * *

"When's your next day off?" he asks as they're driving into the park the next morning, Friday.

"Tomorrow," Dana says. "Then Tuesday. You?"

Gabriel hides his relief by checking his mirrors, changing lanes. "Monday and Tuesday, but they've got me in costume all weekend."

"I could see if someone wants to swap with me. Maybe get Monday in exchange."

"Nah, don't do that."

"It's no fun having a day off without you."

"Crowd Saturday is going to be massive," Gabriel says. "Fourth of July weekend bad. If I could get out of it, I would."

"Talk to Eduardo. Maybe you and he can swap?"

"That's a good idea. I'll ask him."

Friday night, Gabriel uses the same excuse, is almost out the door when Dana stops him. "These are the same army pals?"

"Yeah."

She gnaws her lower lip, eyes searching him, concerned. "You're okay?"

"I'm fine."

"It's just, last night. You know."

"It brought up a lot of memories."

"I figured that was it. I figured that was what happened." She steps closer, puts a hand on his chest, palm over his heart, earnest. "You know I'm yours, right? If you ever want to talk, if you ever need anything. I'm yours."

Gabriel smiles, kisses her mouth lightly. "I know."

"Breaks my heart when I see you sad."

"Am I sad?"

"You seem it. I think your friends made you sad."

"Old friends can do that," Gabriel says.

"Motherfucker!" Vladimir shouts. He's using Russian, grabbing Gabriel in a bear hug, and hoisting him off his feet. The transition from one language to another creates a lag, leaves Gabriel briefly disoriented. Vladimir sets him down. "Motherfucker, Matias! Look at you, you cock!"

There's an awful moment of vacancy, Gabriel looking at this man, this person he knows he knows, unable to remember him, to place him. Then the language clicks, the memory locks, and Gabriel laughs, genuinely surprised to see him, this brother in arms, here, in this place, at this time.

"Vlad! You son of a bitch!"

They're down in Laguna Beach, another business park, but no hotel this time. The recession is still a deafening echo here, and driving in tonight, Gabriel passed storefront after empty storefront, sign after sign offering lease and rental. It's a good place to hide, a good place to stage, the spaces big and private and nondescript, and maybe this one they're in now was used for gymnastics or something like that, because aside from the darkened front office, it's nothing but a great cavern here, a giant cube of poured concrete with rubber mats covering the floor, six long folding tables set against one wall. Rucksacks, sleeping bags, and the smell of pizza and beer to round it all out.

Along with Vladimir and the Uzbek, there are another fifteen, all of them with the looks of hard men from back home. It's been six years, but some of the faces, Gabriel thinks he recognizes them, men on the periphery of his old crew, perhaps, or men he'd crossed paths with somewhere along the line. All of a kind, and even Vladimir's got it, too, and Gabriel realizes they're soldiers, every last one of them.

Vladimir himself, damn if he doesn't look the same. Maybe a little older, a little harder, a little more muscle. He stands relaxed, and there's a difference to his posture, too, not the cocky in-your-face-I-dare-you stance of youth, but now it's more controlled, as if he's proven everything he needed to prove to himself, and in so doing has proven it to others. All that, but the grin on his face, the eager expression—that's the same.

Vladimir jerks a thumb back at where the Uzbek is standing, watching them. "He didn't say anything about you, Matias! This is your thing? This is what you've been doing all this time?"

"It's my thing. It's good to see you, Vladimir."

The Uzbek clears his throat. Gabriel, Vladimir, the rest, all of them turn their attention to him. Then the Uzbek makes them wait, removes his glasses, begins cleaning them. Holds them up to check the lenses in the weak light. Puts them back on. Then he looks at them, taking his time, eye contact with each in turn, all but Gabriel, until the end.

"Gabriel—Matias—has command," the Uzbek says. "You are now operational, and on the timetable. From this moment forward until conclusion, you follow his orders without question, without hesitation."

General assent from all the voices, and Vladimir is beaming, happy.

"There is a plan in place, this much you know. You know your parts within this plan, but you do not know the whole. Gabriel knows the whole. Remember this: his decisions are my decisions, and my decisions come from…"

The Uzbek grins, letting the statement dangle. A ripple of laughter, the joke understood. We do not speak of That Man, the One to Whom We All Now Answer. The Shadow Man, the Man of Silence, and it's not a long walk from such names to call him a demon, an agent of darkness, or, worse, the Devil Himself. Gabriel hears these men laugh, Vladimir and fifteen other hard men, and he hears the truth behind it, too. These are powerful men, dangerous men, and this man whom—as far as he knows, at least—none of them have ever met can make their balls climb into their bellies and their cocks shrink to nubs.

Gabriel sometimes wonders if this man the Uzbek works for exists at all, in fact. If the Shadow Man, this Lucifer, isn't some fabrication, a blind for others to hide behind. But knowing what he knows, knowing what lies in the metal case on the table behind the Uzbek, Gabriel doubts this. Whomever the Uzbek answers to, he is real enough, and Gabriel knows with the certainty of a penitent's faith that as much power and as much strength and as much skill as stands in this room now, the Shadow Man must hold a hundred times again that much, if not more.

The Uzbek motions Gabriel over to him, turns to the metal case. The other tables have weapons and equipment arrayed upon them, almost twenty pistols and eight submachine guns, ammunition for all of them—radios, NVGs, MREs, binoculars, flashlights, gas masks, and white Tyvek suits. This case sits on a table alone, a gunmetal gray cube with a handle at the top. It is the kind of case one uses to transport camera equipment, perhaps; used for the movement of something delicate, sensitive, precious. The Uzbek uses a key to unlock it.

"Sourced from Iran," the Uzbek murmurs as he lifts the lid. "Two ounces. Assemble it once you've secured your perimeter, placement as discussed."

Gabriel looks at the tiny lead-lined container, the symbols and red-painted warnings. He nods, raises his eyes to meet the Uzbek's. The other man has never been easy to read, and this time is no different, but Gabriel thinks he sees, perhaps, the hint of a question, the touch of doubt.

"No change?" Gabriel asks the Uzbek.

"No, as we discussed."

Gabriel looks back at the contents of the box, this seed that can be watered, coaxed to bloom and spread a pollen of illness. Carried by the wind to leave its touch wherever it might fall. Right now, only potential—and it is that potential, more than anything else, that has concerned him, confused him. The instructions here are clear, and yet, through their clarity, indecipherable. Gabriel does not understand.

The Uzbek senses this, puts his mouth to Gabriel's ear. "Place. Do not arm."

"Place, do not arm," Gabriel echoes.

The Uzbek straightens. "Do not concern yourself with the reasons. Concern yourself with the execution."

The Uzbek shuts the box, locks it once more. Gabriel feels the eyes of sixteen men on him as he takes the key. He turns to Vladimir, asks, "You've been briefed?"

"We've all been briefed."

Gabriel Fuller looks at the box holding the makings of a very dirty bomb. He looks at the Uzbek, and at the sixteen men once more.

"Let's go over it again," he tells them.

Chapter Seven

THE FIRST thing Bell does is argue with himself. He tells himself that WilsonVille is a popular vacation spot, that people come from all over the country, all over the world, even, to meet there. Family reunions and birthday parties and wedding anniversaries and, yes, of course, school trips to celebrate graduations or team victories or even the end of another year of education. He knows this, it's not open to debate, it does not require someone to convince him. Summer, too, sees the highest number of visitors to the park, and again, school trips are often scheduled during the summer vacation for all the obvious reasons.

All these things are true, but still, he cannot bring himself to accept his daughter's impending visit at face value. Whether he's being paranoid or simply cautious, he doesn't know, but at the least, due diligence is required. So Bell checks with WilsonVille reservations, asks them to look up the Hollyoakes School for the Deaf, and a bright-voiced woman named Vitoria confirms it for him within minutes; the Hollyoakes school has had their reservation and deposit down for almost twelve months now. Well in advance of his own placement in the park.

That should do it for Bell, that should satisfy, but it's

not enough, and now he knows he's being paranoid, thinking that the reservation could be backdated. He needs a harder confirmation, and that's easy enough to find in his position as the deputy director of park safety.

Tuesday morning, he collars Shoshana Nuri as soon as he's in the office.

"Have a job for you," he says.

"Sure."

"Verify a school trip this weekend, the Hollyoakes School for the Deaf, based out of Vermont."

"Should be in the database."

"It is in the database. I want a verbal, I want you to call the school."

"And say what?"

"Whatever you like, I just want the verbal confirmation. I want a confirmation on the dates, when they made the plans. Tell them you're double-checking, whatever you like. Do it now."

Shoshana Nuri raises an eyebrow, puzzled, then shrugs. Bell goes to his office, is just settling in when she sticks her head through the doorway.

"They confirm," she tells him.

Bell nods, and she holds a second longer.

"My daughter's school," he says.

"I see."

"Come in, close it," Bell tells her.

She does, standing just in the doorway.

"Here's my problem," Bell says. "My problem is I don't want them coming."

"You have new intel?"

"I have the same intel you do." He fixes his eyes on hers. "Unless you're holding back."

"I am not."

"I have the same intel you do."

"So you're being paranoid."

"It's my daughter and ex-wife." Bell pauses. "Of course I'm being paranoid."

Nuri considers this for a second, then nods. "Yes."

"I'm sending it up the line."

"To do what?"

"To put a stop to it."

Nuri shakes her head. "You'll compromise us."

"It's my daughter and my ex-wife, you think I care about that?"

"I do, yes."

For a moment, Bell thinks he might hate her, beautiful, young, smart, and absolutely right. He feels caught, a sudden surge of dread that is almost sickening rising in his gullet. The helplessness of watching an accident unfold with adrenaline clarity, the illusion of slowing time, without the grace of attendant speed.

"Think this through," Nuri says. She comes closer, approaching the desk, and Bell rises abruptly, suddenly wanting to maintain the space between them. "You think you're being played, you're being compromised, but it checks out. The timing checks out, makes this legitimate. This is a flat tire on the Humvee, this is a broken radio, this is a dead battery. That's all this is."

Bell doesn't speak.

"You send this up the line, you're compromised. They'll pull you out and have to scramble someone into your place and that will draw attention, will demand questions be asked and answers given. Operational security will be destroyed. They'll pull you out, and that'll expose your man, that'll leave me here, alone, high and dry. I am not a shooter, Mr. Bell. I am not a shooter."

"I am compromised. I am obligated to inform Brickyard. One way or another, I am obligated to inform."

She looks at him, her jaw clenching for a second. A nod, reluctant.

"You do what you have to do."

She leaves, shuts the door behind her.

Wednesday night, the Yard House, louder, and the volume on the televisions is up. Ruiz is waiting at the bar, a long oblong island in the middle of the space, and Bell squeezes in next to him, displacing a squadron of secretaries. Hears one of them remarking on his ass, loud enough to know it's a come-on, and all it does is annoy him.

Ruiz waits for him to order another of the same IPA, and they detach from the rail, move to a newly vacated standing table. Bell gets a good look at Ruiz's expression, and the colonel is not looking like a happy man.

"Are you asking me to pull you out?"

Bell has been wondering the same thing. Wondering the same thing and feeling, yet again, the same conflict that destroyed his marriage, the same conflict that divorce was supposed to remove.

"What's the intel?" Bell asks.

"Same as before. Are you asking to be pulled?"

"You can't cock-block them? You can't shut this down?"

"Not without exposure. I need an answer."

Bell shakes his head, arguing with himself. Too

many ifs, and if he knew, if he was certain, he could answer, and as he thinks that, he has his response. They're coming, Amy and Athena and the rest, they're coming regardless, unless he goes and stops them himself, and there it is.

Because if, God help him, it comes down this weekend and he's *not* in the park, he will never forgive himself.

"No," Bell says.

Four minutes past eight on Bell's watch, it's Saturday morning, and he hears them coming. Deaf children vocalize with joy, and without restraint, without self-censorship, without care. Then they grow, and they discover judgmental eyes, and self-awareness gives way to self-consciousness. They learn that their voices are unwelcome to many who hear, and they censor themselves. That he can hear them now, Bell knows, speaks to their excitement and their happiness.

Bell raises his head to see Athena and Amy and a man who must be Howe leading a pack of five other teenagers toward the faux-wrought-iron gates of the VIP entrance. He can almost recognize Athena's classmates—some of them, at least—young men and women with whom his daughter has grown up and who probably know her far better than he ever will. But the sight of her here and now, the distinctive sound of her laughter, her fingers flicking and flying in silent banter with her friends, banishes the guilt and the regret and, at least for the moment, the paranoia. Despite everything, Jad Bell is glad to see his daughter.

Amy spots him first, says something to Howe, takes

a stutter step forward, picking up speed. Athena reacts, follows her mother's line of motion toward Bell, and the smile on her face flashes into a scowl. No face reveals emotion like a teenager's, and the anger is still there in hers, but it fades as Shoshana Nuri unlatches the gate. Then his daughter is racing forward, eager, passing Amy and straight toward him, and Bell catches her. In that moment, in the early sunshine, in her hug, everything is forgiven. She squeezes him tightly, like she's six and not sixteen, lets him go, looks up at him. Brushes strawberry-blond hair from her eyes, gleeful.

"Hi, Dad." Athena speaks the words aloud, eager and atonal.

"Hello, Gray Eyes," Bell says.

She reads his lips, hugs him again, even more tightly than before, and then remembers that she's sixteen and that her friends are watching. Her hands slip away from him and she steps back, casting her eyes down in a moment of embarrassment. Bell sees this for what it is, turns to his ex-wife in an attempt to spare his daughter, leaning forward and giving Amy a kiss on the cheek. She accepts it with a smirk.

"Jad."

"You look good, Amy."

Her laugh is self-effacing, dismissive of the compliment as insincere, though he means it as anything but. A year younger than he, fit and healthy, she's more lovely than ever, Bell thinks. It's with some heartache that he recognizes that maturity has given her a confidence that was lacking in their youth. She's carrying a backpack over one shoulder, adjusts it as she gestures to the man who, presumably, is Howe.

"I don't think you two have actually met," Amy says. "Martin Howe, Jad Bell. Jad, this is Marty."

Howe offers his hand. He's two inches shorter than Bell, and slender, wearing khaki shorts just below his knees and an open blue oxford over a white T-shirt with the Hollyoakes school seal printed in navy at its center. Black hair that's a little too long, stubble that's almost verging to beard, black with touches of copper to it. When they shake hands, he squeezes a little harder than necessary, smiling, eager.

"Nice to meet you, Jad. Very nice to meet you at last."

Bell returns the pleasantry, frees his hand. Like Amy, Howe has a backpack of his own, similarly slung. Past them, Athena's classmates shuffle impatiently back and forth, silent conversations coming to a halt one after another as they await entry to Wilson-Ville. There are three boys, two more girls, most of them in jeans, a couple in shorts. All wear the Hollyoakes shirts.

"If you want to come over here?" Nuri says. She's speaking to Howe. "And have everyone line up?"

Howe nods, turns to the class, relaying the instruction in sign. The students fall into line, Athena giggling as she and one of the boys shoulder one another for position. The boy in question is African American, a hand taller than she, hearing aids visible in both ears. Athena glances to him, sees her father looking, looks away, and Bell is wondering just who this boy is when Amy puts a hand on his arm.

"I did everything I could," she says quietly. "But we couldn't just up and cancel without a good reason, Jad. It wouldn't be fair to the class."

Bell feels the tension return as if pouring from a pitcher into his breast. He forces a smile on Amy, puts his hand on her back, steering her a half dozen steps away from the group. She allows it, puzzled, then looks past him to where Nuri is speaking with Howe, and through him, to the class. Going through backpacks quickly, handing out the CELEBRATION! buttons for everyone to wear.

"So who's she?" Amy asks.

"Shoshana? She works with me. Listen." Bell faces her, head bent, and Amy looks up at him, and if it were twenty years ago, the next thing he would say would be "I love you" and then he'd be kissing her. But it's not, it's Saturday morning, closing on the end of summer, and there's been nothing from Ruiz, and Chain still hasn't found whatever the hell it was that got Vesques killed, and, for that matter, neither has Bell.

"Listen," he says again. "Stay together today. Don't let anyone wander off. Pay attention when you're on the rides, know where the exits are."

"We always do." Amy searches his expression, frowns. "Is this your normal paranoia or something else?"

"It's me asking you to do this thing, that's all it is."

"I'm thirty-nine, Jad, I think I know what I'm doing. I know it better than you do, in fact. This is no different than running a classroom or taking them on any other field trip."

"I'm not questioning your abilities, Amy."

"Sure sounds like it." She stares at him, the frown gone, mouth turning to a hard line. Bitterness and the memory of countless fights are swirling up between them, they can both feel it, and Bell can't even remember what the fights were about, but the sense of déjà vu is profound, and saddening.

"We all set?" It's Howe, coming up on Bell's periphery, his head inclined ever so slightly forward, almost solicitous. "Everything good?"

Amy, still glaring up at Bell, says, "Everything's fine, Marty."

"Good, great!" He stops beside them. "They're acting like colts in a stable, we should get moving."

Another moment's pause, awkward, and Bell knows that Athena and her class are watching them now—Nuri, too, most likely. He drops his head, breaking the stare with his ex, sighs before straightening up again, turning to look at Howe. "It's going to get busy today. If I were you guys, I'd hit the near attractions first, the Wild World stuff. The animal shows are best in the morning, before they get tired. Then maybe loop around the park counterclockwise. You make it up to Lion's Safari by ten or so you'll have a lead on the rest of the crowds, at least until around noon."

Bell gestures, pointing to one of the pathways that snakes away from where they're standing, to the northeast, skirting around Wild World Live! Howe follows the direction of his arm, nods, then checks the map in his hand. The standard park visitor's map. Nuri probably handed them out with the badges, Bell thinks.

"I'm not seeing anything here designated for the deaf, no services," Howe says. "When we planned the trip, the website said there were services."

"The website's correct. Just check in when you come off the line wherever you are, and as you enter, there'll be a Friend there. Let him or her know what you need."

"Multimedia on a lot of these rides." Howe taps the map. "If they're not captioned, I'd like an interpreter."

"The park utilizes reflective, handheld, and even open captioning, depending on the attraction. Just let the Friends there know, they'll take care of you."

Howe looks up from the map once more. "I was under the impression we'd have an escort, actually. An ASL interpreter."

Bell takes a second, thinking about this man, wondering if he's pushing because he thinks he can or because he thinks he must. If this man, Howe, is a sincere advocate for his students, trying to secure for them the best WilsonVille experience that he can. Bell thinks that if he'd spent the last ten years as a father and not a soldier, he would know the answer.

"I'll see what I can do about getting a dedicated interpreter assigned to the group," Bell says.

Howe smiles slightly, nods, relaxing. There's both a sense of relief and a vague disappointment coming from him, as if he has, perhaps, been cheated of battle. As if this is a fight Martin Howe has joined many times, and will do again. Bell knows the feeling, and it softens him immediately to the teacher.

"I'm in my office or on the grounds all day," Bell says, turning back to Amy. "I'm easy enough to find if you need anything. Just ask anyone in a blue blazer, they'll direct you."

"I think we'll be okay, Jad." She smiles thinly at him, then turns to where the class is clustered perhaps ten feet from Nuri. Amy raises her arm, flaps her hand loosely, immediately catching their attention. Before she's even begun to sign, they're surging forward, unable or unwilling to contain their eagerness. Howe gives Bell another grin, thanks him once more, then moves to join Amy as the group begins to follow her. She's taking the northeast pathway that Bell indicated, and that, at least, makes him feel a little better about things.

Athena shoots a glance back over her shoulder at him as they depart. Gives him another one of those smiles, signing quickly, small gestures.

Thank you Daddy I love you.

See you later Gray Eyes.

Her smile blossoms broader, and then she turns away, heading into the Wild World.

Chapter Eight

THE MAN who employs the Uzbek does not like video, and does not like voice, and does not like e-mail or text. The man who employs the Uzbek would be happier if all communications could be carried out in person, face-to-face, at the time and place of his choosing. The man who employs the Uzbek understands that there is little by way of privacy left in the world, and that there are always people listening.

Yet he also understands that sometimes concessions must be made. This communication with the Uzbek is one of those times, because of all the work this man does, of all the plans and plots and gambits in motion, this one, in the United States, in California, is the most daring, the most bold. And already, by far, the most lucrative.

So he makes the concession, and sits in front of a laptop computer in a rented apartment in Paris that has been acquired for this communication and this communication alone, and watches as the Uzbek's face appears on his screen. The video is one-way, as is the audio. The Uzbek will speak, but the other man will not. He will type, so that there will be no misunderstandings, and so that his own voice, in silence, will be loud.

At readiness?

The Uzbek answers in his flawless English. "We are."

I have no information on the investigation into the man our boy eliminated. That drew attention.

"Without question, but the investigation is centered outside of the location. He was smart about that."

Smart would have avoided the incident in the first place.

"It was bad luck."

Someone was looking. Someone in the line was not as discreet as they should have been. This is not tolerated.

"A job on this scale, someone somewhere is going to notice something." The Uzbek shifts in front of the camera, uncomfortable. Encryption leaves pixelated blocks that drag a fraction of a second behind his movement before resolving again. "I can confirm that security on this end is intact and absolute."

I know.

The Uzbek says nothing.

The problem arose at the source. It has been dealt with, but the damage is done.

"Are we calling it off?"

No.

The Uzbek nods.

The client's result is not our result. The client's result is incidental, as you know.

Another nod.

The client, however, is restless, and must be assuaged. I wish you to speak to him.

The Uzbek's expression does not change, which does him credit. "Is that necessary?"

I require it.

A nod. "Very well. I shall arrange it."

Explain to him that this is the last time I will accept such a request. Explain that to him quite clearly, please.

"Of course." A thin smile. "It will be a pleasure."

Restrain yourself. I am not done with him yet.

"Of course," the Uzbek repeats.

How is the boy?

The Uzbek raises a hand, adjusts his glasses, taking the moment to collect his thoughts. "He thinks he's in love."

Yes, the girl.

"Do you want me to act upon that? That will require more men, but I could . . ." The Uzbek trails off, leaving the implication open, unsaid.

No. Moving against her is coercion, and coercion will break faith with the boy. You have insurance in place.

"As instructed, yes."

Then that is enough. Let him use the girl for his own motivation. We need not do anything.

"Very well."

This is the last communication before action. Inform me upon completion. I look forward to your good work.

"Thank you."

The man who employs the Uzbek, who pulls the strings to Gabriel Fuller and sixteen more men in Southern California—and hundreds, thousands of others around the world—pauses, his fingers hovering above the keys of the laptop. He considers. He smiles to himself.

You're welcome.

These have been busy weeks for the Uzbek.

This last month alone, he has slipped unnoticed in and out of the United States four separate times to co-ordinate delivery and reconnaissance with operatives in Eastern Europe, South America, and the Middle East. He's seen to the paperwork, both legitimate and otherwise, for the operation; he has handled the recruitment for not one but two separate operational elements, of which Gabriel Fuller's is the second, and, frankly, the easier to direct. For the first, he was forced to work via a cutout to preserve anonymity, and this in turn has demanded an even greater vigilance to prevent directions from being misinterpreted or, worse, the exercise of initiative. To this end, he has received the package, the parcel that began its journey some 120 kilometers southwest of Tehran and traveled halfway around the globe, transferred from courier to courier until it was ultimately delivered into his own hands this past Friday morning. He has slept little, eaten poorly, traveled too much, and killed two people, murders that he judged necessary, even vital, to maintain the security and integrity of this operation.

None of these things is as difficult, for him, as dealing with Mr. Money, the client. Mr. Money, a man who doesn't like him and a man whom he does not like. Mr. Money, who demands things he has no right to demand, and threatens things he is foolish enough to believe he can control, and who has met the Uzbek's employer and master only once, and feels that entitles him to more. He does not understand that meeting him once was a gift. He does not understand that meeting him a second time would end with his own death, and that no amount of wealth in the world would prevent that.

"I didn't get where I am today by not knowing what the people working for me are doing, goddamn it."

He says this to the Uzbek on Wednesday, the day before the Uzbek is to meet Gabriel Fuller at the DoubleTree Spectrum hotel. Mr. Money says these words to the Uzbek in Dallas. Mr. Money had wanted to meet at a restaurant a handful of blocks from the Southern Methodist University campus. The Uzbek had refused. The requirement of needing to communicate in person—and *all* communications at this level were only to be conducted in person, because that was truly the only way to be certain beyond doubt that they were not observed or overheard—meant that the Uzbek was racking up frequent-flier miles. And each trip meant another set of papers burned, all so Mr. Money could feel that he was still vital and involved in what he had put into motion.

The Uzbek, personally, and with a growing passion, wanted the man dead. But that was bad business, at least as of now. Still, it was only at his master's order that he took the meeting, this last time, that he went to meet Mr. Money face-to-face to assure him that what he desired would come to pass, and come to pass quite soon.

But not in a restaurant; the Uzbek had refused that,

and refused (and marveled at the man's arrogance to even suggest such a thing) a second time when Mr. Money had offered to meet in his own home. It had been the Uzbek himself who had finally arranged the place and time for their meeting, an evening soccer match between FC Dallas and Toronto FC played at Pizza Hut Park.

In the cheap seats.

"Twelve thousand people and change here," Mr. Money said. "How is this better?"

The Uzbek shook his head. If the man didn't see anonymity in a crowd, silence in the noise, it wasn't worth explaining. In point of fact, he suspected that the man understood perfectly, and was simply annoyed at being asked to follow directions instead of issuing them himself.

"This will be our last contact," the Uzbek lied. "After this, further communication from you will be ignored. All the channels you have used to contact us are, as of this time, closed. I have been told to relay that to you explicitly. Should the need arise, we shall contact you, not the other way around."

"You were told? You were fucking told?" Mr. Money made a face, squinted out at the pitch, feigning interest in the game. "That man you work for, he should damn well have the courtesy to come in person, considering how much I'm paying for this."

"He pays you the courtesy of sending me, sir. Were it my decision, you would have been ignored entirely."

"I have a right to know what's going on."

"You do not." The Uzbek paused, leaning forward in his seat to watch a corner kick play out right of the near goal line. The ball curled wide, then was headed out of play. He sat back once more. "You have a right to a result, that is all. Knowing how that result will be achieved only serves to compromise you."

"I hope that's not a threat." The man squinted behind his tortoiseshell sunglasses, glanced at the Uzbek.

"It's the furthest thing from it. But you have contracted for a result within parameters that you yourself defined. This result cannot be achieved hastily, and it cannot be achieved haphazardly. You must give us time to work."

"I have given you time to work. I've given you the better part of a goddamn year to work."

"The result, as I said, is not one that can be achieved in haste."

"There's an election coming up."

"You're an American. There is always an election coming up."

Mr. Money grunted, resumed watching the game playing out beneath them, or at least feigned interest in doing so. Then he slapped his thighs with his hands, grunting again, climbing to his feet. The man squinted behind his sunglasses, glanced the Uzbek's way. He was short, and growing old, and physically there was nothing intimidating or even powerful about him. But when he spoke next, he did so with the confidence of a man half his age and twice his size.

"You fuck me around, I will most surely fuck you back. You and your boss. Neither of you is as insulated and mysterious as you might think." Mr. Money tapped at his temple with a long index finger. "You've got reach, but I do, too."

"You have paid for a service," the Uzbek said, looking up at him. "You will have your result."

"I damn well better have it."

Taking the last word, the older man began edging his way along the row to the aisle. The Uzbek watched until he was descending the stairs, then stole a glance at his watch before turning his eyes back to the match. If traffic was with him, he could stay until the half before catching his flight to Anaheim.

Chapter Nine

GABRIEL FULLER ducks through a FRIENDS ONLY door on the northwest side of Town Square at six minutes past ten o'clock, out of sight and traffic and into a small, ten-by-ten-foot courtyard, walled by buildings on all sides. The sun isn't quite high enough to beat the angle, and there's shade here, and he puts his back to the wall to his right, to stay out of the way of the Friends moving back and forth.

He wrestles his hands free from his paws before pulling Pooch from his head. The end of his second shift already, and as the headpiece comes off and he tastes fresh air, he can feel his heart pounding and the sweat running down his back. It's hot today, already hot, but that's not why he's perspiring, that's not what's making his heart race.

He cuts between a Royal Flashman and a Smooch the Baby Elephant emerging from the doorway opposite, makes his way down the stairs into the Gordo Tunnel. There are more Friends here, some in character, but mostly just custodial staff and service personnel. He nearly runs over a guy in a Star System Alliance maintenance uniform, mutters an apology to him, turns into one of the common areas, and then into the Gordo South changing area. Most of the characters are already out in the park, and the room is empty but for a single Betsy. She's an Asian woman, and her un-masked head looks absurdly small as it pokes up from Betsy's cartoon-width shoulders. He's guessing she's in her early twenties, and she's just sitting there on one of the benches, holding the headpiece to her costume, staring into Betsy's eyes.

"Fucking awful out there today," she says, and Gabriel wonders if she's talking to Betsy or to him.

"Tell me about it." Gabriel drops Pooch's head and the paws on the bench, begins to unfasten the buckles and tabs at his waist.

The woman sighs, rises with a supreme effort. "Once more unto the breach, dear friends, once more..." she says, and her head is disappearing into Betsy's, and her last words come out muffled, but dis-tinct. "And close up this park with the bodies of these privileged dead..."

Gabriel Fuller, half out of his Pooch costume, stares after her, feeling an absurd flare of panic. Can she know? How can she possibly know?

But she can't know, no one knows, he tells himself. *Another out-of-work actor, that's all, every other damn person working here is an out-of-work actor, calm down....*

The clock on the wall here is reading eighteen min-utes past ten, WilsonVille Standard Time. He's still on schedule, still on the timetable. He sits, pulls off the boots, then kicks his way out of the leggings. Then it's the chest piece, and now he's standing there in his sneakers and a body stocking that's drenched with sweat. Dana once told him that she'd heard someone else say that some of the characters go naked inside their costumes, but she didn't believe it, because if that went wrong could you imagine how quickly you'd get fired? The next day, Gabriel had taken her down to this same changing area and showed her one of the Pooch costumes in all its component glory, including letting her take a whiff of it. It had been freshly laundered, too, and it still smelled ripe.

No way would I ever want to be naked in that, he'd told her.

No way would I ever want you to be, she'd said, laughing.

He moves to the locker where he's stowed his clothes, works the combination with quick presses of the keypad, listening to the chirp as each digit is acknowledged. He peels himself out of his bodysuit, glancing around once more. He's on duty for another three hours today, and if a manager comes by and recognizes him, he doesn't want to explain why he's changing clothes or, worse, why it is he's committed the near-capital crime of leaving Pooch in pieces on the floor.

But nobody comes by, nobody interrupts him, and the clock is now reading twenty-one minutes past ten, WilsonVille Standard Time, as he straightens from tying his boots. He gives Pooch a shove with one foot, knocking the costume further under a bench, then moves back into the hallway, turning north, along the Gordo Tunnel. Walking like he knows where he's going and like he belongs here, both of which are true, he steps to the side of the hallway as two custodians come rushing toward him, past him, paying no mind. One wheels a mop bucket, the other a garbage can, and he knows they're racing to clean up a "protein spill," and from the way they're hustling, whoever blew chunks topside chose to do it at an inopportune moment or in an inopportune place or, conceivably, both.

The tunnel hits a T intersection about thirty meters further along, where it's bisected by the Flashman Tunnel, and Gabriel makes a right, heading east. Overhead, in the park, he's approaching Flower Sister country, and the traffic in the tunnel reflects that. He passes two Lavenders in whispered conversation, another Friend in a navy blazer escorting a forty-something woman who is weeping openly, and since she's too old to be lost, Gabriel figures she's about to be arrested for something. It occurs to him that what's going to happen in the next seventeen or so minutes may, possibly, be seen as a favor to her of sorts.

But probably not.

The Flashman Tunnel, like the Gordo Tunnel, has maintenance hallways branching off it, their designations painted on the walls at each juncture. He turns south, opens the door on his right, and steps into the Flashman E-5 compressor room. The lighting in here is even dimmer than in the tunnels, and he gives himself a couple of seconds for his eyes to adjust. Then he moves forward, skirting around the main ductwork that juts from the center of the floor and the hissing, thrumming machinery that closes in on three sides. The noise is enough that he doesn't trust his ears to warn him, and so he takes another look over his shoulder, just to be certain he's alone, before dropping to his belly and reaching beneath a snarl of machinery for the duffel bag. There is a moment—just a moment—with his arm extended and his fingers closing on nothing when he thinks it isn't there, that it's been discovered. Then his fingertips are stroking ripstop nylon, and he's pulling the bag free, unzipping it.

He assembles the pistol, then loads and chambers his first round. Next, he takes out the radio, switches it on. He has to hold it to his ear when he keys the transmit button twice in rapid succession, saying nothing, listening for the slight *squelch* that tells him it's working, even if, below ground, sending or receiving any radio transmission is hopeless. He gets to his feet, tucking the pistol into his waistband, smoothing his shirt down. The radio he leaves on, but, returning to the duffel, exchanges it for the cell phone.

He sees the knife then, closed, where he left it, and takes it out, turning it in his hand. In the light here, he can't be sure, but he thinks he sees the dried blood from the man he had to kill. The man who made it necessary to move this cache.

The man had fought like a lion. The man had fought for his life.

He clips the knife in his pocket, zips the duffel closed, pulls the straps up his left arm, onto his shoulder. With purpose, he leaves the compressor room, turns back into the Flashman Tunnel, retracing his steps. He passes other employees, then a clock, and it's now thirty-nine minutes past ten, WilsonVille Standard Time. He'll be cutting it close, he knows it.

He reaches the T intersection again, turns south once more onto Gordo, walking back in the direction he came as quickly as he dares. Friends, custodians, safety officers bustle about, moving in all directions, the energy and crowd above reflected in the motion and purpose around him. Voices seem louder, though he thinks that might be adrenaline. He reaches one of the ramps up to the surface, emerges into the courtyard behind the Dawg Days Theatre, on the north side of Town Square. There's a blue-blazer Friend here, his job to make certain nobody wanders around backstage who shouldn't, and he gives Gabriel a nod of greeting, and Gabriel returns it. Through the walls, he can hear the sound effects of one of the Pooch cartoons playing in the theater, a ripple of delighted laughter from the audience.

He steps outside, into sunlight that's shocking in its brightness and that renders him blind for an instant. A rush of noise accompanies it, the sound of the crowd and the clatter of cars racing along the wooden slats of Pooch Pursuit, rising up above and behind him, almost two hundred feet away. Shrieks of gleeful terror and piped music and voices jabbering and laughing.

Gabriel turns right, coming around the side of the building, looking across Town Square. This time, he checks his watch, and it is now a quarter to eleven precisely. On schedule, everything going to plan. Even with the crowds, the vendors, the Friends in costume signing autographs, he can be where he needs to be, easy.

He sees Dana.

She's walking with a woman, and Gabriel can tell that the woman is a guest by the CELEBRATION button on her shirt, visible even from here, big and sky-blue, with the letters in pink. The woman is maybe forty, attractive, wearing the expression of a harried mother. Dana's wearing one of the navy blazers, and her posture shows that she's listening hard to this woman, nodding, answering her, friendly and reassuring.

His first urge, almost uncontrollable, is to go to her, to take Dana by the hand and pull her after him toward the front gates, to get her out, to get her out *now*. Six minutes, now five, and even as he thinks that, he knows he can't do it, that it'll pull him off the schedule, that it will indict him.

She'll be all right, he tells himself. *She'll be fine.*

But his stomach is turning like flesh-eating worms in his belly, and he feels helpless and sick, and Dana and this woman are still walking together, heading north. North, away from the front gates. North, heading in his direction.

He turns parallel to their course, as if heading for the great big Wilson Restaurant, where there's already a line formed for late brunch or early lunch. The menus are posted, and he can pretend to look at them as he watches out of his peripheral vision. Lilac's Vegetarian Delight and Hendar's Double-Patty Melt and Pooch's Treat, an ice cream sundae big enough for three to share. Dana's still talking to this woman, and he thinks he can hear her laugh above the voices all around as they come closer, closer, and then he hears the woman speaking.

"Well, they're teenagers, so they never listen anyway. Being deaf is just a convenient excuse..."

Dana laughs just as she passes behind him.

"I'm sure it'll be all right."

"You're fluent with ASL?"

"I am, yes, started learning sign in high school and continued with course work when I got to UCLA. I'll be a senior in the fall..."

He loses the rest as someone demands to know why the hell this line isn't moving. Steps back, watches Dana and this other woman continuing northeast now, along one of the main walkways that feed into Wild World. Then they're swallowed by the crowds that seem to ebb and flow like tides on the way to the Euro Strasse.

He checks his watch. He's burned three minutes, almost four.

It takes another two and a half to get across Wilson Town, to cross Town Square from the northeast to the southwest. He's jostled and cursed at, and he can't run, because first, there's not enough room, and second, running would draw attention, especially running against the prevailing foot traffic. So he's weaving, moving as quickly as he can, until he reaches the entrance to the Olde Tyme Arcade, just north of the Sheriff's Office. Inside, he can see the place is perhaps half full, mostly young men and boys playing at pinball machines and refurbished video game cabinets. He turns, casting an eye at the front of the Sheriff's Office, then back to the square.

He pulls out the cell phone, not his personal phone, but rather the one from the duffel, and switches it on, waits for it to find a signal. When the clock syncs, he can see that he is in the right place, at the right time. Gabriel works the keys, bringing up the first of four designated calling groups. With one press, he can send multiple calls, a feature designed, he assumes, for conference calling or mass texting, but now repurposed, albeit slightly. He has four groups, north, south, east, and west, and to do this properly, he has to know the wind.

He licks his lips, closes his eyes. Turns slowly, trying to feel the breeze, if there even *is* a breeze. He feels the skin on his lips tighten, the moisture evaporating. He opens his eyes once more, and finds himself facing north-northeast. Bunting and banners, WilsonVille flags sway slightly, confirming the wind, barely felt, coming in from the Pacific, entering the park from the west.

Thumb on the button, Gabriel Fuller brings the phone to his ear, pretending to listen as he calls group four. He hears the ring in his ear, then abrupt silence, as each phone answers and instantly commits suicide. Holds it for a second longer before hanging up, turning toward the arcade once more. Groups one and three will need to be next, and they'll need to go off in quick succession for maximum effect.

It took six weeks to place each device, each carefully wrapped bundle of powder, phone, and charge. Brought into the park a little at a time, hidden on his person or in his backpack, and the phones he didn't even bother to hide at all. So he was carrying two cell phones, big deal, and nobody even noticed, nobody ever commented.

Now he's moving up the west side of Town Square, passing the carnival games, the ringtoss, the baseball throw. There's a soda vendor at the corner, and he buys himself an overpriced bottle of water, doesn't bother trying to get his employee discount. He looks southward, watching the entrance to the Sheriff's Office. Presses the button on the phone, dialing group one, then just as quickly hangs up and dials group three.

For almost four minutes, there is no activity from those doors. Nothing at all.

Then they are opening, now a flood of navy-blue blazers emerges, radios in hands, and Gabriel can tell just by the way they're moving that they're scared. They scatter in all directions, some of them pushing through the crowd for the main gates, some heading in his direction, then past him, going deeper into the park. And one, a middle-aged black woman, heavyset and urgent, heading his way, and he can hear what she's saying to the people all around him as she moves. She's waving for attention, pointing toward the south.

The music in the square stops, followed by the crackle and shriek of hundreds of hidden speakers switching to PA. It gets attention, calls for silence, and there is just an instant, then, when WilsonVille seems to freeze, only the sound of the rides still running filling the gap. Gabriel checks the phone in his hand, bringing up group two, the last half dozen charges. Thumb poised over the SEND button.

Your attention, please.

A man's voice, and Gabriel thinks that he's hearing the strain in it, the stress, and he can't stop himself from smiling.

Your attention, please. This is Eric Porter, director of park and resort safety. With regret, we announce that due to unforeseen difficulties, WilsonVille will be closing for the day, effective immediately. Friends will help you make your way to the nearest exit. Please follow their directions in a calm and orderly fashion. We apologize for the inconvenience...

Gabriel Fuller doesn't bother looking down at the phone in his hand. He just presses the SEND button one last time. Eric Porter is still speaking, repeating the announcement, and behind him he hears another voice over the speakers, and he can't hear the words, but he recognizes the tone, the anxiety in it, and it gives him a strange, wonderful sense of satisfaction and power.

He's not the only one who's heard it, either. All around him, people are beginning to react, some still listening, others already in motion, and some are trying to be calm, some are trying to be orderly. But not all of them, not the ones who are thinking that the way they came in is the quickest way to get out, and voices are starting to rise and still Eric Porter is on the PA, and Gabriel thinks that he can hear that strain in his voice even more now.

The man never uses the words "evacuation" or "emergency" or anything that might cause a panic.

He never, ever says the words, "toxin" or "gas" or anything like that.

Gabriel Fuller doesn't say those words, either, despite the momentary, perverse pleasure the thought gives him. Like shouting "Fire!" in a crowded movie house or "Bomb!" in an airport security line. That is not the plan, however, that is not what the Uzbek is counting on him to do, and the thought of what the wrong word could now cause has him thinking of Dana again. Dana, who should be at their apartment, taking the day off, and not here because she can interpret for the deaf.

He doesn't want anything to happen to her. It would kill him if something happened to her, he realizes. So a calm, orderly evacuation, and by the time the authorities know what's really going on, Dana and everyone else will be outside the gates, and they'll be safe. Then all he'll have to do is get through the rest of this day. Get through this day and into the night and he'll disappear for a few days after that, and then he'll make his way back, back to her.

Now he's being carried along in the press of people, and they've passed the Sheriff's Office, coming up on the WilsonVille Store, so many people, and they're being herded, so tightly together. He almost misses his chance, fakes stumbling, rights himself, allows himself to be turned around. Stumbles again, and then he's through the door of the store, and just as he knew it would be, it's already empty, already cleared. Racks and racks of official WilsonVille Wear, and he drops low, out of the sight line of the windows, but more important, out of the sight line of the cameras watching the store.

Belly-crawling his way to the main bank of registers, a broken circle of counter smack in the middle of the room, pushing his duffel ahead of him as he goes. He takes it slow. With the evacuation running, he can't imagine that anyone who's still watching the video monitors in the command post is paying attention to the interior of any store, let alone this one. Still, he keeps his movements deliberate and controlled, for fear of catching anyone's eye.

The cabinets beneath the register are locked, and Gabriel has to go into his pocket, comes back with his knife. It's a horrible thing to do to a blade, a disrespectful way to treat it, but it's the only tool he has. He snaps it out and forces it into the gap, working it up and down until he hits the latch. It's a tight fit, and he slams his palm into the base of the handle, and wood splinters as metal is forced into the gap. He twists, wrenches, thinking the knife is going to snap. There's a crack as the lock gives way.

He stows the blade, opens the now-broken doors. There's the squat tower for the computer that runs the register, still powered. A snarl of cables running from it, and then, beside it, the blinking green lights of the router. He pulls it free, turns it in his hands, and God bless WilsonVille Technical Services, because each port is clearly labeled with a small white printed sticker. There are two marked VIDEO, and he pulls the cords from each, turns the cameras watching the interior of the store blind.

He replaces the router, tries to get the doors to close again as best he can, then is into the duffel, now removing the carefully folded Tyvek suit, the gas mask. He's breathing quickly, heart racing, hearing the voices outside as he changes, and then, just sitting there, back to the counter, gas mask in his lap.

He just wants this to be over. He just wants to get through this. Then he'll have done what the Uzbek wanted, what the Shadow Man has required, and he can make his way back to Dana, and never leave her again.

He can make his way back to Dana, and be Gabriel Fuller for the rest of his life.

If he can just get through this day.

Chapter Ten

BELL HAS just signed the authorization allowing time and a half for Dana Kincaid, the ASL interpreter he's brought in for Athena and Amy and Howe and the rest, when Nuri shoves his office door open. There's no knock, and he looks up and sees it in her eyes, and before she's finished speaking he's out of the chair and moving, feeling the dread bursting in him like exploding glass.

"The Spartan," Nuri says, backing up as he approaches, then pivoting, falling into step. "Alarm just spiked in the southwest of the park, near Terra Space."

"Bio or chem?"

"It's reading botulinum."

A cold fear latches onto Bell's back, begins trying to claw its way into his chest. "Got to be a false positive."

"And just wouldn't that be nice? Struss is running a diagnostic now, but we don't know how long it's going to take."

"What's the wind?"

"Blowing from the south-southwest, about three knots."

"Botulinum?"

"Yeah." Her voice is flat, the doubt and the concern canceling one another out, Bell imagines.

They're coming down the stairs, now, from the third floor to the command post on the second, and Bell is taking them two, three at a time. Nuri, a handbreadth shorter but long-legged, nonetheless struggles to keep up. Bell runs the numbers in his head, three knots an hour, 156 acres, converts to metric, says, "Little over eight minutes before it covers the park."

"Closer to seven, if we assume even distribution, constant wind speed, which we can't. But we're talking about an unknown, it could be less, could be more."

Nuri leans ahead of him, shoves the door open into the second-floor command post. Heads turn, and Bell can see the fear, hear the silence of the room as he moves to the air monitoring station, where a middle-aged Norman Struss is working a shift that's on the verge of turning into a nightmare. Bell ignores the man, feels eyes on him, Nuri's among them, as he stares at the monitor. The Spartan's screen lists chem and bio agents in columns, has its own section for radiation, and it's flickering through readings as though it were flipping through a slide show. Then it settles, displaying an image much like an EKG, with multiple color-coded lines running across a horizontal axis. Negative anthrax, negative sarin, negative cyanogen, negative radiation, negative, negative, negative, negative.

Except this one, this line that is flexing and spiking and pulsing in bright red, marked BOTULINUM. A callout, recording estimated concentration per sample taken. Lethality is measured by median lethal dose, or LD50, the amount of any given agent that will kill 50 percent of a population exposed to it. Bell is thinking about botulinum, thinking about context, remembering VX nerve agent. A lethality of roughly thirty micro-grams to one kilogram of human being, or, to put it another way, in aerosol form, one breath of it delivers enough toxin to kill 150 people.

That's VX, Bell remembers.

But botulinum toxin, appropriately weaponized, has a theoretical LD50 of three nanograms per kilogram. That's a thousand times more lethal. This is the same stuff that Aum Shinrikyo tried to manufacture before giving up on it and switching to sarin when they at-tacked the Tokyo subway system. They gave up on it because they could never get the vector to work prop-erly.

A problem somebody else seems to have solved.

It's not an instant death. Symptoms on average be-gin to present at six hours to two days after exposure, but there have been cases of incubation within two to three hours, and within as long as four days. Unlike VX or sarin, which cause seizure and paralysis, bo-tulinum causes muscle atrophy, loss of control, and, inevitably, respiratory failure. Victims suffocate, their diaphragms literally unable to work their lungs.

Bell doesn't know how many people are in the park today. He doesn't know how many people are at Dis-neyland, or Knott's Berry Farm, or even how many live in Irvine and its environs. But he's pretty damn sure that if the Spartan II is reading botulinum and if it's telling the truth, then there's more than enough traveling in the air to spread far and wide beyond the confines of WilsonVille.

Nuri has the phone ready, hands it to him as he

reaches out, then puts an extension to her own ear. Bell doesn't look away, staring at that monitor. The Spartan II that he just doesn't trust. The Spartan II that maybe is lying to him, but is maybe telling him the truth, and he has to push, and push hard, to keep the thoughts of Amy and Athena from overwhelming his reason. Nuri at his elbow, and she's watching him carefully, and he shakes his head just barely.

Marcelin's voice on the line now. "Jad? What's going on?"

"Waiting on Porter," Bell says.

"I'm here. We've got alarms relaying through the office, I was just about to—"

"The Spartan tripped for airborne botulinum, now at forty-three micrograms per sample."

"Jesus Christ," Marcelin says.

"We've got a diagnostic running, but it's going to be"—Bell looks at Norman Struss, who holds up his left hand, shows him five fingers, then five fingers again, then five fingers a third time—"fifteen minutes before it's completed, before we know whether it's a system fault or not."

There's a fraction's pause, both men at the ends of the lines absorbing, digesting. Marcelin speaks before Porter, his voice controlled. "Could it be a false positive?"

"No way to tell at the moment."

"It doesn't fit the profile," Porter mutters, speaking more to himself than to them. "It doesn't fit their profile, you can't just weaponize botulinum, it's not something you can do in a high-school chem lab, it's not in their profile."

On the monitor, the pulsing line jumps, the machine bleats again, repeatedly. Norman Struss taps keys quickly, silencing the Spartan. "New readings, now central north side, from Fort Royal to the coaster. It's spreading. Jesus, it's spreading."

"You guys hear that?"

"It doesn't make sense. If this is retribution, they'd take a suicide run at the gates, blow themselves and take whoever they can with them, go out like true believers shouting it to the clouds. Run a truck loaded with ANFO into the parking lot, that's the profile. This doesn't make sense!"

"How long will it take to evacuate the park?" Marcelin asks.

Bell looks to Nuri, about to ask her, sees that she's been writing on a piece of paper. She holds it up before he can ask the number: 49K AS OF 1030H.

"We're over forty-nine thousand," Bell says into the phone. "Best case, we can clear the park in twenty minutes. That's best case, Matt. And I'd want to second-sweep for stragglers."

"Shut it down, evacuate the park," Porter says. "Jesus Christ, shut it down now, Matthew!"

"Jad?"

Bell is still staring at the monitor. His head believes what he's seeing, but he can feel it in his gut, there's something not right about this. Something about the way the sensors are tripping, the way the toxin seems to be spreading, but he can't articulate it, can't find words to fit the feeling.

"You're going to have to intake, treat, nearly fifty thousand people," Bell says, the image, unbidden and imagined, Athena lying on a gurney, pumped full of antitoxin, unable to even gasp for breath behind a bag valve mask. "You're talking about men, women, children, the elderly, all the staff—"

"You want to take that chance?" Porter is quietly ferocious. "You're thinking about WilsonVille, I'm thinking about Southern fucking California. This shit doesn't care where the park ends, Bell!"

"If that's what it is."

"What else can it be?" Marcelin asks.

"You want to take the chance it's a false positive? You want to take that chance? Because I sure as hell won't."

"I agree," says Bell. "Doesn't matter, Eric's right. We have to clear the park."

"Do it," Marcelin says, and there's no hesitation or doubt in his tone.

Immediately, over the line, Bell can hear Porter shouting for Wallford. Send up the balloon, local, state, federal, call them all, we've got a biotoxin event originating in the WilsonVille theme park.

Marcelin continues, "Eric, get on the PA, make the announcement. Jad, get my park empty and then get yourself and your people out of there."

"On it."

"Make it happen."

Bell hangs up his phone, sees again all the faces watching him, this room of twenty-odd people, twenty-odd Friends. All of them, plus one, a new addition, and everyone feels it, wondering if it's already seeping into their lungs. Wondering how much time they have. Nuri is at the duty officer's desk, has the big blue binder out, and nobody else is moving, waiting for him, waiting to hear it. He knows what he says now matters, and he hopes to God he can get it right.

"We are evacuating the park," Bell says. "We are evacuating the park. Hear me, hear what I'm saying. You know what I know. You know what it *might* be. What it *might* be, not what it is."

Nuri is back, opening the binder and setting it on the console in front of him. Bell can read the heading on the open page: PROCEDURE IN EVENT OF EVACUATION. She looks at him, and he nods, and she moves away, toward the line of radios locked down and sitting in their chargers.

"I'm going to give you your posts," Bell says. "Take a radio, take a light, take your posts, clear the park. That's all you have to do, just that. Just that, and one thing more.

"You cannot lose your nerve. Not a single one of you, not now. We have to get this right. The wrong word will start a panic. The wrong word will get people killed. You know that word, you've heard that word, but that's all it is right now. That's all it is, just a word. It's just a word."

He stops, feels that he's spoken too much, that his own words—just words—are inadequate. But people are watching him, and he sees the resolve, a few of them nodding. They're getting to their feet, and Nuri has the radios out, ready to distribute them, and so Bell takes the binder, and starts calling people by name.

One by one, he sends them out into the park with nothing but a flashlight, a radio, and their courage.

*   *   *

The room clears, is all but empty, when Nuri moves to Bell's side, opening her mouth to speak. He holds up a hand, indicates Norman Struss, still manning the Spartan II, still trying to gauge the machine's potential duplicity; Heather Heoi at the network station, on the coms; and finally Neal Bailey, watching the surveillance monitors. All of them are grim, all of them focused on their work, but Bell can see the beads of sweat shining on Struss's balding head, and he knows how frightened all of them must be. He cannot fault them for that.

"Right, get outside, help with the evac," Bell tells them.

The Spartan begins bleating once more, and Struss quickly silences it with two keystrokes. The man's shoulders slump, then rise once more, and when he turns in his seat, the expression he's wearing is both apologetic and somehow resolved. Bailey refuses to glance away from the monitors, and Heoi is looking at him almost sadly.

"Someone's got to babysit this thing," Norman Struss says. "Someone has to wait for the diagnostic to come back."

"I've got a job to do," Bailey says simply.

Heoi nods slightly.

"Doesn't have to be you guys. Grab a radio and get outside, help with the front gate."

"I appreciate what you're trying to do, Mr. Bell," Bailey says. "But this was my job today. Wouldn't be right for me to leave another to do it. You need eyes here, anyway, someone to check and make sure everything gets cleared out."

"I'll take it," Nuri says.

"Not your job, either, Miss Nuri."

Bell is scanning the monitor banks, the surveillance video. A time stamp in the upper corner of one of the screens tells him it's been all of five and a half minutes since Nuri fetched him from his office. The evacuation is already in progress, people moving en masse, and he can see it on the screens. There's a Hendar leading a young man by the hand, one of the concession Friends waving the glow sticks he sells above his head as he leads a cluster of confused and anxious parents with their children. He's seeing all this, but Bell is not seeing panic, and that's maybe the best he can hope for.

He is also not seeing any sign of the group from Hollyoakes school. If they'd done as suggested, they should be on the north side of the park, guided to either the northwest or northeast service exits, and out into the employee lots. Further along the bank of screens, he can see a view of the gates in question, visitors flooding through them. In the northeast lot, one of the first responder teams has already arrived, a fire engine and a group of what looks to be six men suiting up for hazmat work, white jumpsuits and gas masks.

He still doesn't see Athena, still doesn't see Amy.

And he still can't shake the feeling that something about this isn't right, isn't what it seems at all.

Norman Struss, Heather Heoi, and Neal Bailey are all looking at him.

"Second it comes back, you contact me," Bell says to Struss.

"Second it comes back, you'll know," Struss says.

They're coming off the stairs and into the fake police station, finding it deserted, hearing the muffled noise from the foot traffic outside, when Nuri says, "What're we doing?"

Bell has his cell phone out, the real one, the secured one, not the office one. Presses it to his ear, ignoring Nuri, listening as it rings once, twice, is halfway through its third, when Amy picks up. There's ambient noise over the line immediately, and he can hear someone shouting for people to stay calm, to follow him.

"Jad?" Amy sounds calm, if a little breathless. "Jad, what the hell is going on?"

"The park is being evacuated. Do you have Athena with you?"

"What?" The noise over the line swells, a background of multiple voices, the reverb of Porter on the PA. "We're—hold on—we're being evacuated."

"Is everyone with you? You have everyone with you?"

"Yes. We're with that girl, the one you got for us. She's leading us out. There are park people everywhere."

"She'll get you out, just follow her directions. I'll be in touch."

"Jad? What's going on?"

"I'll call you later."

"This is why you didn't want us coming, isn't it? This is—"

Bell hangs up, hits another button, raises the phone again. Nuri has moved away, she's now standing by the double doors, looking out as she speaks on her own phone. She glances his way, and from her look Bell has a good idea just who it is she's talking to, and maybe even what he's telling her.

"Chain, Warlock. Sitrep."

"Assisting southwest evac. You inviting me to this dance or am I going stag?"

"It's not that you don't look pretty in a dress," Bell says. He's moved closer to Nuri, now lowering her phone. Bell looks out the windows of the double doors, and the mass of people beyond is like a moving wall of flesh and anxiety. A man passes, pushing a stroller, wife with diaper bag right behind, pulling a little boy along by his hand. The boy is in tears, dragging a stuffed Rascal doll by its tail. As he watches, someone steps on the monkey, the boy losing his grip. He wails in protest, but his parents don't stop.

"What we got?"

"Something in the air."

"I need to hold my breath?"

"Too late for that."

Nuri makes a noise, shakes her head. Bell ignores her.

"Am I coming to you or you coming to me?"

"Neither," Bell says. "Heading for the Keep."

"You're bringing the Angel?"

"Negative."

"Roger that," says Chain, and the line goes dead.

"That was some mighty macho bullshit," Nuri says. "You want to tell me what you're thinking?"

Bell tucks his phone away. "I'm thinking that if someone had aerosolized botulinum you or I or some-one we know would've heard about it. I'm thinking if someone *has* done it, we're all dead anyway. I'm thinking it's a hell of a good way to get a park all to yourself, and I'm thinking that I've never seen a dispersal pattern that uniform in twenty years of looking at worst-case scenarios."

"Funny."

"Funny?"

"I was thinking the same thing. Minus the twenty years part."

"Good, then you'll love the next bit. Get back into the command post and keep an eye on things."

Her jaw tightens. "I'm coming with you."

"That's a negative. Real or not, there's someone on the inside, someone who planted the botulinum or mind-fucked the Spartan. If that someone is upstairs right now, they have access to all our intel, our coms, our eyes, and all of it is compromised. I need someone I trust upstairs, and Chain's not here, so I'm stuck with you."

"Those aren't my orders."

"They are now, Angel. What's the word of the day?"

Her eyes are more brown than hazel in this light, and anger flashes in them. "The word of the day is 'buzzsaw.' You don't trust me?"

"The word of the day is 'buzzsaw,'" Bell agrees. "I've got mission coms in my office, in the desk, middle left, back. You get a chance, plug in. Chain or I will contact as soon as we're on the net."

"You didn't answer my question."

Bell pushes on the doors, feels the wash of heat, the sunlight, the noise of the evacuating park.

"Of course I don't trust you," Bell says. "You're CIA."

Then he wades into madness.

Chapter Eleven

ATHENA DOESN'T like most hearing people.

They're too much trouble, and they don't *get* it, and pretty much all of them have no idea how to treat the deaf, anyway. Some of them freeze up and some of them just pretend there's nothing different and sometimes, some of them, they act like it's contagious or something. Like they can somehow *catch* deaf, like Athena can pass it on, which would be a trick and a half, especially because she doesn't know how or why she lost her hearing, can't remember if she really ever had it, and nobody else does, either. That's not uncommon, Mom told her, the same time she told her that something like 90 percent of all deaf kids are born to hearing parents.

It just happens, Mom said.

So she doesn't like hearing people that much, most of them, and the jury is still out with this woman Dana, but it's looking pretty good for her. Dana signs a little slow, and it's hard not to get impatient talking to her, but she's been nice and she's funny, and she doesn't break eye contact the way most hearing people do when you try to talk to them. People who can hear, Athena has learned, don't like it when you keep looking them in the eye. They get uncomfortable the longer you do it. People who can hear don't understand that it's the eyes and the face and the thousand microgestures and movements coming from each that make up communication.

Best of all, Dana doesn't do any of that bullshit silly embarrassed awkward stuff that people do when they're uncomfortable around Athena and her friends. Dana's going to be a senior at UCLA and she wants to be a teacher of the deaf, and when they were talking after the Timeless River Cruise, she told Athena she has a boyfriend who works here in WilsonVille, too. When Dana told her that, she kind of blushed, and it made Athena laugh. Dana laughed, too, and that scored her major points, because sometimes when Athena laughs, people stare, and she understands why; her mother explained that to her once, too.

Because of how you sound, Mom said. *A surprising sound to them.*

Bad?

No! Not a bad sound, Mom said, and she spelled out "no" instead of just shaking her head, totally meant it. *Never! Beautiful sound your voice even if you cannot hear it you laugh when you like all you like. Anybody has a problem with that they can take it up with your father and me.*

Athena had smiled when she said that, and not just because Mom is fierce, but because Dad wasn't at home; he was someplace he wouldn't ever tell them, fighting Bad Guys. There was a lot about her dad that Athena didn't understand, not even now, but she understood one thing, and she understood it without ever having to be told. Her dad was a soldier, he was a warrior, and he went to fight a lot of Bad Guys, and he always came back.

Bad Guys did *not* want to mess with her dad.

Dana didn't even make a face or anything when Athena laughed, didn't even try to tell her or any of them to quiet down. Dana grinned at her and winked when she saw Joel holding her hand on the Timeless River, as Mr. Howe and Mom had their backs to them. After, when they were getting smoothies at Thyme's Fruit Stand, Dana caught her eye and signed to her, keeping it close, whispering through gesture.

Joel's cute.

Athena nodded, sneaking a look at Joel, who was joking with Leon and Miguel. Signed back to Dana, *Yours cute?*

To me!

They couldn't decide where to go next, because the boys all wanted to go to the Pyramids of Ke-Sa, but Athena and Lynne and Gail all wanted to visit the Euro Strasse and maybe buy some stuff, and then go on Lion's Safari. So the boys said they should vote and the girls said there wasn't a point, because it'd still be a tie. Mr. Howe suggested they split up, that he could take the boys to the Pyramids and Mom could take the girls to the Euro Strasse, but Mom vetoed that right away. Then Dana said she'd be glad to take one of the groups, and that seemed to Athena to make fine sense, but Mom shot that down, too. So then Mr. Howe asked to talk to Mom, and the two of them stepped off by the side of the Forest Friends Feed Shack to have "a conversation."

Athena didn't catch all of it, partially because they

were far enough away to make it hard to see their mouths, and also because she didn't want to be obvious about trying to read them. Mom knows how well she can read lips, too, and so when she's saying something she doesn't want Athena reading, she turns away. But Mr. Howe doesn't know or maybe he forgets, and Athena caught enough, guessed enough, to make her uncomfortable.

Because she's pretty certain that Mr. Howe and Mom were talking about Dad.

She didn't know what to think of that. It made her tense, made her angry, and she wasn't sure whom she should be angry at. Then they came back, and Mom had the fake smile, the one that's too bright, and she told them that they'd all go to the Pyramids first, because the girls had gotten to choose already. This was true enough. They'd gone into Wild World when they arrived, and that's about when Dana had joined them. She had said that if they wanted to see the Flower Sisters Mystical Show, going early was best, because the animals got tired later in the day. The boys had objected, but they'd been overruled. Dana had been right about the show; it had been awesome. There was a jaguar, and a lion cub, and Athena had fed a real meerkat with Lilac's help. Joel held a python— he wanted to hold the cobra but nobody thought that was a good idea except Joel—and they'd all gotten to meet Lilac and Lily and Lavender and have their pictures taken with them. When the show was finished, and since they were already in Wild World, they went to Lilac's Secret Garden, and then, after that, on the Timeless River Cruise.

So it wasn't that Mom was wrong about it being the boys' turn, and Athena knew that. But she was angry anyway, even if she couldn't exactly say why, and when Mom tries walking with her, Athena ignores her and then takes three quick steps to catch up with where Dana is walking with Gail and Leon, leading the way across the bridge into Desert Oasis. Leon is really trying to impress Dana, and Athena can tell he's already got a crush on her.

Dana looks at her, then cants her head, showing the question. *Something wrong?*

No.

Angry?

No.

No? In WilsonVille I know when someone is angry or sad. My job to know. I can lose my job if you do not tell me why you are not happy.

Athena gives her a look, or tries to, but there's the hint of a smile in it. She can tell Dana's lying, too, that she won't lose her job if they're not all having a good time.

I see you smiling. Tell me.

Athena sighs, throws up her hands. *Because my mom and my dad are stupid divorced and I think* and she stops here, throws a glance over her shoulder. Mom is walking beside Mr. Howe, at the back of the group, and they're talking to each other. Mr. Howe has that same expression he uses on the class when he's telling them to be reasonable. The look on Mom is the same one she wears when she argues with Athena about what she's wearing to school because she thinks it's "inappropriate."

Athena turns back to Dana, continues, *I think Mr. Howe likes my mom* and she spells the word, because she wants this absolutely and unequivocally clear. *G-R-O-S-S.*

Dana puts a hand to her mouth, trying to hide her laugh. Lowers her hands, asking, *Your dad?*

What about Dad?

Dad where?

Here.

Dana looks at her curiously. They've come off the bridge, and there are palm trees and fake ruins here, and rising behind them are the tips of three pyramids in a line, the center one the tallest. There are plenty of people about, but it's not so crowded that they're interrupted every time they talk. Sometimes that happens, when Athena's somewhere and it gets really busy, people will cut in between her and Mom or her and Joel or her and whoever she's trying to converse with, not realizing that it's the exact same thing as if Athena had just decided to interrupt their own conversation by putting her hands over their mouths.

Here what do you mean "here"?

Here he works.

Dana shows surprise. *His name?*

J-A-D B-E-L-L but J-O-N-A-T-H-A-N real name.

Him I know! Dana nods quickly, smiles. *Very important man! Here in the park very important!*

Athena looks aside, feeling herself blushing, not sure why she's doing that. The anger is abating, still nameless and insubstantial. She shakes her head, then has a horrible thought and glares at Dana suspiciously.

Not your boyfriend!

Dana jerks her head back. American Sign Language is conveyed as much through expression as through gesture, and Dana's expression is perfectly eloquent. Surprise and amusement and just a touch of disgust at the suggestion, so that when she's shaking her head, Athena already knows what she is saying, what she is going to say. *Too old!*

Athena laughs, relieved, amused, and she thinks Dana is, too, from the look of her. Someone nearby looks their way sharply, surprised, but Dana ignores it and Athena doesn't care. It's her hearing that's gone, not her voice. Now Joel is tapping her arm lightly, and Athena turns to face him. He had cochlear implant surgery a couple years ago, when they were all in ninth grade, and he's supposed to talk aloud when he signs now, but sometimes he forgets. Not this time, and Athena can see his lips moving as he points.

"Come on come on come on!"

He holds out his right hand for her, and Athena smiles, takes it, and they're running together toward the pyramids. Because Dana's with them, they get to avoid almost every line, led instead along private paths that parallel the regular queues. Dana makes them wait for Mom and Mr. Howe, and then they're plunging into the shade.

From the shadows, Athena sees Agent Rose watching them. Joel points and she just catches a glimpse of Flashman—she can't remember which one it is, the boys know that stuff—jumping from an overhang and disappearing into the pyramid. Agent Rose sees him, too, pulls a pistol from beneath her coat, firing at him, shouting something after him. Athena can't hear her words, of course, because of the comedy-tragedy mask that Agent Rose wears, but she totally understands what she's saying, just from the way she shakes her fist.

I'll get you, Flashman!

Agent Rose disappears deeper into the pyramid, and they follow. Around them, fake torches flicker, and the air is turning cooler on her bare arms. Beneath her feet, Athena feels a thrum, a rumble, a vibration moving into her body, and it makes her eyes widen. The whole pyramid shakes, and then there are spiders, great big hairy evil-looking spiders, dropping down from the ceiling all around them.

Athena feels herself shriek, and now they are being led down a passageway by a man who looks like the same Flashman she saw before but she thinks probably isn't. Air blows past Athena's face, kicks her hair up, and a ghastly ghost appears above them, swoops down low. Everyone ducks. She doesn't scream so loud this time, because she kind of was expecting something, and she's also laughing, and then Flashman is turning to Dana.

Get in cat!

Dana leans forward to whisper to Flashman, and he nods, takes a half second, then indicates a different direction.

Get in those cats!

She lip-read that wrong, she must've, but Dana is nodding, and she signs as quickly as she can—still slow, but she's trying—and indicates the side, and Athena gets it then. The ride itself, the cars, are shaped kind of like miniature sphinxes, but with a canopy top, and they all tumble into them. Dana makes sure everyone is in their cars, moves along the line, checking seat belts.

Everyone is buckled up? Good. Keep your hands inside and do not get out until the ride ends!

She climbs into the back of Athena's car, so she's sitting behind her, and Athena has Joel to one side and Gail on the other. There is a sense of urgency that leaves Athena breathless and excited, and she knows that's silly, that there is nothing real about this, that it's all an illusion. Joel is laughing, looking all around, trying to see everything at once, and Gail is squeezing her arm, pointing and signing, smiling big and delighted. Then their sphinx-car shudders, lurches, and suddenly they're diving into darkness.

A bright light bursts before them, and Agent Rose appears, floating in the air ahead and above. It's the same Agent Rose from the movies, and even though the one they saw before looks the same, Athena knows it wasn't *this* one, the real one, because this one has removed her mask. She's a projection, but all the same, she's very pretty, but a little scary, too, her hair flowing out behind her in a blood-red nimbus, her black trench coat flapping. She holds a big red gem in both hands, the Eye of Ke-Sa, that's the source of the light, and she's raising it high above her head as she speaks. On the windshield of their sphinx-car, closed captioning appears. It's well placed, high enough for Athena to read it without having to ever look away.

AGENT ROSE: YOU FOOLS! I HOLD THE EYE! YOU WILL NEVER LEAVE THIS PLACE ALIVE! I HAVE THE POWER! I AM INVINCIBLE!

Then Agent Rose lowers the Eye and looks *right at them* and smiles this very sinister, kind of sexy smile. Gail's grip on her forearm tightens.

AGENT ROSE: YOU WILL SERVE ME...FOR ALL ETERNITY!

Then, out of nowhere, Flashman is there, swinging down from high above on a rope. Like Agent Rose, it's not the same Flashman, another projection, and like Agent Rose, it's the movie Flashman, too, played by that actor that Lynne has all those pictures of, the one who keeps going to rehab. He has a revolver in his hand, and he's pointing it at Agent Rose.

FLASHMAN: ROSE! DON'T MAKE ME DO IT!
AGENT ROSE: YOU CAN'T STOP ME!

A beam of light shoots from the Eye of Ke-Sa, just as Flashman fires his gun.

(SOUND OF A GUNSHOT. AGENT ROSE SCREAMS.)

The light goes out, total darkness, and the car dips, turns, it feels like they're spinning out of control. For a second, Athena actually thinks they're going to flip over. More ghosts race past them, dressed in tatters and dripping decaying flesh; one of them actually seems to be *inside* their sphinx-car, and then the ride begins in earnest. They race along the track as pieces of pyramid fall all around them, as snakes hiss and spit, as animal-headed gods and goddesses pursue them through twists

and turns. Athena can't tell if she's laughing or screaming now, out of breath, buffeted by the ride. At one
point, the canvas canopy of their car is torn away by an
unseen claw, and she sees above them a sky of blood-
red, clouds boiling away into an infinite darkness.

The sphinx-car judders to a sudden, sharp stop.

Joel, Gail, Athena, they're all thrown forward, so
hard that those seat belts Dana made sure they fastened
dig into hips and waists, keep them from smashing
into the windshield. Around them, the darkness flickers. All of them are turning in their seats, catching their
breath as they crane their necks, trying to see a hint
of what will happen next. There's dim light in the car,
and Dana looks puzzled. From that, from the expression and the posture and the way her mouth has just
tightened like *that,* just a little, Athena knows this isn't
right.

Something is wrong.

She looks the question at Dana.

Stay seated.

Athena shrugs, shrugs to Gail, to Joel. The closed
captioning on the windshield returns, this time with an
image of Gordo, Betsy, and Pooch.

PLEASE REMAIN SEATED. WE ARE EXPERIENCING
TECHNICAL DIFFICULTIES.

Nothing else. Just that message.

Athena's starting to get a little nervous when the
lights come on, dispelling the illusion of the Pyramids
of Ke-Sa. Now Athena can see other sphinx-cars all
along the track, cars that had been hidden in the dark-

ness. Mom is in the one right behind them, riding with Mr. Howe, Leon, Lynne, and Miguel. Everyone is looking around, curious and confused. Joel taps her shoulder and then points at a mass of snakes on the ground ahead of them. They're inert, rubber-looking, surprisingly fake in the light.

Movement on her periphery, and Athena looks about quickly, this time at all the other cars. People are straightening up, their chins raised, and she knows there's a voice talking to them that she can't hear. Then the car shifts slightly, and Athena twists around, watches Dana climbing out. There's a man dressed like a jungle explorer, with a radio in one hand and a flashlight in the other, coming their way. She can't read what he's saying, but then Dana is facing them, signing.

Everyone get out follow me.

What? Athena asks, the question in her expression more than in her sign. *Something wrong?*

Dana shakes her head.

The park is closed.

So the man in the jungle explorer outfit, he walks them through a doorway marked EXIT that's almost hidden off to one side, and then into a tunnel that doesn't look like the interior of the Pyramids of Ke-Sa at all. Lots of people are here, filing out, and now they're mostly walking with their heads down again. Athena sees Agent Rose and Flashman, standing together, and they're pointing the way to go, no longer playing at being enemies.

It takes less than a minute before they're out of the

ride, eyes readjusting to the sunlight. Athena can feel it as much as see it; something's changed in the park. There are more people about, but unlike before, they're all moving in the same direction. Men and women in park uniforms, directing people, and there is a tension, too, totally different. Before, the park felt like fun. Now that's gone, and people are looking confused, and they're looking scared, and some of them are upset, not only the little kids. She sees someone dressed in a Gordo costume, standing on the bridge they crossed, and he's directing traffic back toward them. The man in the jungle explorer costume is talking to Dana, and he points, the same direction that Gordo is pointing. Not toward the entrance but in what Athena thinks must be the opposite direction.

Mom is beside her, holding her phone to her ear. She puts her other hand on Athena's back, resting her palm between her shoulder blades. Mr. Howe flaps his hand for their attention, then begins to sign, but she's only watching him peripherally, instead trying to read what Mom is saying. She's talking to Dad, and it's over, and Mom is looking at her phone, and she says a word.

Bastard.

Mom sees Athena looking at her. Forces up a smile, indicates Mr. Howe, and both of them turn their attention back to him. He talks as he signs, so she can read his lips at the same time. His hands are saying, *Do not worry. All good. The park is closing.*

His lips are saying almost the same thing, but there's a word there Athena can't make out, and she signs to Mom, tries to spell what she saw, curious. *What word this "v" word?*

Mom gives her the sign for "evacuate." *Everyone must leave.*

Dana has joined Mr. Howe up at the front, and now they're leading the way. Both keep looking back, Mr. Howe to make sure they're all still together. Dana seems to be searching for something or somebody, frowning, though when she sees Athena watching her, she tries a smile. It's not a real smile. It's the kind of smile you use when you're worried, and Athena knows that she's looking for her boyfriend.

Why evacuate? Mom why evacuate? Dad coming?

Mom shakes her head slightly, hand still on Athena's back, the pressure a little more than just guiding her. They've fallen behind, are being passed on both sides. There's another group ahead of them, a big one, and there's a woman wearing a navy blue blazer. She looks in their direction, calls out something that Athena cannot read at this distance. Dana raises her arm, and the woman nods, then turns and hurries to catch up with the larger group.

Athena looks back, over her shoulder, and she sees nothing but an empty park. It's unnerving, to see nothing where before there had been so many. To see the Timeless River with an unmanned boat floating on it, to see the big wooden roller coaster with no cars running, abandoned.

She catches her mother's eye, asks the question again. *Where Dad?*

Mom's mouth tightens, a look in her eyes that Athena can't understand, because it's not anger, and it's not love, and it's not concern, but it's perhaps all of them. Or perhaps it's something else. Mom doesn't sign in response, just shakes her head once.

She doesn't know. She has no idea.

They follow Dana. Walk along a pathway that would've been crowded before and is now empty and spacious. There are signs on wooden posts, directing them to Lion's Safari to their right and the Pyramids of Ke-Sa to their left, and the Euro Strasse to their south, but they keep going. Everybody else is gone, Athena can't see anyone, thinks they must be some of the last people still here, heading this way, at least.

Dana stops at these giant wooden gates, like the kind of gates you'd imagine finding in a jungle for a fort. The gates are open, the space through them narrower than the path, and Mr. Howe stops with her, and Athena can tell they're both counting everyone, making sure they're still all together. Then they're moving through the gates, no longer in the park proper, but instead in some sort of service area. There's three little golf carts parked here, all with the WilsonVille logo painted on them, and some bundles of plastic painted to look like wood, and lots of big oil drums, and a sign on a little building that says AUTHORIZED PERSONNEL ONLY. Behind that, there's a concrete wall, easily three times as tall as Athena herself, and it stretches to the right and the left as far as she can see, curving gently out of sight in both directions. She can see cameras on narrow posts on the wall, the kind you see in banks.

Dana walks them along this narrower path, a black asphalt road that radiates heat, running between the concrete and the fake wood. It narrows further, and now only four, maybe five can walk abreast. The road curves, and Athena thinks they must be following the top edge of the park here. There's nobody ahead of them now that she can see, and she realizes they're all walking a little faster. Mom's palm is pressing even more firmly on her upper back. Mr. Howe turns to speak to Mom, and Athena reads something about hearing sirens, perhaps there was an accident or something?

Athena sees the man in white coming around the bend, points, but Mom has seen him, too, and so has Dana, and they all stop. Athena thinks it's a man, at least, wonders if it's a costume. He's wearing white coveralls, and it really does cover almost everything, except maybe some of his face and his hands, and even those are hidden. He's wearing a mask for breathing, black and lumpy, and his hands are covered with shiny black gloves, and he's holding a black duffel bag in one of them.

He raises his free hand, and Athena thinks he's speaking, but she can't see his mouth, doesn't know what he's saying.

Mom's hand moves up to her shoulder, pulls her back into her, a little closer. Mr. Howe starts to step forward, and so does Dana, and Dana is gesturing back in Athena's direction, clearly talking about the class. The man in the mask shakes his head, still holding out the one hand, the sign he's giving perfectly clear. Stop. Do not move.

Behind the man in the mask appears another one, dressed the same way, even carrying the same bag. Then come two more, until there are four men, all in white, faces behind masks for breathing, blocking their way.

Athena is pretty sure they aren't wearing costumes.

Dana's gestures are coming faster, broader, and even if Athena can only see her from behind, even if she can't read the words, she can read the body language. We have to go. Why are you stopping us? You have to let us go. Mr. Howe joins her, his gestures even grander. He's getting indignant, she's seen this before, when he feels he has to defend them.

The first man in the mask hoists his duffel bag up in front of him, holding it between himself and Mr. Howe and Dana. Unzips the top with a shiny black hand, reaches inside. Athena feels Mom's fingers dig into her shoulder, feels herself pulled and turned against her mother's breast. She twists her head as Mom tries to put a hand to her cheek, to keep her from doing just that thing, but she isn't in time, and Athena sees what Mom didn't want her to see.

Sees Dana's hands flying up to her face, turning to Mr. Howe, her eyes wide and her mouth open. Sees Mr. Howe take a step backward, then try to take another one.

Sees him falter, then collapse.

There is an ugly hole above his right eye.

There is blood.

The other men in masks are reaching into their duffel bags. The other men in masks bring their shiny black-gloved hands out again, and each of them is now holding a pistol.

They point their guns at Athena and Mom and Dana and Joel and all of them. She knows they're talking, saying something, but she doesn't need to read their words now. The one in the front, the one who just shot Mr. Howe in the head, who just killed the man who has been teaching her and her friends not just ASL but science and history and literature and art for the last three and a half years at the Hollyoakes school, that man, he points his gun at Mom.

He gestures.

Turn around. All of you, turn around and start walking.

Back into the park.

Chapter Twelve

ELEVEN MINUTES and twenty seconds Gabriel Fuller has been hiding in the circle of cash registers at the center of the official WilsonVille Store, back against the cabinets, radio in one hand, gas mask in the other. He's listened to the sound of the park emptying, the muted voices passing by outside, the sounds of the evacuation. The announcement on the PA has changed, changed about a minute and a half ago, now it's something recorded. There's a string of music, the signature Gordo, Betsy, and Pooch theme, and then a sweet-sounding woman's voice.

> We regret to inform you that WilsonVille is closing. Please make your way to the nearest exit. We apologize for the inconvenience and hope you have a pleasant day.

His radio burps out static, twice, quickly, then twice again. He presses his own transmit button two times in answer, then hooks it onto his Tyvek suit at the waist, pulls on his gas mask. Carefully, he leans out from the side of the counter, looking past the racks of clothing and toys, into Town Square. He's only got a low view, but from what he sees, it's cleared significantly. He uses a rack of WilsonVille fortieth-anniversary sweat-shirts as cover to get to his feet, takes another peek.

It's an odd sight, to be sure. A cluster of perhaps seven or eight visitors is heading his way, toward the main gates, approaching from the east side of the square, being hurried along by two of the navy blazers. Further back, just passing the Soda Shoppe, he can see another group, smaller, similarly led, this time by a Skip Flashman wearing twin six-guns and chaps, his cowboy hat, as ever, atop his head. Coming from Wild Horse Valley, Gabriel expects, where Skip most often resides. He watches as each group moves closer, then out of view, passing the store.

Now Town Square is empty. Emptier than he's ever seen it, even after hours, even after closing, and it's a strange sight, to see it barren in daylight. At closing, after hours, there's always someone, a maintenance crew doing touch-up paint or repairs to the streetlights or hanging new banners or something; a custodian, sweeping the sidewalks or watering the grass around the statue of Gordo, Betsy, and Pooch. A navy blazer, making rounds.

This time, there's no one and there's nothing.

Gabriel reaches down for his duffel, taking it in his nondominant hand, then moves to the door. He stops again, checks to his right and his left, and then again, and when he looks left a second time, he sees four men in Tyvek suits identical to his own carrying duffels twice as large as his, wearing gas masks and gloves. They stop about a dozen yards into the square, looking around. These are his four, his element for this stage, and he doesn't know their names, but in his mind he's already named them Gordo and Betsy and Hendar and Stripe, though he'll be damned if he lets them know that.

They see him the instant he emerges from the store, and he gives them a nod, exaggerating and slowing the gesture so it carries through the mask. They fall in together, heading toward the Sheriff's Office. At the doors he nods to the one he's named Hendar, the tallest of the four, and the man steps up and pushes his way inside.

The room is empty.

Gabriel points to the front desk of the fake precinct with one hand, then moves to the half-concealed interior door that leads to the stairs that, in turn, lead to the command post on the second floor and the safety offices on the third. When he gives the door a push, he's not surprised to find that it's locked.

The one he's calling Betsy is at the front desk now, vaults it lightly, disappears behind the counter. Gabriel looks up at the surveillance cameras, raises a hand in greeting, indicates the door. He and the others wait for what seems like a painfully long pause. If they've been picked up on the cameras in here, then someone will be coming down to let them inside, certain that they're here to help. If they haven't been seen—and why would they be, when all eyes should be watching the exterior, watching the evacuation of the park?—so much the better. But whatever the case, they will have the element of surprise.

There's a subdued clunk from within the wall at Gabriel's elbow, and Betsy is coming back over the counter, rejoining the others. Gabriel waits until he's ready, has his bag back in hand, and then shoves the door open, leads the way into the stairwell. Quick glance up the stairs, all around, and not a camera to be seen here. Five of them in the hallway is a tight fit, and he presses his back to the wall, trying to make enough room for them to spread out. The gas masks leave their ears uncovered, and Gabriel knows they're moving quietly, very quietly, but the rustle from the Tyvek suits sounds too loud all the same.

The door swings shut on its hinges, the bolt again latches in place. Gordo and Stripe have their pistols out of their duffels, are screwing the suppressors into place at the end of each barrel. Finished, they hoist their bags onto their backs, then give Gabriel a thumbs-up with a free hand. Gabriel returns it. He can feel perspiration beginning to slide down his spine, feel the tightness in his chest that reminds him of patrols in Afghanistan. There's a slow cloud of condensation beginning to rise in his gas mask, and his pulse is strong at his temples.

The door at the top of the stairs has a sign affixed to it that reads SAFETY OFFICE—AUTHORIZED PERSON-NEL ONLY. There's the hint of noise beyond the door, a voice, then another. Gabriel, still in the lead, turns his head so his uncovered ear can be that much closer to the sound. Two, maybe three people, but he can't make out the words, the conversation subdued.

Gabriel straightens, looks to the four men waiting behind him. He points to Gordo and Stripe, then to the door, and each man nods. He moves, presses his back to the wall to give them room as they pass him, now in front, entry positions, and their entry positions aren't that far from what he was taught in the army. Betsy and Hendar have their weapons out now, too, ready to act as the second wave. The sound of conversation in the room beyond stops, and for a moment, Gabriel can imagine whoever is inside has sensed what is coming.

But they haven't. The moment they're through the door, Gabriel knows that the two men and the one woman reacting to their entrance never saw it coming at all.

Gordo takes out the coms first, the woman, the one wearing the headset, before she's even finished turning toward them, just as her eyes go wide. Then the gunshots, soft snaps from the suppressed pistol, and she slumps in her seat, topples to the floor at the same moment as one of the men, balding and gray, falls backward against his bank of monitors, collapses like overcooked pasta. The third one, he opens his mouth, and then Gabriel sees his body jerk, both Stripe and Gordo putting shots into him, and then this man, too, falls, sinking to his knees before pitching facedown to lie on the floor and twitch.

Stripe steps in, takes a position to the left of the door, on one knee, as Gordo mirrors the movement. Betsy and Hendar follow, remain standing, their weapons out and ready, swinging a slow track about the room, searching for the next target. There's silence but for the whir of the machinery, the bleat from one of the monitors. Then Stripe raises a hand to Gabriel, motions him forward.

"Sweep," Gabriel says, voice dulled by the gas mask. "Make sure we're clear."

Stripe nods, gets to his feet, moves off toward the door at the back of the room, the flight of stairs that leads to the third floor. Gordo is up just as quickly, moving from body to body, pausing only long enough to dump a round into each head. Gas masks start coming off, and Hendar takes one of the headsets from the communication console, presses it to his ear. Listens for a moment, then nods to Gabriel, gives a new thumbs-up. He drops the headset, hoists his duffel, pulls a slim black box from inside, and sets about connecting it to the radio set on the desk.

Gabriel takes another half second to absorb the room. His only visit prior to this had been during orientation, on his way up to the second-floor conference room, down the hall from here. It's an impressive array of surveillance equipment, almost overwhelming, and it takes several more seconds before he can decipher the layout, before he understands what he's seeing on multiple screens. Coverage is comprehensive, and if there are gaps anywhere, he certainly doesn't see them. Exterior views from the gates, all the exits, are showing crowds milling about outside, still being shepherded by WilsonVille Friends. The parking lots seem to be the main gathering points, and Gabriel sees a couple of new fire engines arriving.

On one camera, the one covering the northeast access, there's already an engine parked, just as planned. That was Vladimir's element, and on an adjacent monitor, he can see what must be Vladimir's group entering the park, dressed in their Tyvek. They're just coming through the gates, and people are giving them a wide berth.

Gabriel removes his own gas mask. Gordo is already settling himself in front of the surveillance monitors, and Betsy is helping Hendar. One of the machines is bleating, and on its screen Gabriel can read the botulinum alert. It takes a couple of seconds before he can figure out how to silence the machine.

"We have their coms," Hendar says. "Secure and scrambled."

"Contact all elements, tell them we have control."

"We still have people in the park," Gordo says, indicating several of the monitors. "Stragglers."

Gabriel looks over his shoulder, can see clusters of park guests still making their way to the gates. More Tyvek suits, too, and he sees that Vladimir's group has taken hostages already, is moving southward, crossing one of the bridges that spans the Timeless River. On another monitor, he can see a Lilac trying to encourage a small group of people to follow her, another element in Tyvek closing on their position. A man in a suit is jogging past the camera by Nova's Tower, roughly in the same area, and he can see still more staff, this one in a Terra Space mechanic's suit, walking quickly by the now-stopped Race for Justice.

The one in the suit earns a double take. Nobody comes to WilsonVille wearing a suit, not like that. Navy coat and tie, park-approved wear, but a business suit on a ninety-degree day at the end of July? The only people who dress like that while in the park are management, upper management.

"That one," Gabriel says, pointing at the monitor. "Can you give me a better view?"

Gordo takes a moment, flicking through monitor settings, and then manages to pick up the same man again, now turning north. He's still jogging along, looking around, clean-shaven, early forties, perhaps. No radio, no flashlight, but with a phone to his ear. Then he's out of camera, the next view distant, devoid of detail.

"Hey," says Betsy. "Where's Dmitri?"

They find him upstairs, the man Gabriel had named Stripe.

He's lying on his back beside the desk in the largest office on the floor, his tongue swollen between blue-tinged lips, his cheeks puffed and his eyes open, wide and staring, broken blood vessels painted in dead white orbs. His gun is gone. One hand is at his throat, and when Gabriel moves it away, he can see that the man's trachea has been crushed, or, more precisely, cracked.

He feels the pistol in his hand, turns and looks at Betsy, is about to speak, when his eye catches a photograph on the desk. He steps closer, sees the same man he saw earlier, the one on the monitor. It's a picture of him with a woman and a girl, all of them smiling, the girl a strawberry blonde, the woman with hair the same shade. He casts an eye over the desk, the paperwork that has been scattered there, and it doesn't take long to find the name, the name of the man who belongs to this office. Bell, Jonathan, Deputy Director of Park Safety.

Then he sees something else. An authorization form, signed, granting Dana Kincaid time and a half for today's work.

This may be a problem, Gabriel thinks.

Chapter Thirteen

BELL'S PHONE bleats at him, the two-tone alert that says Brickyard is calling. He doesn't break stride as he answers. "Go for Warlock."

"Sitrep."

"Biotoxin alarm in the park, evacuation in progress."

"Can you confirm?"

"That's negative."

"Assessment?"

"I think we're dealing with something else. Trying to figure out exactly what right now."

There's a flicker of a pause, long enough for Bell to hear the background static-and-whine characteristic of secured communications. Then Ruiz says, "I'm en route to Marcelin. Let me know as soon as you have something. Out."

Bell lowers his phone, rounds the south side of Flashman's Laser Light Show. Ahead, working along the path that'll take them to the northwest exit, he can see a Lilac trying to rush a group of three along with her. They're just kids, two boys and a girl, and as he comes closer he can see that all are near tears, their meerkat companion trying to comfort them.

"We'll find them once we get outside," Lilac is saying. "I'll stay with you the whole time, I promise. And you know I always keep my promises!"

"You lied to Hendar that time," the girl says through snuffles.

"That was different. I did that to save Lavender." Lilac sees Bell, stops. "They were on the carousel, got separated from their parents. We're going out the northwest, is that way still open?"

Bell slows, falls into walking with them. All the kids look at him, and one of the boys, the older one, dark-haired and dark eyes shining with tears, reminds him of another boy, playing soccer in a dusty square. He gives them his most confident smile.

"Should be," Bell says. "I'll keep you company."

"See?" Lilac tells the kids. "You find friends every-where you look."

"Everyone okay?" Bell's phone is still in his hand, and he brings up Chain's number with a glance, think-ing to tell him that there's a change. "Everyone feels all right?"

"It's a little scary," the youngest boy says softly.

"Why is the park closed?" This from the older boy, who cannot hide his disappointment. "You guys never close."

"You know what a gas leak is?" Bell asks. "Natural gas? It's not dangerous alone, but you have to be care-ful."

"There's been a gas leak?"

"That's how it looks." Lilac is watching him as she holds the hand of the younger boy, the one who admit-ted his fear, tear tracks streaking his cheeks. There's doubt, maybe curiosity in Lilac's expression, and Bell is about to ask if anybody is having difficulty breathing when ahead of them, cresting the slight rise onto the bridge that crosses the Timeless River here, he sees one of the hazmat responders.

That's the moment, that's when he knows. Every suspicion crystallizes, every doubt, every question. The instant this man first comes into view, thirty-odd feet away, as Bell sees who else is with him. Sees Tyvek suits and gas masks and black boots and black gloves and black gear bags. He knows. He knows that the Spartan was spoofed, that there is no aerosolized botulinum toxin wafting through WilsonVille. He knows it was a lie, and that this is something else, something different.

Something even more dangerous.

Because walking toward them, this man dressed for hazmat response, with another following just behind and to his left, there's a group of six other people. Six other park guests, men and women and another child, and in the rear, two more dressed as hazmat responders, same as the first two to the last detail. Confused and frightened expressions on the evacuees, no conversation, and the way those six guests walk, he knows that walk. Never mind that they're heading the wrong way, that they're heading deeper *in* rather than making their way *out*. He knows that walk.

Those six, they're not walking like evacuees. They're walking like prisoners.

His thumb presses down, dialing Chain, but he doesn't raise the phone, just drops it into the pocket of his coat. Takes two steps forward, putting Lilac and the kids to his back, raises his free hand in greeting.

"You guys got here fast," Bell says. "Only the four of you? I'd have thought there'd be more. We've got most of the park cleared out already."

The group comes to a silent stop in front of him, the nearest only fifteen or so feet away, at the foot of the bridge. In his mind, almost unconsciously, Bell has marked the four men in hazmat gear: Tango Four, rear left, Tango Three, rear right, Tango Two, near right, Tango One, near center. Four and Three have spread out slightly at the back of the group, still on the bridge itself, albeit barely, and now Three is putting his hand on the shoulder of the young woman nearest to him. He turns her slightly, using her to obscure Bell's view. Sunlight bounces off the black rubber glove, and the woman flinches, just a bit, easy to miss, but if Bell had any doubts left, she's just burned them away.

The same part of him that has numbered and named each Tango has prioritized targets, has counted out sequence, movement, shots; has shown him the motion, crystal-clear; drawing the weapon riding just back of his right hip, up into his hands, safety down, firing. It isn't a compulsion, neither is it an automated response, neither is it quite instinct. Yet it is all these things. But that same training, that same tactical brain is also telling him something else, is telling him that there are three children behind him and six hostages in front of him, and he does not know which Tangos are weapons-ready and which are not.

So Bell does not move, not yet, but instead repeats himself. "You guys got here fast."

Tango One is closing, and Tango Two is raising his free hand, putting it to his left ear. On coms, and that makes sense, this is coordinated, which means, in turn, someone is coordinating, probably someone in the park, perhaps the same inside man who managed the botulinum spoof. A flicker-fast thought: Nuri back at the command post, but she had damn well better be able to take care of herself.

Not his problem, not right now.

"You need to come with us," Tango One says. His voice is thick, dulled behind the gas mask, and Bell can't discern an accent. The Tango's eyes flick to the kids and Lilac before returning to him. "You have to be screened."

Lilac says, "We have to get these children back to their parents."

"After they've been tested," Tango One says, not looking away from Bell.

Tango Two has lowered his hand. "We take all of them." He indicates Bell. "That one's management."

"Deputy director of park safety." Bell smiles.

"You all are going to have to come with us." Tango Two reaches to unzip the top of his coveralls, and Bell's back-brain immediately reprioritizes targets, moves this man to the front of the line. At the same time, he registers movement in the background, just below the crest of the bridge, at the railing to his left. Chaindragger, dripping with water from the Timeless River, pulling himself up and over to position himself a dozen yards or so behind Tangos Three and Four.

"Turn around."

"Sure," Bell says, and he takes it slow, pivots about to face Lilac and the children. Confused, scared faces, but they don't understand, not yet. They don't see it. They don't know.

Bell feels very tired, suddenly.

"Do what he says," he tells them. "Now."

Lilac is the first to react, the first to realize, and maybe she's seen something, the gun that Bell is positive is about to be leveled at his back. Maybe she sees something else, but she pulls the youngest around with her, reaches out for the hand of the second, the girl, maybe ten years old. The dark-eyed boy, the older one, frowns, his mouth clamped tight.

"We have to find our parents," he whispers.

Bell puts a hand on the boy's shoulder. Says with all the quiet certainty he can, "You will."

The boy turns, and Lilac is starting to move, and now they all are beginning to walk back in the direction they came. Bell follows, one step, another, just walking here, just walking, wrapped in cold calm. Slowing slightly, almost able to feel Tango Two at his back.

He pivots, spins, left hand extending, palm out, his right hand dropping, drawing. Tango Two's gun has a suppressor, and if it hadn't Bell wonders if he'd have been shot again, maybe for the final time. But the suppressor makes Tango Two's pistol that much longer, long enough for Bell's left palm to connect with its side, knock the weapon out of line and up, and there's the muffled report as the man fires on instinct, sends a round skyward.

Now Bell's own weapon is free, and he's running the count in his head. Tango Two, sight, fire one, fire two, both head, can't miss at this range; Tango Two down; left hand to pistol, shifting, barely have to even swing about, Tango One beginning to backpedal, and the friendlies don't even know what's happened yet, haven't begun to react. Chaindragger in motion, covered, bad angles, nobody better miss or else they'll shoot each other, worse, they'll shoot the friendlies, and have the shot; three, four, five, tracking line, upper thorax, neck, head; Tango One down.

Bell sidesteps left, the .45 high and ready, looking for Tango Three, Tango Four, and Chaindragger has done what he was called to do, both are down. Gunshots echoing, fading, then gone. Friendlies are stunned, they still don't quite know what's happened, one of them covering his mouth with both hands, the woman Tango Three had handled standing stock-still. Then she's shaking, silent tears beginning to fall. The woman beside her wraps an arm about her shoulders.

The entire action has taken less than two seconds from start to finish, from four live Tangos to four dead ones.

Digging out his phone again, Bell turning in place, gun still in hand. Lilac and the others have stopped, staring back, and she's doing what she can to keep them from looking. The older boy is staring at the bodies on the ground.

"Turn around," Bell orders. "Turn around."

The boy does. Bell kills the still-open call to Chaindragger, jabs another button, wishes to God he was on mission coms already.

Nothing.

He remembers thinking that she could damn well take care of herself, and he feels foolish and stupid.

He hangs up, tries again, gets the same, hangs up

again. Looks around, feels midday sunlight burning his vision. There's no one else around that he can see, just six friendlies plus Lilac plus three kids and four bodies spilling red into white Tyvek suits and onto WilsonVille cobblestones.

Chaindragger is coming up beside him, his own weapon held low-ready in both hands. Water from his dip in the Timeless River drips from his Star System Alliance Defense mechanic's coveralls, pools at his feet, makes his rich brown skin shine.

"Top?"

"Angel was in the command post. No response."

"Meaning we don't have eyes."

"Meaning they do." Bell scans the immediate area, looking high, for hidden camera placements. He finds three, knows he's missing at least that number again. Knows that whoever is in the command post is watching, has seen them, will be reacting.

"We've got to get these people out of the park."

"They have our eyes." Bell indicates one of the bodies. "You see any more of these on your way here?"

"That's a negative."

"Check them." Bell holsters his pistol as Chain drops to one knee, begins searching bodies and bags. Lilac is watching him warily, the boy and girl clinging to her. "You with me? Lilac? Are you with me?"

Lilac nods, hesitantly at first, then again, with resolve, and maybe it's calling her by her character name that does it, but she takes a breath, stands a little straighter. She is Lilac the meerkat, the heart of the Flower Sisters. Fierce and loyal, yet kind at heart, and she will do what must be done.

"Yes," she says. "Yes, I am."

"You get them to the main gate, don't stop until you're outside," Bell tells her, then turns, directing his words at the others. "You understand? All of you, follow Lilac. Follow Lilac. Don't stop. Run."

"Lily runs," the girl says softly. "Lilac dances."

"Not today," Lilac says. "Today, we run so fast that Lily won't believe it when we tell her. Right?"

The girl nods, wide-eyed.

"Go," Bell tells them.

Chapter Fourteen

RUIZ IS racing his Mustang through traffic at speeds no one would call reasonable or safe, listening to the duty sergeant in his ear delivering the bullet. What they know, and more, what they don't, and then the interrupt he's been waiting for comes at last.

"I've got Warlock," the duty sergeant says, her voice as implacably calm as ever. Ruiz used to wonder if anything would faze her or the others of her kind, those who staff ops rooms and duty posts in bases and secret and secured rooms all around the world. All hell breaking loose in WilsonVille, worst fears being realized, and that didn't do it, which makes Ruiz believe nothing ever will.

"Put him through." A pause.

"Warlock, go for Brickyard." Hiss-click on the line, background whine of the scrambler, then Jad Bell's voice.

"Brickyard, I'm in the park. It's a take."

"What do you have?" Ruiz asks, wrenching the wheel around an F-150 driven by maybe the only person in Southern California who is actually slowing to stop at a yellow. Horns blare, and Ruiz stomps on the accelerator.

"It's a take," Bell repeats. "Chain and I have four

neutralized, repeat four neutralized, estimate at least three times that number left in the park, cannot confirm."

"Assessment?"

"They're taking hostages and they're taking the park."

"Can you confirm they have hostages?"

"Cannot confirm, but highly probable. We have ten, repeat ten, freed and heading out now." Bell pauses. "We've lost contact with Angel. May have been taken when hostiles took the security offices."

"KIA?"

"Cannot confirm."

"They have control of the surveillance?"

"Affirmative."

Ruiz spins the wheel about, the Mustang embracing its notorious heritage, fishtailing into the Wilson Entertainment corporate lot. In the rearview, he can see one of the security guards in the gatehouse he just blew past running after him, yelling into a radio. He's killing the engine and climbing out as he continues speaking to Bell. "If they're taking hostages, the botulinum is a hoax."

"Agreed."

"I'm putting Bone and Board into play, should have them on the ground and staged for you in three hours. This is the opening move, Warlock, not the endgame. We need to get ahead of them."

"Understood. Out."

"You," Ruiz says as the line goes dead in his ear. He's facing the visibly jumpy Wilson Entertainment security guard closing on him. The man is unarmed but

for a radio, but Ruiz holds out one hand anyway, showing an empty palm, while his other dips into his jacket.
Wearing blue jeans and a black T-shirt and a wind-
breaker, he lacks the authority of a uniform, knows he
has to make up for it with his voice and manner.

"Colonel Daniel Ruiz to see Matthew Marcelin. I
am aware of the situation in the park. Take me to him
now."

The security guard hesitates, tries to be clever about
it, reaching out for the ID. Ruiz shakes his head.

"I need to see that, sir."

"Son, you have a terrorist incident developing in
your park," Ruiz says. "What you need to do is bring
me to Matthew Marcelin, and you goddamn need to do
it now."

Ruiz starts toward the entrance of the building, not
quite running, but strides that force the guard into a jog
to catch up, then keep pace. The man falls in, glancing his way, but doesn't speak, and at the doors he's
there first, pushing them open and then running ahead,
clearing the way. There's a mural of the Flower Sisters
looking sweet on the wall, cavorting with friends, and
there's a crowd in the lobby, executives milling around.
Ruiz suspects that the building is being cleared, security protocol, perhaps, fear of another attack or a
response to the biotoxin threat.

A threat that is unequivocally false, Ruiz is now certain. The security guard is holding an elevator for him,
and he steps in, finds Jerome Wallford inside on his
phone, sport coat and slacks and mop of blond hair,
looking ten years younger than Ruiz knows he is. Wallford acknowledges him with something like a nod, the

guard reaches around, presses a floor, then backs out. Doors close.

Wallford covers the mouthpiece of the phone, still at his ear, with a hand. "You confirm mobile in the park?"

"I have two shooters in the open, they have engaged and neutralized one element. The botulinum—"

"Bullshit, yeah."

"They lost contact with your girl."

"*I've* fucking lost contact with my girl." Wallford uncovers the mouthpiece, says, "Then get onto NSA and shut it down before it starts a panic. Anything else, you call me."

"Shooting down the balloon."

Wallford lowers the phone, scowling. "Twitter, Facebook, everyfuckingthing."

"This won't stay quiet."

"It's already not quiet, it's already being shouted from the mountain. Media is en route both here and to the park."

"My man says they're taking hostages. Means something else is coming."

"Something else is most definitely coming," Wallford agrees. "The question is what."

For a man trying to ride chaos, Ruiz thinks Matthew Marcelin is doing a damn fine job of not losing his head. He's standing in his outer office, tie loosened and collar open, a Bluetooth in his left ear and a landline held to his right. When Ruiz and Wallford enter, he cuts off midsentence, staring at them.

"You I know," Marcelin says to Wallford. "Him I don't."

"Colonel Daniel Ruiz. Master Sergeant Jonathan Bell belongs to me."

There's a heartbeat's pause, and then Marcelin says the same thing to each of his phones, "Call you back." The landline goes to one of the assistants standing in the room, the Bluetooth comes out of his ear, and Marcelin gestures to his office, moves to enter without waiting for them to follow.

Wallford shuts the door behind them once they're inside.

"You bastards knew this would happen?" are the first words out of Marcelin's mouth. "You *knew* this would happen to my park?"

"If we knew it was going to happen, we'd have stopped it before it could start," Wallford says. "Believe me."

"You placed your man in my organization." Marcelin points at Ruiz. "You knew something was coming."

"Sir," Ruiz says. "What we suspect and what we know at any given time are often, regrettably, radically different things. We suspected some sort of incident, and our analysis showed that in such an event, WilsonVille would be a priority target. How seriously we took the threat is measured by the presence of two of my very best people in your park, not to mention one of Mr. Wallford's."

Marcelin's jaw clenches, as if to literally keep himself silent, and this lasts for several seconds as he processes what they've just told him, what he already knows, what he must now conclude. Outside the office, phones are ringing, voices overlapping.

"Doesn't matter, not now," Marcelin says, finally. "What can you tell me?"

"Bell confirms that the botulinum alarm was faked, we don't know how yet."

"Thank God for that."

"Yes, sir," Ruiz agrees. "However, he further confirms the presence of hostiles in the park, and that they are taking hostages."

Any relief Marcelin feels vanishes. "How many? Do we know?"

"We do not."

"What do they want?"

"Unknown. What I require from you is an accounting of your personnel working in the park today, and some means of confirming if they're out or not."

"What about the guests?"

"Personnel is the priority."

"You think someone's on the inside?"

Before Ruiz can answer, Wallford snorts. "Something like this? At least one, maybe more."

That gives Marcelin pause, forces him to look aside as he digests the implications. He draws a breath, again bringing himself back to point, asks Wallford, "And where's Porter in all this? He in on this with you?"

"Eric Porter is not part of my operation," Wallford says.

"Operation." Marcelin echoes the word, displeased by it, then moves to his desk, where he lifts the handset to his phone. Dials with an index finger, then adjusts his glasses with his thumb. "I need someone in personnel."

Wallford takes the moment, turns half away from

Marcelin, leaning in to Ruiz, says in a lowered voice, "The hit on this is going to be massive. This is minutes away from blowing wide. There's not a corner of the globe isn't going to hear about this."

"Which is the only reason to do it. Why do it *this* way is the question."

Wallford glances to where Marcelin is still on the phone. "It was always the question. Unless there are an incredibly large number of hostages inside, suicide run at the front gates would've pulled a bigger body count. So it ain't about the body count."

"Someone's making a statement."

"A suicide bomb is a statement. And on American soil? What this is, this is a *different* statement, Colonel."

Two-tone beep, and Ruiz puts a hand to his earbud, and even before he does, Wallford's phone is demanding his attention, too. Coincidence is no longer in the offing, and Ruiz knows as he answers that whatever bad news is coming his way, Wallford is getting the same from a different source.

"Charlie Foxtrot," the duty sergeant says with the same complacent calm as ever. "Hit the BBC first, but it's spreading, CNN just got it. Video uploaded to YouTube, NSA is already onto it."

"Tell me." Ruiz picks up the remote control resting on the edge of Marcelin's desk, points it to the flat screen on the wall. The television flicks on to the WilsonEnt channel—WE!—an animated sword fight between some rough-and-tumble pirate and a host of shambling one-eyed beasts. Begins flicking channels quickly, the line still open in his ear.

"Hostages, ultimatum, and demands," the duty sergeant says. "Hostage numbers are unknown. Demands, as follows, quoting, 'the release of all unlawfully imprisoned soldiers of God held at Bagram, Guantanamo, and those secret installations around the world.'"

"Soldiers of God?" He doesn't look away from the screen, wondering just how many goddamn channels he'll have to wade through before he can find anything like information. Marcelin has hung up his own phone, coming around the desk to his right.

"That's the line, yes, sir."

"Or else?"

"They claim to have a radiological device they will detonate if their demands are not met within twelve hours."

"Direct quote?"

"Affirm. They're giving us until just before midnight."

The flicking pays off, a ticker running beneath a talking head who stands in front of a glowing world map, and Ruiz thinks they're so early that the news networks haven't even had time to work up their graphics. He's been channel surfing on mute, but he doesn't need the sound up to know the words being spoken by the earnest beauty staring anxiously, meaningfully into the camera. Then she vanishes, replaced by a video.

"Hold," Ruiz says.

"Holding."

He brings up the volume, taking in the image on the screen. Minor pixelation from the video camera, but it's simple, straightforward. If the analysts will draw anything from the image, Ruiz can't imagine how. White-wall background and a ski-masked man standing before it, dressed in black from head to toe, even his eyes hidden behind mirrored sunglasses. Not a bit of flesh to be seen. The voice that perhaps belongs to this figure speaks in English, is heavily digitized, has been run through filter after filter, warped and stretched. Ruiz wonders at the polish on display, the lengths to which whoever has crafted this message has gone to preserve anonymity. This is something new, he realizes, an order of magnitude above the terrorism he and his men have faced for the last several years.

That, as much as the figure's words, worry him.

The grotesque monument to the depraved and decadent blasphemy that is America, exporter of corruption and lust, the land where the pigs and dogs of the United States come to bloat themselves on sin, WilsonVille, now belongs to us.

We demand the immediate release and repatriation of those soldiers of God imprisoned by the immoral government of the United States and her allies. Those men now tortured and trapped in Guantanamo, Bagram, and elsewhere, held in secret prisons around the globe, are to be freed.

Unless these demands are met by twenty-three hundred hours, we will detonate the radiological device we have planted in WilsonVille. The yield of this detonation is large enough to render the park and the surrounding area uninhabitable, and will scatter radioactive material along the I-5 corridor, as far south as Camp Pendleton and San Diego, and as far north as Los Angeles and the Valley, as well as into the Pacific, to be carried along the coastal tides.

We hold hostages within the park. Any attempt to retake WilsonVille will result in their summary execution and the immediate detonation of our device. We are willing to die for our cause. We will not negotiate. This will be our only communication. We will know when our demands have been met.

God is great.

Video flicker, an edit, and the figure in black is gone, and there is, again, the glimpse of the white wall, and then there is nothing. The talking head reappears, manages to get as far as saying, "Local authorities are urging residents around WilsonVille not to panic—" before Ruiz turns the television off.

There is a moment where none of the men speaks.

"Mother of God," Marcelin finally says.

Ruiz looks to Wallford, finds the CIA man watching him. His expression mirrors Ruiz's thoughts.

"You have two shooters in the park," Wallford says. "Can they confirm there's a dirty bomb on the ground?"

Ruiz shakes his head slightly. "Only by eyeball, they're not geared for it."

"Your shooters." Marcelin is speaking carefully. "You've got to get them out. If they're spotted... they'll get the hostages killed."

"They already took down four," Ruiz says. "Too late for that."

"You heard what he said."

"I heard what was broadcast, yes."

"They'll get the hostages killed," Marcelin repeats.

"If there even are hostages," Wallford says. "We have no confirmation."

"You can't take that risk! *I* can't take that risk!"

"The demands are bullshit, pardon me, Mr. Marcelin," Ruiz says. "If the time frame was longer, I would accept it as plausible. As it stands, twelve hours is impossible, and whoever put this together, whoever had the wherewithal and technical expertise to mount this operation, to spoof the botulinum attack, they have to know that."

Marcelin meets Ruiz's gaze. "Then they have the technical expertise to hide a dirty bomb in my park, too, Colonel."

"In which case," Ruiz says, "my two shooters are the only people who can make certain that device, if it exists, never goes off."

"If you're wrong—"

"If he's wrong, we are thoroughly and completely fucked," Wallford says. "And that's all there is to say about that."

Chapter Fifteen

COMPARED TO a nuclear device, even a pocket nuke, a dirty bomb is still heavy, and this means Gabriel Fuller is lugging serious weight into the heart of WilsonVille. He's on coms from the command post, listening to the updates from Hendar, and when the call comes that one of his teams has met the deputy director of park safety, Jonathan Bell, with a group of three kids and one Friend, he's almost relieved.

"Pick him up," he tells Hendar. It's not because the man's management, though that may prove useful. It's not because, apparently, Jonathan Bell killed Stripe with his bare hands and then got out of the building without them noticing, though that marks him as far more danger-ous than Gabriel had any reason to believe WilsonVille security might be. It's not even because Gabriel is angry at Jonathan Bell for bringing Dana into the park today, something he knows is irrational yet feels nonetheless.

It's none of those things, and all of them, and the feeling he had when looking down at Stripe's corpse. This is going to be trouble. This man, he's going to make things hard.

When he hears the gunshots, then, he knows. As the echo fades in the park, before Hendar is squawking into his radio, Gabriel Fuller knows. He was right.

"Fuck!" Hendar says. "Fuck, that guy, he and another one, they just took down Bravo."

"Where are they now?"

"They're splitting up, he and another guy, some black guy, they're heading west, north of the river. The rest of them are running for the gate, ten of them. I can pull from Charlie to intercept."

"How many are we holding?"

"Alpha and Charlie have reported. Holding twenty-seven."

"Negative."

"Say again?"

"Negative. Charlie proceeds as ordered, let the ones heading for the gate go." Gabriel hops down from the platform beside the parked roller-coaster cars. The shots came from the east, and where he's standing, he can just catch a glimpse of the fleeing hostages before they vanish from sight. He turns northward, but rides and buildings are blocking his view, and even if they weren't, the foliage bordering the Timeless River would prevent him from seeing anything more. He moves to the control booth for the ride. "Track the other two, I want to know where they go. Are they leaving?"

"Doesn't look like it."

"Track them. Keep me posted."

"On it."

Gabriel stows his radio, stares down at the control panel for the coaster. It's idiotproof, a battery of meters and monitors reading the status of each train of cars, their speed and positions, a handful of switches and one lever to control release and pace and movement. One large red button, marked for emergency stop. He

186 • GREG RUCKA

reaches for the lever, ready to release the first train, then pauses, goes for his phone instead.

The Uzbek is answering before the first ring has sounded. "Status?"

"We have a problem," Gabriel says. "We have hostiles in the park, two of them."

"Do you indeed?"

Something in the Uzbek's tone makes Gabriel hesitate. "They just took down Bravo element."

"You've placed the device?"

"I'm about to run it up."

"How many hostages are you holding?"

"Twenty-seven."

"Break them up into smaller groups. Pick one, put a bullet in his head, and dump the body outside."

"We separate the groups, I'll have to break up the elements."

"I am fully aware of what it means. Give the order, and then take who you need and solve your other problem."

Gabriel doesn't speak. Solving his other problem—he understands that, he has no problem with that. There's no choice, and this Jonathan Bell and whoever is with him, they've got to be stopped before they can do more damage to the operation. But shooting a hostage, he can't help it, he doesn't like it. He doesn't want to do it.

"Matias? Is there a problem?"

"The hostages, they're mostly women and children."

"That is not a problem. That is a benefit."

The Uzbek hangs up.

Chapter Sixteen

THERE ARE fourteen of them in here, not counting the men with the guns.

There's Mom and Dana and the rest of the class, and a half dozen other people—three kids and their parents and someone dressed as Xi-Xi, the panda that Lilac, Lily, and Lavender made friends with when they visited China. All of them are sitting on the floor with their backs to the wall, and everyone is scared, though Mom and Dana are maybe doing the best at trying to hide it.

Athena can tell, though. She would be able to tell anyway, even if her mom wasn't holding her hand so tight and so hard that it hurts.

It's hot in here, too, no air-conditioning, even though there's this big machine that's been vibrating nonstop since they got here. They're inside Hendar's Lair, back in the Wild World, where they'd started the day, though Athena and the others hadn't actually gone on this ride. It's supposed to be a kind of interactive haunted house, except it's not a house but a cave, and it's not even really a cave because it's Hendar's Lair, which means it's decorated for some reason like a cross between an Arabian prince's tent and an old dungeon.

The man who shot Mr. Howe led them in here, just pushed the FRIENDS ONLY door open and then the three other men with their duffel bags filled with guns herded them all inside. They came in through the back, Athena thinks, past all these crates and boxes of equipment and supplies, and then into the heart of the ride, where Hendar's got his bedroom with all the gleaming treasure and silks and so on. Up close, she can see that the glittering treasure is Mylar and glass, and the silks are made of plastic.

They all had to stand in a line then, and the man who shot Mr. Howe searched them while the others pointed their guns. He took wallets and purses and bags but he didn't seem to care about the money, only cell phones. He wasn't nice about it, and Athena thinks he likes them being scared of him.

When he searched Mom, Mom tried talking to him. She saw her lips, knew she was trying to explain that Athena and Joel and Leon and Lynne and Gail and Miguel, that all of them were deaf. Dana tried, too, but whatever the man who shot Mr. Howe said in return made them all stop speaking. He finished searching Mom and pushed her, pointed to a space on the floor, and Athena found herself moving forward without thinking about it to push him back, but Dana caught her arm. Mom just shook her head, sitting where she'd fallen by the big fake bed that isn't as soft as a real bed should be.

Then the man who shot Mr. Howe gestured to the bed, and he must've said something, because the other three with guns laughed. He stepped closer to Athena, and Dana still had hold of her arm, and her fingers tightened on it. Athena didn't look away, trying to see this man's eyes behind the mask, but the light inside this little cave and the glass or plastic or whatever it is that covers his eyes made it impossible. She could feel her heart racing and she knew she was scared, but she was angry, too, and she wouldn't look away. Then he put his hands on her, to search her, and they weren't kind, and he touched her in places that she'd never let anyone touch her before. When he put a hand between her legs, he must have said something else, because Dana moved, then, just enough that Athena could read her lips.

Don't you dare you leave her alone.

The man who had murdered Mr. Howe left his hands where they were for a moment longer. Then he shoved Athena in the same direction as he had Mom, and she was sitting on the concrete floor painted to look like cave stone, smooth and cool, but not cool enough to keep her cheeks from feeling like they were on fire, or to keep the tears from pushing up in her eyes. Mom put her arms around her.

But Athena didn't look away, and she saw that when he searched Dana and took her phone away, he was even more cruel than before. He put a hand behind her head, and lifted her hair, and he kept one hand on her breast when he put his other between her legs. Dana didn't speak that Athena could see, but her jaw was clenched so tightly that the muscles in it trembled.

He did the same to Gail and Lynne, too, and when it was done and all of them were seated on the floor in a line, Athena could feel the anger and the shame.

All the worse because the men, the boys, they wouldn't even look at them, not even Joel.

Then the men with guns, all of them, moved away, to the other side of the room. Heads inclining just enough, and Athena knew they were speaking, and then the one who murdered Mr. Howe said something, gestured, and all of them were taking off their masks. Mom was holding her hand then.

She thought he would look evil, or ugly, or mean, but the man who had murdered Mr. Howe didn't look that way at all. Younger than Athena had thought he would be, maybe in his midtwenties, but that's only guessing, she really didn't know. But his face was smooth and almost handsome. One of the other men saw her looking at him, and he said something, and she missed most of it, but she thought she caught his name.

Vladimir.

Whatever else he said, Athena didn't know, but it made Vladimir look her way. Then he smiled.

Mom's grip on her hand got even tighter.

The men take off their white suits and open their duffel bags. They have guns of different kinds and radios. They don't talk to each other very much at all now, and when they do, Athena can't see their words.

Once, Mom turns her head to say something to Dana, and Vladimir with the smile points his gun at her. He doesn't seem angry and he doesn't seem to shout, and he's even smiling.

No talking.

Mom takes a deep breath, leans back against the wall, pulling Athena in closer. Vladimir lowers the gun in his hand, then turns his head sharply, and Athena is watching very closely as he picks up a radio and seems to listen to whatever is being said. Watching his mouth with every ounce of her focus, to see what he says in answer, but it doesn't help, because all she is sure he says is one word.

Understood.

Then he sets the radio down and points to two of the others, and they begin zipping their bags closed again, hoisting them up. Vladimir turns to look at them, all fourteen of them in a line against the wall. He smiles the not-kind smile again, points to Mom and Dana, and then to Joel, Lynne, Miguel, and the dad and one of his kids, a toddler. Last, he points at the woman dressed as Xi-Xi.

Up, Vladimir says. *Go with them.*

Mom and Dana start talking at the same time, each of them signing as they do.

Wait what are you doing? Mom is signing and saying.

Deaf, Dana is almost shouting. *They need an interpreter you can't break them up!*

Vladimir considers.

I only need one.

He grins. He points at Mom.

Up go with them.

Dana starts to get up. *I go.*

The grin gets bigger. *Sit down.* He looks at Mom again, motions with the gun in his hand for her to get to her feet. *Up now.*

Mom looks at Dana, at Athena, and her expression is nothing Athena can recognize, so beyond anything she has ever experienced from her mother that it takes her a moment before she can name it. Fear, yes, but that has faded in the face of this, and it is the look of someone who is helpless, who doesn't know what else she can do.

She lets go of Athena's hand, starts to rise.

"No!" Athena feels herself say, pulling on her mom's arm, trying to draw her back down, trying to get up with her. "No no no!"

Vladimir starts to come forward, and Mom shouts something to him, and he stops. She's on her feet, Athena standing with her, still holding onto her arm. She can feel the tears again trying to push their way free, and she shakes her head, repeating herself over and over again until Mom is facing her, bringing her hands in close to her chest.

Dad comes, Mom signs. *Dad comes soon.*

Athena silences herself, feels her lips trembling. Feels an ache in her breast and the pressure behind her eyes. She signs quickly.

Mom please mom no go please.

All okay Dad comes soon all okay.

Vladimir puts his hand on Mom's shoulder.

Love you.

Vladimir pulls Mom away, then pushes her to where the two men are gathering the other half of the group. Mom and the family and Xi-Xi together. Vladimir motions to them, says something that Athena can't see. One of the other men goes to the door, pushes it open slowly, peering out. Then they're all moving, being shepherded out the door, and Mom is looking back. From the way her mouth is moving, Athena knows that she's mouthing the words instead of speaking them.

It'll be all right baby, she mouths. *It'll be all right Daddy is coming Daddy is coming.*

Then she's gone, and Vladimir turns back to Athena.

And he smiles.

Chapter Seventeen

CHAIN CRACKS the service door on the east exterior wall of Valiant Keep while Bell covers their rear, his weapon in both hands, constant scan of overwatch. But there's been nothing, no movement, no contacts since the four hostiles they burned on the bridge. Bell's counted the cameras as they've made their way, thought about dumping a round into every one he saw, but two things speak against that tactic.

First, as of this moment, ammunition is precious.

Second, he wants his command post back, and there's no point in reclaiming it only to be blind.

"Clear," Chain says, and slips through the doorway, pivots, gun raised, covering Bell as the larger man ducks past, into the deep shadows of the still-under-construction keep. Chain shuts the door, moves past him, motioning to be followed.

They shadow the outer wall of the keep for twenty feet, then down a short flight of faux-stonework stairs to a large "oak" door that is neither oak nor large, the actual access being concealed in its face. Again Bell covers their backs as Chain checks, motions them through.

Bell backs in, still weapon-ready, feels the sudden temperature drop that comes from moving from above ground to beneath it. He's starting to turn when he hears the movement, feels Chain snap his weapon up, catches the glimpse of movement.

"Friendly," Nuri says. "Buzzsaw, friendly, friendly."

He turns to see the woman emerging from one of the side tunnels, clinging to shadow, gun in hand.

"Took you fucking long enough," she says.

Bell and Chain move forward, holstering their weapons as Shoshana Nuri does the same. Subdued tunnel lighting makes her skin and hair seem that much darker, part of the shadows she's been hiding in.

"We made contact," Bell says. "Four down, no idea how many left to go. Tried raising you, no response."

"Make it five," she says, reaching out with her free hand first to Chain, then to Bell, dropping an earbud into each man's palm before falling into line with them. Chain fits the bud to his left ear, stepping ahead to lead the way. "I was in your office when they hit the command post. Had to take one of them down to get out, headed straight into the tunnels."

Bell taps the earbud he's just fitted. "And out of coms. No reception down here."

"No radios, no phones. No way to contact you unless I went above ground. Staying put for the moment seemed wisest."

"No question."

"There's one benefit. No cameras down here." Nuri digs into the pocket of her blazer, comes out with a broken, warped piece of plastic that she offers to him. "Take a look."

Bell does, fragments of plastic and circuit board, with a strip that curls up and away from the underside.

A cell phone, he thinks, and he holds the pieces up to one of the light fixtures for a closer examination. Maybe a plastic wrap or a bag that fused to it, melted, and there's a cloudy, off-white film adhering to it. He hands the pieces back to Nuri.

"That how they did it?"

She nods, barely. "Think it is, at least. Cell-phone IED, inside some sort of wrapper or container holding the botulinum spoof. I could smell the plastic when I got down here, found it near one of the air-con compressors."

"If it's not botulinum, what is it?" Chain asks.

"It probably *is* botulinum, just not weaponized. Maybe derived from Botox. The toxin has seven distinct subtypes. If you're not actually weaponizing it, just making it *look* like you have, it's conceivably a relatively easy task to make something that would spoof the Spartan."

"Easy?" Chain shakes his head. "You Company girls."

"Relatively easy, I said." She looks to Bell. "What do we know?"

"Minimal. They're coordinated, and they've taken hostages." He indicates the remains of the IED in her hand. "They're resourced, and smart enough to do that and to fake weaponizing botulinum."

Nuri makes a small noise, almost approving. "Hostages to keep the assault force at bay."

"Big park, lots of places to hide people."

"And by the time any team breaches and locates where they're being held..."

"The hostages could be dead and cold."

Chain has moved on, taking it slower now. Bell is feeling calm, methodical, and while all their guard is still up, the cool and dim of the tunnels is welcome. For the time being, at least, for these next few minutes, they all know what they need to do.

There's a door along the west wall, and Chain unlocks it with a key he takes from around his neck. Pushes it open and reaches along the inside wall, and a weak energy-saver bulb comes to life, too-white light in the small room. Packed with merchandise awaiting the opening of the Keep, boxes labeled for posters, jackets, action figures, comic books. Chain pops his knife and slices one open, scatters a handful of T-shirts before freeing the first of their gear bags. Bell takes it as he digs out the second, and both men drop to their knees, Nuri watching, as they begin breaking out their gear.

"You cached these when, exactly?" Nuri asks.

Bell doesn't need to look up to see her expression; it's all in her tone. "Does it matter?"

"It matters if your people were sitting on intel they didn't see fit to share."

Chain mutters something about the Catskill Institute for Acne, continues pulling equipment from his bag. He's got their long guns out, M4 Commandos, is assembling them with almost magical speed. Bell sits back on his haunches, shucking off his suit jacket, looks up at Nuri. She's watching them with half an eye, the rest of her attention on the tunnel, gun still in hand.

"You with me?" he asks her.

"Of course I'm fucking with you. I'm standing here."

"You geared?"

"Not hardly."

Bell pulls the vest from his gear bag, hefts it up and into her hands. She exhales sharply, taking its weight, thirty pounds of personal protective equipment.

"Put that on."

"You have one for yourself?"

"I will endeavor not to get shot," Bell says.

Chain hands one of the assault rifles to Bell, then begins donning his own vest. "First time for everything."

"Last time I got shot, it was because of you, I recall." Bell finishes checking the rifle, a cursory, automatic survey that has nothing to do with faith in Chain and everything to do with twenty years of habit. He leans it against the wall, begins removing his necktie.

"Blue on blue," Chain says. "I barely touched you."

"How much do you know?" Nuri asks. She hasn't put on the vest.

Bell begins tucking magazines into the pouches of his combat harness, then moves to slip it on. "Right now? Hostiles in the park, and they have hostages."

"I'm talking prior knowledge."

Bell stops, harness open, looking at the woman. "You think we've been banking our intel?"

"There's an inside man."

"That's a given."

"You identified him. One of yours KIA."

Bell shakes his head. "You think we let this ride? I knew who killed Vesques, I'd never have let things get this far. You're thinking like CIA, sweetheart, you're thinking of acquiring assets. You're thinking little fish leads to the big one, but that's not our game. Our game was to keep this from happening, and when that failed, to do what we do now. We shut it down."

"Don't call me that."

Bell finishes his gear check. "FB?"

Chain holds up two of the flashbang grenades.

"Makes four," Bell says, showing two of his own.

"That's the next move?" Nuri asks.

"They took our eyes. We're taking them back." Bell stuffs his coat and tie into the bag, then stows it back in the box it came from. He reloads his pistol. "Contact Brickyard once we're in coms range, get the Sitrep, proceed from there."

"You want to take the CP back," Nuri says. "We take the CP back the hostiles will know, Master Sergeant. They'll know, and they'll drop the hostages."

"I am informed two of our brothers are en route. We'll wait until they're in position before we move. Once we have the CP, we'll be able to locate the hostages. Do what we do."

"One hundred and fifty-six acres of park, you're not going to be able to hit anything fast and hard. You're not thinking this through. We don't know who they are. We don't know who we're up against."

Chain shrugs, now in his own rig, wearing it over the Star System Alliance Defense coveralls. Bell sees it's still damp from the plunge Chain took, wonders if Chain has even noticed. "Doesn't matter."

"It *does* matter." Nuri is almost hissing. "We have no idea of their assets, their capabilities, their agenda."

Chain glances to Bell, raises an eyebrow. Bell notes

it, doesn't return it, still locked up on Nuri. She does not look like a woman who is having a good day, though Bell knows the same goes for the rest of them. Battle banter aside, all of them are aware of the stakes, and more, how many variables are still in play. They all know how much they don't know. And the woman has a point; if these men who have launched their very coordinated, very smart assault on WilsonVille believe their hostages are of no further use, then they'll no longer view them as hostages. Rather, they'll view them as target dummies.

"They want something," Bell says. "You see that? If this was straight-up terrorism, they wouldn't have cleared the park. They'd have just suicide-bombed us and been done with it. But they have the hostages for a reason, because they want something."

"That's what I'm saying." Nuri brushes hair back from her cheek. "Moving on them before we know what they're after, that doesn't track smart to me. There's a larger play."

"Whatever they want, that's going to keep them holding their fire."

"That's a leap I'm not comfortable making."

"It's the one we're taking."

"And you're sure of it, are you, Master Sergeant?"

"Sure as I can be."

"And if—just *if*—what they actually want is to make us look like fools, to humiliate us in front of the world? To wait until we make our move and then murder those same people we're trying to save? What then? AQ tactic is to deliver a first strike then follow up when the responders are on the ground, you know that.

Maybe they're just waiting for us to make our move before they make their next one."

Bell considers.

"We move faster," he says.

They stick to the tunnels, cutting south, common sense dictating that they not emerge where they entered. Moving more slowly now, more cautiously, and the minutes continue to tick. Chain on point with his M4 up and tucked at his shoulder, Nuri, now wearing the vest, center, her pistol in both hands, and Bell watching their backs with his own assault rifle high and ready. They pass abandoned maintenance carts and toppled trash bags, dressing rooms with discarded costumes scattered here and there, left where they were dropped in the evacuation; makeup tables with cosmetics and prostheses on them. The scent of soda pop, caramel corn, hot dogs, and burned plastic mixes with the recycled air.

"How we doing this, Top?" Chain asks.

Bell defers the answer, asks Nuri his own question. "Angel? What route did you take?"

"You mean from your office? Used the access in the service area behind the facades."

Bell considers. The row of buildings that border Wilson Town on the east and west sides are designed to look like individual structures to park guests, but in truth are one enormous building each. Long hallways, hidden from public view and use, run along the rear of both structures, facilitating movement of staff and goods, and each hallway has tunnel access.

"They made your egress, they might have someone watching it."

"And a welcoming committee," Chain adds.

"Problem. All other approaches require covering open ground. Puts us on camera, they move to intercept."

"There's another option," Nuri says. "We have mission coms."

"Effective only above ground. Hold."

They come to a stop, and Bell lowers his rifle, hands it to Nuri, then removes his combat harness. He offers it to her, takes the rifle back while she puts it on, then returns the M4 to her hands.

"I'm not the expert at clearing a room," she says.

"I'll give them something else to look at while you do it. Follow Chain's lead, you'll be fine." Bell checks his watch, the hands faintly luminous in the subdued light of the tunnel. "I have twelve forty-seven. Mark me thirty minutes, move at thirteen seventeen. Contact when you have the CP."

"Thirteen seventeen," Chain echoes. "Hey, Top? Don't get your old-man ass shot again."

"You won't be with me," Bell says. "Think I'll be all right."

Chapter Eighteen

THE UZBEK has been waiting for months, quite literally, to make this call.

It's almost a quarter past one in the afternoon in this room at the Beverly Hilton in Los Angeles, the television on and babbling with anxious glee about the developing situation at WilsonVille. The information is still confused, but the video has done its job, and the media is, as ever, eager to play their part.

The Uzbek's been impressed with the government's response, on almost every level. Local authorities have done an impressive job of cordoning off the area, and already the governor has held a press conference, urging people not to panic, explaining that the situation is fluid, in flux, and there is no reason to believe the claims in the video are true. The White House has released a statement saying much the same thing, assuring the American people that everything can and will be done to resolve this crisis, and adding that under no circumstances will the nation bow before the demands of terrorists. The president is monitoring the situation closely.

Helicopter footage shows, live, the streams of automobiles clogging Interstate 5 and the 405 and the state routes. Most people who are able to seem to be heading east, for the mountains and the desert. There's been some unconfirmed reports of rioting as well, and the Uzbek has listened to two experts on two different channels talking about dirty bombs, about how they're not to be confused with actual nuclear weapons, about their limitations. These two experts have tried to use facts, but facts are of little interest in the face of sensation.

The Uzbek's favorite part, as he eats gravlax and washes it down with a modest prosecco, was when one broadcast was interrupted with live footage, telephoto shots of the front gates of WilsonVille. When two of his handpicked men, long guns slung over their shoulders, still dressed in their Tyvek and gas masks, tossed the body out the front gates. The woman dressed as a panda, who hit the ground heavy and wrong and didn't move. Authorities had imposed a no-fly zone over the park, but one of the news copters violated it and got footage from above, and it made the statement all the more clear, all the more stark.

When that happened, he imagined boys and girls all around the world looking at their own little stuffed pandas in horror and fear. He suspects his master thought much the same thing when he saw it.

Then the broadcast cuts away to more anxious babbling, and the Uzbek turns the television off. He takes out the cell phone he has purchased specifically for this call. He dials slowly, one-handed, using his thumb, emptying his glass with the other, then rises and moves to the window. He has a view of the pool, and, perhaps unsurprisingly, there are still several people around it and in the water, oblivious to or uncaring about what's happening less than a hundred miles to the south. There are several beauties, wearing strips of fabric that are, at best, coy, and as the phone rings in his ear, the Uzbek wonders if he could fuck one of them. Times like this, he wishes he could fuck them all.

The phone rings several times before being answered. "Jamieson residence."

"I need to speak to Lee Jamieson," the Uzbek says.

"Mr. Jamieson is unavailable." The voice belongs to a man, the accent vaguely Hispanic. "I can take a message."

"Give him this message, exactly. I will call back in exactly three minutes. I am calling to speak to him about a dead panda."

The Uzbek hangs up, then powers off the phone, tosses it onto the bed. Checks the time, then takes the second phone, also purchased precisely for this call. He opens the sliding glass door, steps out onto the balcony of his room, smells the smog and heat, hears the water and the laughter and splashing below. There's a blonde lounging poolside, sunglasses and golden tan. Her legs are long and her breasts barely contained by her top, a belly flat and smooth, and he can almost taste her from here. He watches her unabashedly, obviously, and after a few moments she reaches up and adjusts the strap at her shoulder, then lowers her sunglasses just enough to show him her eyes, meeting his gaze. The Uzbek grins at her, and she returns that, too, lazily. Tilts her head to the side, where it lies against the chaise lounge, and he can feel her looking him over.

The Uzbek raises his free hand, shows her three numbers in sequence, his room number. She seems to laugh. The Uzbek closes his hand, opens it again, five fingers this time.

Then he turns away and dials once more. This time, there is only one ring, and Mr. Money is answering.

"Why the fuck are you calling me? You said there'd be no more contact, you Russian fuck! Why are you calling me?"

"I lied to you," the Uzbek says, not bothering to correct the man. "You have been following the news?"

"Jesus Christ, yes." The man sounds breathless, as if he's taken a beating to the stomach. The Uzbek wonders how he'll sound in just a few more moments. "What the hell are you people doing? This isn't what I paid for, I didn't pay for that! That woman, they just *dumped* her—"

"The device is in place," the Uzbek interrupts, voice mild. If Mr. Money thought that WilsonVille could be taken and held without loss of life, he was actively deceiving himself. He steps back into the room, leaving the door open behind him. "Exactly as you requested. In order to effect the result you commissioned, you understand that the device had to be legitimate, yes? It has to do what we claimed it would do. And it does, I assure you. It does *exactly* what it is supposed to do."

There is a pause, just a moment, and the Uzbek admits he is surprised at how quickly Mr. Money puts two plus two together.

"You motherfuckers."

"Hmm." The Uzbek might be agreeing with him. "You will pay, as before, the same sum, as before, or the device will be armed and detonated. Do you understand?"

"You…motherfuckers…." Mr. Money is breathing heavily, almost wheezing into the phone. "You would, wouldn't you? You sons of bitches, you…you would…"

"Of course we would," the Uzbek says. "You're the one with an ideological agenda, sir. We are simply a business."

"I can't free that sum, not in this amount of time, not…not without it being tracked. You'll expose me, you'll—"

"Do you think that concerns us in the least?"

The wheezing stops, the line going silent for long enough that the Uzbek wonders if Mr. Money has suffered a heart attack or some similar event. Then his voice returns, trembling in its rage, or perhaps in its determination.

"I refuse. This isn't what I paid for; I paid for the statement, the message, not this."

"I would urge you to reconsider."

"No, you listen to me. You were paid, your people, they were paid."

"Your answer is no, then?"

"I wouldn't even if I could."

"Hmm," the Uzbek says. "Very well. I wish you a good day."

"Wait just—"

The Uzbek hangs up. Purses his lips, checks his watch. It's coming up on one thirty now. There is a knock at the door. He opens it, and there is the blonde, her towel wrapped about her hips, chewing her lower lip in nervous affectation.

"Hi," she says. "I'm Taylor."

"Taylor. Please, come in." He steps back, sweeping his arm and ushering her inside, closing the door after her. She steps in slowly, leaning forward to look about the room, and the Uzbek takes the opportunity to slap her towel-hidden backside. She jumps, squeaks, turning to grin at him.

"You don't waste time."

"Nor do you, I think," the Uzbek says. "Make yourself comfortable. Pour yourself a drink. I have one more call to make."

"Comfortable, huh?"

He nods her toward the bed, then ignores her entirely. He can feel his erection, already full and determined, and he wonders what is thrilling him more: the thought of fucking this woman who is giving herself up so easily, or the thought of fucking all of Southern California, the United States of America, and that piece of shit, Mr. Money.

He dials Matias's number, thinking that it's all fucking the same things.

Chapter Nineteen

BELL MOVES quicker alone, sacrificing stealth for speed, heading back up the Gordo Tunnel and then turning again onto the Flashman Tunnel, heading east. Jogging easily, pistol in his hands, south again at Betsy. Maybe he should've kept the rifle, but appearing on camera with a long gun and full combat rig, that would have tipped his hand, maybe even warned whoever was on the cameras that more were coming, geared and ready. With the pistol, Bell hopes to look like the same threat he was before, hopes his presence alone will be bait enough. Trying to remember the camera emplacements above ground, where he'll be most easily spotted. The highest concentration is, logically, in the zones around the park perimeter, tapering off the deeper one goes into the park.

He wants to be seen, and Bell figures Wild World Live! is probably his best bet; it's close enough to the entrance that he'll have cameras, but far enough from the Sheriff's Office, the command post, that—presuming that's where the hostiles are staging from—they'll need to cover some ground to reach him. There's the added benefit that it's a theater, backstage areas outside of surveillance, with plenty of cover and room to move.

The mixed scent of the animals greets him as he

makes his approach, slowing at the foot of the ramp. Their noise comes next, the anxious chitter and chirp of creatures used to constant tending and near-constant attention, abruptly abandoned. Perhaps they've sensed that something has happened, perhaps it's simply the breakdown in their routines, but they don't sound happy.

He holds in the shadow of the ramp that feeds into the backstage, checks his watch, and finds it's nine minutes past one. Chain and Angel should be in position and holding, and he frees one hand to press at his earbud.

"Chain, Angel," he murmurs. "Warlock, coms check."

No response, which he interprets to mean they're still below ground, still waiting on the clock. As they should be, and it's what he expected, but it was worth a try. He frees his phone next, sees that it has, once again, acquired a signal. Still holding in the shadows, the noise of the animals in the background, he punches up Brickyard.

"Brickyard, go."

"Warlock. Chain and Angel are in position to take back the CP, ten minutes."

"We have new information," Ruiz says.

"Tell me."

"Confirm hostages on the ground. One has already been executed. Hostiles are claiming they have a radiological device, will detonate if demands not met, will detonate if any attempt is made to retake the park. Bone and Board are en route to my location, estimate deployment fourteen forty."

Bell leans back against the wall, eyes on the mouth

of the tunnel, up the ramp. There's been no movement, but still, he won't look away, even as he considers what Ruiz is telling him. A dirty bomb changes things, and changes them radically, but it throws a whole new sheet of doubt up, as well. Whoever these people are, they're savvy enough to have coordinated taking the park, to have put at least one person on the inside, to have spoofed the botulinum. Bell can believe in their ability to construct and place a radiological device.

But believing its existence and then believing that, whoever these people are, they're willing to set it off— that's something else. Unless they're willing to die for their cause, they'll be exposing themselves to the same radioactive debris as their targets. Outside of immediate ground zero, a dirty bomb does slow work, attacks economies far more effectively than it does individuals. Contamination from the debris would take years to manage, cost literally billions to clean up, and even then, the park's reputation would be destroyed. A dirty bomb detonating in WilsonVille would kill the park just as thoroughly as if it were shot in the base of the skull, and would kill Wilson Entertainment with the same slow inevitability as cancer, the same cancer hundreds of thousands might contract as a result.

Death might come slowly, but it would come all the same, to friend and foe alike.

"Are they true believers?" Bell asks.

"They talk the talk," Ruiz says. "But they're walking funny."

Bell wants to grin at that, but can't bring himself to do it. "The CP has the Spartan. We get it up and running, we can scan for radioactive material."

"You trust that Spartan?"

"Either that or wait. Are you telling us to hold?"

Ruiz answers without hesitating. "They're killing hostages."

"Understood."

"Out."

WilsonVille itself isn't equipped to house the animals who perform in the Flower Sisters Mystical Show and Wild World Live! on-site. Rather, they're brought into the park each morning, escorted by their staff of handlers and overseen by the chief vet. For every animal used in the show, there's at least one, sometimes as many as four, left to figuratively—and often literally—wait in the wings. Three separate jaguars are required for Real Live Hendar, for example, none of which are allowed to work for more than thirty minutes a day. A tired cat is a dangerous cat, and, from a management point of view, a lawsuit waiting to happen. The same can be said for the lionesses that perform as Real Live Lavender, though as Bell understands it, there are only two gazelles because, as it was explained to him, gazelles are actually really fucking stupid.

He's not sure about the snakes.

He's thinking about all this as he comes off the ramp from the tunnel and into the animal holding area of Wild World Live!, hears the growl from one of the big cats hidden nearby. It's a wide, sunken space, feeding into backstage, covered overhead by a massive awning meant to shield those below from the sun. The holding areas themselves are separated by sixteen-foot-tall curtains, and he imagines this is done to keep the animals from eyeing one another, though clearly it does nothing to hide their scents. The cat—or perhaps a different cat—growls again, and maybe the beast is smelling Bell, or maybe it's just pissed off at having been left alone on this scorching day.

It's a sound that sinks through flesh and awakens primal warnings that evolution has done nothing to dull. It's a sound that makes his muscles tense, and draws his attention unconsciously from what he's doing and where he is to the more urgent need to be certain—absolutely certain—that some pissed-off jaguar or indignant and hungry lioness isn't about to make a meal of him.

This is why Jad Bell doesn't spot the Tango until it's too late.

This is what he tells himself later, at any rate.

He's coming around one of the holding pens, this to his right, the heavy, high curtains blocking the sight lines of one animal to another. The stage is to his left, the literal backstage, and another curtained block lies dead ahead. He hears a snarl, this one unquestionably a warning, a declaration, catches the scent of fresh blood and offal, all suddenly clear; the ammonia tang of urine. He hears what he thinks is the sound of a baby's whimper.

The curtain beside him flutters, parts. Head turn, a quick flash, a cage, a jaguar, a dead gazelle torn open stem to stern, organs spilling into a burgundy pool on the concrete ground. And the Tango, most important, the Tango: Caucasian, no more than his midtwenties, still in Tyvek, no mask, no gloves, black hair and startlingly blue eyes. A submachine gun in his right hand,

and Bell identifies the weapon without thought, an MP5K. The man is grinning, opening his mouth to speak in the moment before he realizes Bell is standing, unexpectedly, in front of him.

Bell pivots, raising his weapon and trying to take a half step back all at once. The Tango is fast, or maybe he's panicked and *that* makes him fast, but his left snaps up, into Bell's hands, knocks the .45 out of line and out of his grip, sends the gun clattering to the concrete. Mouth opens, and he starts an inarticulate shout of surprise, but Bell is now stepping forward, snapping his forehead into the Tango's nose. The cry is stifled, turns to a choke, his nose shattering, and he staggers back.

Bell presses, pursuing, trying to put his fingers through the man's trachea. But the Tango is swinging the submachine gun up, wild, and the weapon begins to speak and spit even before it's in line, and Bell throws his left forearm up instead, blocking the swing. He's inside the man's guard, drives his right at the Tango's throat, hits his chin as the other man instinctively tries to protect his neck. Still surging forward, smashing the Tango's back against the bars of the cage. The jaguar within roars, meal threatened.

The MP5K shouts again, another rattle of shots, wild, deafening in Bell's left ear. He shifts, moves from the waist, gets his right onto the Tango's wrist, slips to a finger, twists and pulls, feels bone snap. The Tango shouts as he loses his weapon, pounds his left down, trying to catch Bell at the back of the neck. Misses, the punch just low, hitting the spine and the mass of muscle. Bell grunts, right forearm rising to cross, again going for the throat, and now each man has a grip on the other; Bell can feel the Tango's fingers clawing at his face, straining for his eyes even as Bell tries to force the man's head back, tries to crush his windpipe with his arm. The Tango drops his weight, Bell's purchase vanishes, and he feels half his wind rush free as his back collides with the cage. Punches with his left, hard and fast twice to the man's midsection, and the Tango takes both punches and is now trying to crush the back of Bell's head against the bars, through the bars. The jaguar roars again, and Bell feels a searing heat blossom at his lower back.

There is an awful clarity, a pristine knowledge, that comes to Jad Bell then and there. He is getting old, he is getting tired. He is a hard man, a warrior soul, a soldier, but this man, this Tango, is younger and faster and maybe stronger. This Tango, he fights like they taught Bell to fight; he fights dirty, for his life, and to win.

Jad Bell is about to lose this fight.

He strains to move his head against the Tango's pressure, turns his mouth enough to find the meat at the side of the man's hand, bites. Tastes sweat, copper, feels his teeth tearing skin, struggling to meet. This time, the Tango screams, uses his other hand to punch Bell in the face, breaking the bite, lurching backward. Bell lunges, again trying to press his small advantage, and the two are grappling again, out of the pen, into the open, clutching at each other, pulling at clothes and flesh.

Tango twists, using Bell's momentum, trying to shake him, swinging him about. Bell hangs on, lungs burning, gasping for breath. This much exertion, sweat is pouring off him, pouring off the other man. World spins, peripheral information, all the things that fight-or-flight take in when fight is at full. He can discern the velvet-like fabric of the black curtains, sees a new set sweeping wide, revealing another Tango, armed, cage behind him. People in that cage.

He thinks he sees Amy.

Then they're gone, out of sight, heavy fabric enveloping him, opening, as he and the man trying to kill him spin into a new pen. The Tango brings his knee up, sharp, catches Bell in the hip, frees one hand, follows the blow with another attempt at the neck. Bell shields, catches it on the jaw, light sparking behind his eyes and blood spilling in his mouth, and his grip is gone and he smashes into something hard and smooth. Feels it give way and an instant later, the shattering of glass.

He hits the concrete, feels the abrasion on his cheek, the weight of the Tango falling on him as he tries to roll. Vision clearing, and he snaps an elbow back, catches the other man a glancing strike to the head, too high for the temple. Rolling over broken glass, hearing it snap, and Bell sees dirt and rock and branches spilled on the ground, the cases on their stands, the snakes in their cases.

He's on his back now, the Tango over him, feels his vision burst again, a rock-heavy impact and another, punched twice more in the face. Trying to bring one leg around, to lock the other man, but he doesn't have it left in him, there is not enough air, there will never be enough air, and sweat stings, drips off this Tango into Bell's eyes. Feels the hands at his throat, the cloud pressing into his mind, slowly trying to blind him. He flails, right hand straining amid the debris at his side, broken glass beneath his fingertips.

Something hisses like steam escaping a relief valve, the hood of a cobra spreading in the corner of Bell's eye. The Tango's grip loosens for a moment, the man looks, he can't not, and the shard of glass is cold under Bell's hand. He feels it cutting his palm as he takes hold, pours all the strength that remains into his right arm, striking up and in, feels the sadly familiar sensation of stabbing a living body. The Tango's eyes snap wide as Bell shoves the piece of glass into the man's neck, driving it upward, carotid, jugular, trachea, twisting it to make the wound crueler and quicker.

The Tango dies, blood pouring out of him and down Jad Bell's arm. He goes to dead weight, and Bell wants to stop then, wants to stop there, hurting and breathless and aching, knows he can't.

Because there's one more Tango, and he thinks there's Amy, too, thinks he can hear her voice calling for him.

He hears the cobra warning him again, angry, and Bell shoves the dead man off him, toward the snake, struggles to his knees. More broken glass on the ground and no weapons but for the knife on his person, and he's about to go for that when the cobra rises, swaying, swings toward the curtains that are suddenly sweeping apart, reacting to the sudden motion. The remaining Tango, another MP5K, searching, seeing them.

In one move, Bell grabs the cobra above the tail, flings the snake at the Tango even as the creature tries to arch, to snap back at his hand. Flies through the air, a writhing length of cord, the Tango panics. His weapon hits the ground, hands coming up, trying to shield and catch and backpedal all at once, through the curtains. Bell dives, finds the submachine gun with both hands, sliding forward, beneath the edge of the curtain. Sights and fires, a three-round burst that lands groin, gut, thorax.

The remaining Tango drops, still holding the cobra, the snake's fangs latched at the man's collar, pumping venom into a corpse. Bell thumbs the selector down, aims, and takes its head with a bullet.

There is an aching, awful silence, broken at first by his ragged breathing.

He hears Amy.

"Jad! Jad! God, please, Jad! Answer me!"

Bell knows what she's going to say next. Knew it the moment he saw her, but didn't have the time to realize it. What has to be, because she's here, knows it the same way he knows that these two Tangos thought putting the hostages in the gazelle's cage, and putting the gazelle in with one of the jaguars, made perfect sense.

Makes perfect sense.

"Oh, God, Jad." Amy, hidden from view, and her voice, trying to stay steady even as the words themselves betray her. "They have our baby, Jad. They have Athena."

Chapter Twenty

WHEN THEY lost them at Valiant Keep, Gabriel considered going into the tunnels in pursuit, but he didn't consider it for long. He'd spent too much time beneath WilsonVille already, and the thought of a gunfight down there wasn't just stupid, it was suicidal. He'd either end up playing cat and mouse, or pouring his people into a fatal funnel. Less than three hours into the operation already, and he'd lost five of his men. He didn't want to spend any more of them unless he was certain of the result. Army tactics: engage the enemy on your terms and your grounds, pick your battle.

Fighting fair gets you killed. So you don't fight fair.

That meant waiting, hard to do already, harder still after he'd heard the gunshot, after he knew that one of the hostages had been killed. He was making his way back to the command post, Hendar still on coms, Gordo and Betsy still on surveillance, watching for a sign of Jonathan Bell and his friend, but after the execution, Gabriel had to ask.

"Who was it?"

"Some woman," Hendar said. "Dressed like one of those bears, you know, from China?"

"Xi-Xi."

"Whatever."

Whatever, Gabriel thought. Whatever.

And then he thought that maybe he knew this Xi-Xi, maybe they had exchanged words in some changing area, or backstage at some show. Shared a joke, a drink of water, maybe bitched about management, and he stopped that line of thought as quickly as he could.

Not quickly enough.

Not knowing where Jonathan Bell might emerge, Gabriel has Betsy join him outside Dawg Days Theatre. He'd have preferred to draw another shooter off one of the remaining teams, thinks he can probably afford to do it, but he doesn't like the idea of leaving any of the hostages under weak guard, especially now that Alpha and Charlie have been broken into separate elements. Up until now, he's kept the faith in the Uzbek's plan, trusting that both he and the Shadow Man know what they're doing, that there is a purpose to everything they have asked Gabriel to do.

Now, for the first time, Gabriel Fuller is beginning to have doubts. Seventeen men to take and hold the park? A dirty bomb that might or might not be real, that might or might not be armed? Almost thirty hostages, but no orders to ransom or release them, and one of them already murdered for display?

It doesn't make sense. None of it makes sense. He doesn't understand.

And the nagging, persistent, and now growing fear that the egress plan isn't much of a plan at all. That despite the Uzbek's assurances that Gabriel is too valuable to leave to die here in WilsonVille, his escape is anything but assured.

All these things, and this variable, this Jonathan Bell and his friend in the Star System Alliance Defense coveralls. Friends and Management, bullshit. They were in the park, they were armed, they took down Bravo before any of Gabriel's own people could fire a shot. That means only one thing.

That means someone knew they were coming.

There was never supposed to be opposition *inside* the park. All the things they accounted for, all the details they covered, and they never considered opposition within the park, because that was never, ever, supposed to happen. They were to clear the park, hold it, use the hostages as a deterrent. They were to place the device, not arm it. They were to take the command post to monitor any approach to WilsonVille, any effort to breach the walls, and they were to shoot dead anyone who got too close. Then they were to wait until the Uzbek contacted Gabriel to say their demands had been met and to tell him to prepare the egress.

Thus far, Gabriel has done everything right, everything the Uzbek ordered. He's done everything right.

But it feels like it's all going wrong.

The only thing to do, then, is to kill Jonathan Bell and his Star System mechanic friend, and hope that puts the plan back on track. But he's down five men, and he can't spare any from the hostage groups, so finally he orders Betsy to join him, and tells himself that, when the time comes, they'll have the element of surprise.

Don't fight fair, Gabriel Fuller reminds himself. *Fight to win.*

They wait in the foyer of the theater. Betsy has

brought the submachine gun that Stripe was using, has one of his own. Gabriel watches as the other man leans back against the wall, beneath a painting of Willis Wilson with his arms spread wide and welcoming, pulls a pack of cigarettes from a pocket, and knocks one free. Betsy lights it, then offers the pack to Gabriel, who just shakes his head, thinking that there's no smoking allowed in the park.

He keys his radio. "Any movement?"

"Nothing. No sign of him or the other one anywhere."

"Check the teams. I want their status."

"Hold on."

Betsy flicks ash onto the royal blue carpet, squints out the open doors at Town Square, sunlight kicking back off the bronze heads of Gordo, Betsy, and Pooch, where their statues stand at the heart of Wilson Town. Gabriel shifts the submachine gun in his hands, looking down at the weapon, not quite seeing it. It was the same when he was in Afghanistan. The waiting is always the worst.

"Charlie has broken into two groups," Hendar says. "Six and seven hostages each. Alpha's the same. Have three of the elements on camera as well, so we can monitor."

"Why only three?"

"Alpha Two, the one that took the panda, they're holding their group in one of the backstage areas of some animal show, out of camera. Why the fuck aren't there any cameras backstage?"

"The same reason there aren't any cameras in the tunnels." Gabriel stops for a moment, steps out from the theater a couple of steps, into the sunlight, looking around. The sun beats down so hard it feels like his hair is aflame. "The cameras are for the guests, not the Friends."

"The Friends?"

"Employees. Staff."

Hendar chuckles, says, in Russian, "Fucking Americans."

"Keep it in English," Gabriel snaps. "Tell Alpha Two to move into camera range. We need to see them."

"Understood."

"Just two guys," Betsy says, stepping up beside him and flicking his butt away. "You're too tense. Just two guys, we can take them."

Gabriel gives him a look that says exactly what he thinks of this unsolicited opinion. Betsy shrugs.

"We may have a problem," Hendar says slowly.

"What?"

"Second Alpha element...they're not responding."

Immediately, Gabriel starts running, cutting between the Wilson Restaurant and the Sweets Emporium, Betsy close on his heels. "Get them on radio!"

"That's what I'm fucking trying to do!"

Betsy stays close at his heels, following as Gabriel vaults the turnstiles at Cannonball Plunge, runs alongside the waterfall, feels its spray on his skin, feels the water evaporate almost instantly. Cuts between two concession stands, submachine gun in his hands, legs pumping. Hendar is silent in his ear, the whole park silent, and he realizes he hasn't heard gunfire, no shots, and for a moment he can allow himself to believe this is just a coms error, a clusterfuck breakdown. It could be perfectly innocent, if innocence still manages to re-side anywhere within WilsonVille.

This doesn't have to belong to Jonathan Bell.

Then he hears the gunfire, the reports rolling through the park, distant, its direction impossible to determine. But he knows where it's coming from, he knows where it has to be. Just as he knows the source, and the reason.

"Still no response," Hendar reports. "Nothing, not a thing—"

"Watch the perimeter!" He's rounding the cluster of giant mushrooms that house the toilets between the two live animal shows, realizes he doesn't know which one he's heading for. "Where are they? Exactly!"

"The animal show, they're—"

"There are two of them!"

Hendar says "Shit" in Russian, shouts to Gordo. There's another battery of shots, this time quicker, a three-round burst, and Gabriel immediately cups one of his ears, closes his eyes. A breath later, a single re-port, and he *thinks* it's south of where he's standing now. Sets off again as Hendar comes back, still no idea where, why the hell aren't there cameras backstage?

"Watch the perimeter," Gabriel says. "Watch the fucking perimeter, I don't want any more surprises!"

Then he's threading the chain-marked queue at Wild World, half spinning as he comes through the entrance at the side of the amphitheater. He pauses here, presses himself against the wall just outside the seats. Benches rise along one side of the bowl, allowing an unob-structed view of the stage below. There's no move-ment, no motion that he can see. With his left hand,

Gabriel signals to Betsy, orders him to move around to the other side, to take a flanking position. He hears an echo, faint, the source lost in the acoustics of the amphitheater; metal clanging on metal, then nothing more.

"Tell me you have something," Gabriel hisses to his radio. His hands are perspiring around the submachine gun, and he shifts his grip, wipes his palms against his T-shirt. "Tell me you have something."

"Nothing, no movement."

Across the bowl, opposite him, Gabriel sees Betsy raise a hand in signal, in position. He raises a fist in response, indicates the direction he wants Betsy to take. Settles his grip on the submachine gun, begins to advance in parallel, both men working their way down the aisle, toward the stage. Closing, he catches the scent of the animals, hears them in the distance. The radios have gone silent, no traffic, and Gabriel feels the same adrenaline apprehension he would feel on patrol, in the dust and scrub. Search and destroy, and the environs have changed, but he realizes the mission is the same.

They flank the stage, holding at the stairs on either side for a moment, each of them again checking their surroundings, listening and looking. Only the sound of the animals, and even they seem subdued now. Another exchange of hand signals, and together they mount, turn, weapons raised, advancing to the scrim, splitting off at the wings, and still there's no one and nothing, and they come around into the backstage together, overlooking the depressed holding area, the curtained cages, and Gabriel knows they're too late.

One dead man on his back, with a dead snake to keep him company. No weapon, no radio. Parted curtains and an open, empty cage. Broken glass and another body, likewise missing his gear. A jaguar with a bloodied muzzle, watching them with yellow eyes as it lies beside the torn form of a gazelle.

"Fuck," Betsy says.

Gabriel pulls his radio. "Anything?" he asks Hendar.

Hendar doesn't respond.

"Delta One, respond," Gabriel says.

Dead air.

Betsy is looking at him.

"Coms check," Gabriel says. "Alpha One, respond."

"I have you," Vladimir answers. "Loud and clear."

"Stand by. Delta One, respond."

And nothing.

"Could be power, maybe?" Betsy says. "They would cut the power to the park, right?"

"Park's on its own generators." Gabriel shakes his head. If this was a bank, something else, sure, the authorities would have cut the power long ago. But WilsonVille can't afford a power outage, not when hundreds of people may be on roller coasters and inside haunted houses when a blackout occurs. WilsonVille has its own power.

Hendar isn't responding, and it's not because coms have gone down.

Then the phone in his pocket begins to vibrate, and Gabriel Fuller knows the Uzbek is calling.

And he doesn't know what to tell him.

Chapter Twenty-one

MATTHEW MARCELIN is back from his second press conference, gulping water from a bottle while one of his assistants tries to apply another powdering of makeup in preparation for his third. Looking past his shoulder to the television, Ruiz sees the man again, standing outside and in front of this same building, behind a WE! podium. The volume is muted, but his concern and his competence are both loud.

"Trouble," Wallford tells Ruiz. "Incoming."

Marcelin's office has become, to Ruiz, the war room, and to Matthew Marcelin, he imagines, the crisis management center. Junior executives and personal aides scurry in and out, the flat-screen monitor on the wall now fixed on one of the cable news networks, more telephones than people, and more noise than Ruiz would like. Warlock in his ear, giving him the bullet: two more Tangos down, Chaindragger and Angel have secured the command post, and he is escorting the hostages through the tunnels for evac.

And the ribbon on the package.

"They have my daughter," Bell says.

"I have the rest of your unit joining me, fifteen minutes," Ruiz says, watching as Eric Porter enters the room. Coming up on four hours since the park was taken, this is the first time Ruiz has seen the director of park and resort safety, and the part of him not evaluating just how compromised his team leader has now become has to wonder just what the hell Porter has been doing in that time, and where exactly he's been doing it. There's a flush to Porter's cheeks, a sheen of sweat, and maybe it's the forty pounds of extra meat the man carries on his frame, and maybe it's the stress, but Ruiz wonders if he'll be smelling whiskey on Porter's breath in just another few seconds.

"They have my daughter, Colonel," Bell says again. "I am securing my wife in the command post, and then I am locating my daughter."

"That is ill-advised, Master Sergeant. Hold for the rest of your team, we will move to free all the hostages together."

"You are asking me to wait, sir. Would you wait, sir?"

"That is affirmative, Master Sergeant."

"Clarify: Are you ordering me to wait, sir?"

"I am ordering you to hold position in the CP until further notice. Confirm."

He hears Bell's breath, a ragged exhale that makes Ruiz wonder if he's been wounded.

"I am holding position," Bell says. "Out."

Ruiz kills the connection, pockets his phone. He's lied to Bell, he knows damn well that if it was his daughter, if he had a daughter, he'd arm up and burn every sorry motherfucker between him and her down to the ground. But he does not have a daughter, he does not have a wife, and right now, that allows him to see with clarity what Jad Bell certainly cannot. They will rescue the hostages, of that Ruiz is sure. But they will do it right, and they will rescue them all.

Marcelin has come forward to meet Porter, his manner a mix between relieved and enraged. "Eric, Jesus Christ, where have you been?"

"Tried to get down on-site when it started, got caught up in the craziness, getting all the guests out." Porter rubs his mouth with his hand, shakes his head ever so slightly. "Went back to my office to see if I could get any information, then discovered everyone was here. Jerry? Where are we?"

"I'll get you up to speed," Wallford says, guiding Porter off to one side, away from the television.

Ruiz turns to Marcelin. "I need a room. Someplace I won't be disturbed. Plans for the park, underground and above."

Marcelin doesn't even ask why, just nods, calls out. "Natasia? Clear one of the conference rooms, and have someone bring up all the plans for the park for the colonel here."

At "colonel," Ruiz sees Porter raise his head, searching for him. Meets his eyes, and Ruiz acknowledges with a nod, and then Porter's attention is back to Wallford, listening intently. On the flat-screen, the news is replaying the footage of Xi-Xi being dumped outside the gates. Marcelin has stopped midconversation beside him, caught by the images as well.

"Jesus," Marcelin whispers. "Jesus, do we need this on? Do we have to have this on?" He turns in place, speaking to the assembled, his voice rising. "Do we even know who that was? Do we know who she was, at least? Has someone talked to her family?"

Staff stares back, mute.

"Can someone get on that, please?" Marcelin asks. "Someone find out who was playing Xi-Xi today, who isn't accounted for. Can we identify her? Can we do that, at least?"

Ruiz turns away, finds Wallford and Porter returning.

"That dirty bomb," Porter says. "Jerry says you've got two shooters in the park. That dirty bomb needs to be their priority."

"We're not certain that threat is real, sir," Ruiz says.

"That threat is real. That threat is as real as the woman they dumped."

"Do you have any proof, sir?"

Porter shakes his head, shakes it again. "You need to put your shooters onto finding that bomb, Colonel. That needs to be their priority."

"Their priority is the safety and lives of the hostages," Ruiz says. "That is standard protocol, and until I receive orders directing otherwise, it will remain so. My people are aware of the presence of the device, and they will take steps to identify and neutralize it once the hostages have been secured."

"We are dealing with terrorists who have made demands, unreasonable, impossible demands." Porter's voice drops as he becomes more insistent, more urgent. "They know we will never meet their demands. They know you have shooters in the park. They will detonate that device, Colonel. They will do it."

Ruiz glances to Wallford, is surprised to see that the man has apparently been paying their conversation no attention, is instead now standing in front of the wall of windows, his cell phone to his ear. They match eyes in the reflection off the glass, and Wallford's expression is dead, mouth moving as he talks, but staring at the colonel at the same time, and Ruiz wonders what the meaning is in this, what the man from the CIA is trying to tell him by not saying anything at all.

"They will do it, Colonel," Porter is repeating. "God help us all if we let that happen."

Marcelin's assistant, Natasia, the one tasked with getting the plans and the conference room, calls out from across the room. "Colonel Ruiz? There are two men here to speak with you."

"If you could have them meet me in that conference room you acquired, I'd be grateful," Ruiz says.

"Listen to me." Porter shifts, moving in front of Ruiz, trying to keep him from leaving for just a moment more. "You have to forget about the hostages. Those are what, ten, twenty lives? We're talking tens of thousands dead, hundreds of billions of dollars wasted."

"Mr. Porter, sir," Ruiz says. "I have my orders, and I will follow them."

"Who's your commanding officer, then?" Porter pulls out his phone. "I haven't been out so long I don't have pull, Colonel. Who's giving you these orders?"

Ruiz shakes his head. "Sir, you do not want to make that call. If you'll excuse me."

"Who? Damn it, who do I need to talk to for you to get this straight? The hostages don't fucking matter!" Porter is shouting, and the room comes to a halt, making his words seem that much louder, and that much more poorly chosen. "Tell me who's giving you your orders!"

Ruiz exhales, squares his shoulders.

"You need to call the White House, sir. Then you will need to ask to speak to the president of the United States. Again, if you'll excuse me, I have men waiting to be briefed."

Natasia escorts him to the conference room where Cardboard and Bonebreaker are waiting, gear bags resting on the floor. Board stands, already studying the blueprints displayed in PowerPoint on the wall. Bone sits, boots on the table, leaning back in his chair, and neither man acknowledges Ruiz's arrival. Ruiz thanks the young woman, waits just inside the door as she turns and leaves. Bone watches her go, craning his head to catch the last glimpse of the woman as she departs.

Then they're alone, and Ruiz closes, locks the door. Bone gives him a nod of acknowledgment, moves to sit beside Board at the table.

"The mission is to rescue the hostages, to rescue the hostages," Ruiz says, indicating the blueprints still being displayed. "Your secondary objective is to locate and verify, and in the event of verification, to disarm the radiological device believed to be in the park."

"We have numbers?" Board asks.

"At this time we believe there are between fifteen and twenty hostages still in the park." Ruiz pauses for a fraction. "There is a complication. Six of those hostages are deaf. Warlock's daughter is one of them."

Both of the men, already attentive, already focused, shift. Boots come off the table, spines straighten a fraction, and Ruiz feels the transformation, the easy slip from professional to personal. Their community is a small one, the bonds between them precious and forged quite literally under fire. What strikes at one comes to strike all, and never more so than when it strikes their Top. Of Warlock's team, Cardboard has been with him the longest, Bonebreaker a year shy of that, Chaindragger the most recent member. Of Warlock's team, Cardboard is divorced with two children, Bonebreaker recently married with one on the way, Chaindragger single.

All of them know Jad Bell, and all of them know Jad Bell's family. All of them know Amy, and all of them know Athena, and Cardboard, in particular, has memories of piggyback rides and birthday parties, his children and Bell's.

This strikes home.

Hard.

"He knows we're here?" Cardboard asks, swipes his hand over his shaved head, clearing it of perspiration. "You have commo?"

"Just cleared. He and Chain burned another two, liberated a group of six, have them safely in the park's security office, used as a command post. They have an additional asset, CIA-placed, call sign Angel."

Cardboard slides a look at Bone, then both men are looking at Ruiz.

"He's holding?" Bonebreaker asks.

"Warlock is holding on you gentlemen," Ruiz says. "Let's not keep him waiting."

Chapter Twenty-two

CHAIN AND Angel moved the bodies before Bell brought the group back to the command post, but coming up the steps and into the room, the group sees that the signs of the killings remain. A battery of surveillance monitors are dark, glass cracked and the screens a smoke-coal shade, the victims of a flashbang that detonated too close to the equipment, perhaps. Still-wet blood staining the carpet, and a handful of spent brass. He can read the room, and he can tell; Chain and Angel never gave the Tangos a chance.

There are five with him, plus Amy.

Amy, who hates him more than she ever has before, because he's following orders.

Bell had found the keys on the second man, the one he'd shot, pulled himself painfully to the cage where his wife and these strangers waited, looking at him anxiously from behind the bars. His throat ached, the sensation of the man's thumbs still upon it, a dull throbbing that was too slowly beginning to recede behind his eyes. One forearm soaked with blood and the submachine gun in his hand, more blood flowing from his lacerated palm, and he didn't blame any of them for the looks they gave. Amy at the front, taking him in, and from her reaction, he knew he was a sight.

"Listen," he said, fitting the key, voice so hoarse he almost couldn't hear it himself. Coughed, repeating, "Listen, there are more of them, more of them coming. You will follow me, you will stay right on me."

He pauses for a breath that hurts to take, that feels like wet concrete in his upper chest. The door unlocked, still closed, and he meets each set of eyes in turn, they have to understand him. An early-thirties couple, husband and wife from their rings and the way they keep their children close, more children, three of them, one only a toddler in arms, a boy, and two girls, neither far into their teens.

"Stay on me, close to me, no talking until we're in the tunnels. Nod if you understand."

They did, they understood, and Bell pulled the door open, Amy pausing to make certain everyone else was out first. He recovered his pistol, stripped the radios and the other submachine gun from the bodies, led the way as fast as he was willing to back to the ramp, down into the Gordo Tunnel, out of the heat. Checking over his shoulder, and they were all with him, Amy taking the rear. He brought them north, skipped the turn onto Flashman, then up to the Nova Tunnel, heading west, until he found the service entrance to the Speakeasy. Through the unlocked door and into the empty bar, and he ushered everyone inside, closed it.

"Wait here. Quiet."

"Who the hell are you?" This from the husband, a short Latino man who reminds Bell fleetingly of Bonebreaker in posture and manner.

"He's my husband," Amy said flatly. In crisis, it seems, their divorce is forgotten.

"What's your name?" Bell asked him.

"Michael."

"Michael, I am the man getting you and your family out of here," Bell said. "Wait here. I won't be long."

He took the short flight of stairs up to the door, threw the silly little spy-hatch slat, looked out, saw nothing and no one. Awakened the earbud and called for Chain or Angel, and it was Angel who came back immediately.

"We have the command post," she said. "Whatever you did, they never saw us coming."

"Do you have the cameras?" Bell asked. "Have you located the other groups?"

"We've located another thirteen. There may be more, we don't have all the monitors. Some were damaged in the take."

"The group of deaf kids this morning, my daughter's group. Do you see them?"

She paused. "Negative."

"I'm en route, have six with me. Find those kids, Angel. I need you to find those kids. Out."

So there are nine of them in the command post now. Angel wrestling with the coms scrambler that was hooked into the park's network, and Chain trying to master the Spartan. Bell hands over the weapons and the radios, then puts Michael and his family in the conference room. He gives them bottled water and tells them that they need to sit tight here, they'll evacuate them as soon as they can.

"We're safe here?"

"This is the safest place in the park," Bell says. "You've got two shooters in the command post and more on the way and no one and nothing is going to happen to you or your family."

Michael nods, takes hold of his wife's hand. She smiles at Bell, a wan, weak smile, but it's there nonetheless, and Bell leaves the room knowing they believe him.

Amy follows.

"They're at the haunted house," Amy tells him. "Hendar's Lair, that's where they took us. That's where Athena is."

Bell yanks the first-aid kit from the wall, heading for the bathroom. "I have orders to wait."

"It's your fucking daughter!"

She follows him inside, glares at him in the mirror as Bell opens the kit on the counter, starts the faucet. He's got bruises rising already on his face, below his left eye, and whatever happened to the small of his back is stinging, the wound still seeping. He unbuttons his shirt, splashes water on his hands and face.

"They have our daughter."

This, Amy says much more softly, almost inaudible over the water. Bell is ripping open the packaging for a two-by-two-inch square of gauze, stops, feels every ache all together, feels tired.

"I know."

"You have to get her. You have to get her and the others, Jad. The whole class is there, all of them. This is what you do. Isn't it?"

"There are fourteen other hostages in the park and

there may be a bomb. Jorge and Freddie are on the way, Amy. Soon as they're here, we'll move, I swear to God. I swear to God we will get Athena back."

"They shot Marty." Amy turns, hands resting on the counter, leans forward. She closes her eyes. "They murdered him right in front of us, right in front of the kids. They murdered their teacher right in front of them."

Bell is bandaging his lacerated palm, flexes his hand experimentally. The cut is not so deep that it reaches tendon, and he is, at least, grateful for that. He begins wrapping his hand in cling gauze.

"What do they want? Who are they?"

"I don't know," Bell tells her. "Help me with this." He indicates the scissors in the kit with his head.

She straightens, sighs, cuts the cling from its roll, splits the end at the center, tearing down to create two lengths. She wraps them around his hand in opposite directions, ties them together, snug. Bell wiggles his fingers, checks his circulation, but of course it's fine.

"Still pretty good at that," he tells her.

"Turn around."

Bell turns, facing the mirror, watches as Amy lifts his shirt free, makes a face at what she sees. "Looks like you got clawed."

"The jaguar."

"New scar."

"How deep?"

"Lean forward."

Bell complies, and Amy runs more water, washes her hands, then digs into the kit. Begins opening new squares of gauze, then takes the bottle of Betadine, squirting it over the wound. Bell feels cool liquid spilling over his skin, down the back of his pants. Then her hands, cleaning the injury with the gauze, tossing it away to cover it with fresh strips.

"Tape."

Bell takes the spool of cloth tape from the kit, hands it back. Watches his ex-wife's reflection as she tends the wound, the tip of her tongue extended just past her lips in concentration, brushing hair from her cheek with the back of one hand. She uses her teeth to tear strips from the roll. He wishes he still didn't find her beautiful.

She finishes and Bell rights himself, feels the tape pulling as he straightens. Tucks his shirt back in, turning to face her. Her expression is the same as he remembers, countless training wounds and little injuries tended, the same look when she discovered a new wound, the dark eyes and somber, gentle sorrow.

Amy leans forward, puts her lips to his, soft and dry, the kiss almost apologetic at first. Then harder, and Bell kisses her back, wraps an arm around her waist, pulls her close, and her palms are against his chest; the kiss breaks, and she buries her face against his shoulder. Like that, he holds her, feels her regaining her strength, feels her body tensing.

Then she is pulling away, shoving free, one open palm beating against his breast, then the other, before she lets her hands fall, unable to look at him. Grimacing in frustration, in pain, in fury. Bell understands. Anger at him, at herself, at the world.

"I asked you…" She shakes her head, swallows, refusing to give up tears. "I asked you, on the phone, if this was what you were afraid of. Did you know, Jad? Did you know this would happen?"

He wants to be angry that she would even ask, almost tries to find it within him to be angry. But he's too tired, and he hurts too much, inside and out, and the kiss, brief as it was, is an ashen memory. That she would think that of him, that he would do this to them, that she could believe him so callous and cold. He understands that there is nothing left between them, the emotional truth of intellectual knowledge six months old finally striking home. She does not love him anymore, because she does not know him.

She does not know him, and she thinks him a monster.

He says nothing. He can't answer. But the silence damns him.

"You bastard," Amy says. "If anything happens to her, Jad Bell, if anything happens to our daughter..."

She can't finish, but she doesn't need to. She turns away, shoves the door open, leaves him alone in the bathroom, with his injuries and his guilt.

Chapter Twenty-three

THE CALL with the Uzbek goes like this:

"Status?"

"Status?" Gabriel echoes. "Status is fuck-awful, that's the status. I'm down another four and lost the second group of hostages. The whole damn thing is falling apart."

"Calm down. Explain."

"We're fucked. We were waiting to ambush them when they came out of the tunnels, but they got around us somehow. They must've split up or, fuck, maybe there are more of them, but they hit the command post and one of the groups. I'm down another four."

The Uzbek makes a clicking noise into the phone. "Very interesting. I thought I'd told you to take care of the problem."

"Why do you think we were waiting in ambush, damn it? You think I'm just letting them fuck us like this?" Gabriel is practically shouting into the phone, and Betsy, still examining the bodies, looks up at him in alarm, gives him a look like he's cursing out a priest.

"Do not lose your nerve."

"My nerve is solid, it's the plan that's fucked, don't you get it? There's at least two of these guys in the park, *at least* two of them, you understand me? They're serious shooters, special forces, I don't know. Don't talk to me about my nerve, your plan is in fucking goddamn pieces!"

"The plan is a good plan, and we will abide by it," the Uzbek says complacently. Gabriel thinks he can hear water running in the background, an open tap, maybe a sink or bathtub, he's not sure. "We are entering the final phase."

Gabriel squeezes his eyes tight shut, tries to calm himself, can't manage to diminish what he's feeling, the yawning lack of control. "The plan never accounted for resistance in the park. That was never part of the plan you gave me."

"There was always the possibility that one intelligence service or another would get wind of our designs. It's immaterial now, and too late as well. Remember who you are and who you work for."

"I don't fucking know who I work for," Gabriel reminds the Uzbek.

"You know enough. Just as you know that names mean nothing. Power, reach, expertise, those are everything. It's all been accounted for, even this. You must trust me. Do you trust me?"

"I'm trying to," Gabriel says, thinking that this might be more honesty than is prudent.

The Uzbek laughs softly. "We have always done well by you, always taken care of you. Do not despair now. Keep your nerve."

"My nerve isn't the problem here."

"Your faith, then. The hostages were only ever to buy time, to prevent a full-scale assault. They continue to serve their purpose. If the opposition has the command post, use the hostages to draw them out and deal with them."

"You mean shoot more of them."

"That is what they're there for. Have your old friend handle it. You have another task to manage."

"We need to talk about the exfil." Gabriel looks to Betsy, sees that the other man is nodding in agreement. "We need to move up the timetable to get us out of here."

"Soon. Not yet. I need you to arm the device. The timer is already programmed. Just arm it, then contact me, and I will initiate exfil."

He can feel the sweat from his ear wet against the phone. Betsy still looking at him expectantly, waiting to hear how the fuck they're getting out of this. Gabriel turns away from the other man.

"Did you hear me?"

Gabriel lowers his voice. "I heard you."

"The device is still under our control?"

"Yes."

"You are certain?"

Gabriel thinks, says, "Yes, I placed it out of sight. They can't have found it. Even if they've got detection equipment, there's no way they could've found it."

"Very good."

"I do this, do what you say…how much time does that give us for exfil?"

"You're worried you've become expendable, is that it?"

"That's exactly it."

The Uzbek chuckles. In the background, the sound of running water stops abruptly. Gabriel thinks he hears a woman's voice, indistinct and faint.

"Let me reassure you. *You* are not. The others are. All of them. Do you understand what I'm telling you?"

Gabriel thinks he does. Gabriel thinks the Uzbek is saying that he is worth time and money and potential to the Uzbek and his shadow master, even now, even after this; or, perhaps, because of all of this. But the others, Vladimir and Betsy and Charlie One and Charlie Two and the twenty-one remaining hostages in the park, they're all meat for the block. Intuitively, he sees that it's those bodies, those lives, that will buy Gabriel his escape.

"I understand."

"Very good. Arm the device, then contact me. I will have the details of your exfil then."

"Wait," Gabriel says. "You didn't answer my question. Once it's armed, how much time do we have?"

"Enough."

The Uzbek hangs up.

"He's going to fuck us, isn't he?" Betsy says.

They're tracking north, above ground, through Wild World, but staying as close to the trees as possible. Gabriel doesn't want to risk the tunnels for the exact same reasons he avoided going into them after Bell earlier, and now, above ground, they're certainly going to be showing up on camera. But he has no intention of making it easy for anyone who might be watching. Each time he spots one, he stops and raises the submachine gun, switches it to single-shot, then puts a round through the housing.

"He says we're almost through," Gabriel answers.

"Just have to do one more job and then we contact him for exfil."

"What job is that?"

Gabriel ignores the question, stops, pulling back. He indicates yet another camera emplacement. Betsy sights and drills a round into it, then a second for good measure, and they continue on, hopping the rail that guards the slope down to the river. It's a gentle enough drop, but it puts them five feet or so below the pathways, will make it that much harder to be spotted on any cameras they might miss.

What job is that? Gabriel is thinking, *It's my fucking job. It's the job where I kill God knows how many people. I'm just supposed to do my job.*

The Uzbek is going to burn them, he knows this. Perhaps he will not burn Gabriel himself, he wants to believe in his value to the man. But now he is all but positive that the others will be sacrificed to whatever end the Uzbek is advancing. They will all die. Bullets or bomb, the Uzbek will spend their lives freely.

Pushing past a fern, he spots another camera, shoots it out, and as he feels the weapon kick in his hands, has a realization.

He cannot do what the Uzbek is asking. He will not do what the Uzbek is asking. It is not in him to do it. Perhaps once, a lifetime away, he was the man who could do it. But that man did not have his life, did not have his dream, did not ever imagine a woman like Dana, who would love him, too. His job? He is the wrong man for this job.

He will leave the dirty bomb as it is, unarmed, inert. The Uzbek is a liar, and nothing he says can be trusted.

As much as Gabriel wishes to believe the Uzbek's assurances, and through them believe that he matters, that loyalty matters, he knows better. Loyalty matters little to men like the Uzbek, and perhaps even less to the Uzbek's master. They are men from that other lifetime, and there, in Odessa, only one thing ever mattered.

Money.

There is no money to be made in getting them out alive. That is an expense, that is not a profit. The Uzbek has never intended for them to leave the park. That is enough to make the decision for him. Gabriel has promised himself he will get through this day, he will put all this behind him, and he will reach Dana again. He will return to his dream, and then he will contact the Uzbek through their secret e-mail account, and he will tell him it is over, it is done. He will tell the Uzbek that he wants nothing more of him or his master, and that he knows enough to know too much. Leave me alone, Gabriel will write, or else everything I have done, everything I know of you, I will give that information to the authorities.

I'm done, he thinks. *Done with all this.*

Gabriel fishes out his radio, hesitates before keying it. Jonathan Bell took the radios from the bodies back at Wild World Live!—he knows that. Any transmission he makes, it could be overheard. They have to switch the coms.

Abruptly, Gabriel breaks right, sprinting toward one of the clusters of mushroom houses near Smooch's Park. Betsy stays on him, helps him at the locked door, the two of them kicking at it together before they manage to snap the lock free of its plate. It's warm and still inside, and Gabriel is almost frantic, urgent.

"What are you looking for?"

"Phone, there's a park phone. Here." He scrabbles the molded plastic box open, pulls the handset free, puts it to his ear. There's a dial tone, and on the inside of the box's door, a listing of numbers. Running his finger down it until he finds Hendar's Lair, and he pulls out his radio again, jabs the transmit button twice, then twice more quickly, hoping everyone listening in understands. Hands the radio to Betsy.

"Get the cameras, make sure there aren't any cameras," Gabriel says, and then he dials Hendar's Lair, listens to the phone ring.

And ring.

And ring.

Until finally, Vladimir answers. "That you?"

"It's me. Our coms are compromised, nothing on the radio, you understand? We use the landlines. You have a cell phone?"

"I have a phone."

Gabriel rattles off his number. "Call me back."

He slams the handset down. He feels out of breath, tries to shake it off, to calm himself. In his pocket, his cell phone begins to vibrate. He frees it, answers.

"Matias, what the fuck is going on?"

"Don't worry, I'll explain in a bit. What's your status there?"

"Everything is good. These deaf kids know how to stay quiet."

The satisfaction, the new confidence, the resolve, all of it trembles, threatens to collapse. Gabriel feels as if

his throat is knotted, the adrenaline flooding his system. The beat of his heart speeding, the hunger of his
quickened breathing. He is abruptly, acutely aware of
the muscles in his right forearm, how they control his
hand, how his hand holds the phone, how his thumb
rests at the side, along the volume control.

"What did you say?"

"They know how to stay quiet."

Gabriel swallows. "How many of them?"

"Six."

"You have seven."

"Yeah, there's a park girl with them, knows how to
sign. She's a mouthy one, I keep telling her she doesn't
shut up, I'll give her something else for her mouth to
do."

Heat blazes up Gabriel's neck. He is aware of Betsy
just outside the door, scanning for more cameras, listening.

"We don't..." Gabriel begins, doesn't trust his
voice, stops. Clears his throat, then tries again, saying,
"We don't have time for that bullshit."

"Fuck, I know that. Maybe we can keep a couple of
them for later?" Vladimir laughs.

"I'm en route. Keep your hands off them. I mean
that."

"I was joking," Vladimir says.

Gabriel thinks maybe he isn't.

It takes another fourteen minutes before they're at the
mouth of Hendar's Lair, another seven cameras dead
along the way, with Gabriel taking just long enough
to reach Charlie One and Charlie Two separately over

the park phone, telling them that their coms have been breached. From here on out, Gabriel tells them, we use the park phones or our own cell phones.

Now Gabriel ducks the chain, climbs over the treasure chest–themed carts stacked in a line at the platform. Music plays, variations of Hendar's theme, much louder than Gabriel has ever heard it before in the absence of crowds and the running of the ride. At the entrance of the tunnel, multicolored lights swirl and yellow, wicked eyes shine in the darkness.

"Tell Vladimir to come out here," Gabriel says. "Take over for him inside. I'll keep watch."

Betsy says, "That Uzbek shit, he's going to fuck us, you know that?"

"I know that."

"You're going to let him?"

"I am not. No, I am not. Go get Vladimir. Don't touch the hostages. We're going to need them."

Betsy nods in understanding. "Yeah. That's good."

The man heads down the tunnel, following the ride's track, disappears into the darkness. The music breaks, Hendar growling, his voice rising, seductively dripping poison into the ear.

I smell you . . . I hear you . . . I see you . . . always nice to have someone drop by for a *bite* to eat. . . .

Another growl that turns into a rich, sinister laugh.

Come in, come in. There's so much I want to show you . . . so much I want to teach you. Why else would you dare enter my domain? I know what you want, and I will give it to you. I will teach you of power. Come...if you dare....

A growl, then a roar, and screams that Gabriel always assumed were from guests, and now realizes are also part of the sound track. He turns to the control console, wondering if there's a clearly marked way to shut it off, just to mute it for a moment, and his eye catches on the flickering black-and-white images relayed from inside. Like all the enclosed attractions, Hendar's Lair has on-site monitoring, similar to the surveillance out of the security office, but local to each ride.

Gabriel looks at the tiny square images, the whites too bright to accommodate the dimness within, and of the eight screens, six show him nothing, just empty trackway. But two of them have angles on the hostages, and he can see Betsy now speaking to Vladimir, gesturing. The cameras are nowhere near as high-resolution as the ones he left in the command post, but he sees what look like six teenagers, seated on the floor and in a line, and a seventh at the end, knees drawn to her chest and an arm around the shoulders of a young woman beside her.

Dana.

Of course Dana. It had to be Dana, and even though the video is blurry, void of detail, Gabriel is certain it is she. The way he was certain the moment Vladimir said the kids were deaf.

He looks at her on this monitor, thankful she cannot see him. Thankful that she does not know he is here, his part in all this.

Fuck the Uzbek and his bomb, Gabriel Fuller thinks. *Fuck him, his plan, his devil master, fuck them all. We are done, we are getting out.*

"Hey," Vladimir says, emerging from the tunnel, the other side, where the cars would exit were the ride in operation. He's got the submachine gun slung, but his pistol is in his hand, and for a second Gabriel wonders if old loyalties count more than new ones, if Vladimir will be with him or against him.

"We lost the command post," Gabriel says. "We're down to eight men now, including you and me."

"Sonny said."

"Sonny?" It takes a half second before Gabriel understands that Vladimir is talking about Betsy. "He tell you anything else?"

Vladimir digs around in his pockets, finds his pack of cigarettes. Unlike Betsy, he doesn't bother to offer Gabriel one. He gets his smoke lit, exhales. When he speaks again, he uses Russian.

"That it's going wrong, badly wrong. That there are shooters in the park, at least two and maybe more. That the Uzbek fucker is maybe hanging us out to dry."

"That's what I'm thinking, too." Gabriel slips into Russian, finds the language stiff and old on his tongue. "I'm thinking he was planning on doing it all along. These shooters, they knew we were coming, Vladimir."

"You think the Uzbek warned them? Why would he warn them?"

"Fuck me if I know. Does any of this make sense to you? He keeps saying there is a plan, but he never tells me what the plan is. I don't even know why we're here.

Take the park, hold the park, plant a bomb but don't arm the bomb. Nothing makes sense."

"He said—"

"I know what he said. But he told me little more than he told you." Gabriel turns to face the man full-on, meets his eyes. "Who are you with? Are you with me or are you with him?"

Vladimir blows smoke, eyes Gabriel. "It's not that simple."

"It is that simple. We stay here, we die here."

Another jet of smoke. "You don't know. The Shadow Man has a long reach and a long memory, Matias. You left and the Uzbek moved in, some of our boys, they got ideas, tried to do their own thing. And the Uzbek, he said that sure, they could do that, good luck with that.

"And they all died, Matias. Not all at once and not fast, but all of them ended up dead. Adam Nikoleyavich, you remember him? You were gone two years, maybe, he got a wife and new baby boy, they found them all dead. What they had done to the baby not even I want to talk about. That is what this Shadow Man does to those who break with him."

"And you are willing to die for him? For a man who maybe doesn't exist?"

"You tell me if he doesn't exist. You were picked by him, that was what the Uzbek said. You were picked to do his work." Vladimir takes a last pull, flicks the butt away.

Gabriel shakes his head. "I have never seen him, never heard him. Only ever was it the Uzbek. For all these years, only ever the Uzbek."

Vladimir's mouth works, lips together, frowning as he thinks. Looking out along the pathways again, and from the corner of Gabriel's eye, he sees the man's fingers open and close around the grip of his pistol.

"We betray these men, we will die."

"We stay here," Gabriel says, "we will die sooner."

Vladimir grunts, perhaps in agreement.

"So what do we do?"

"We make a deal," Gabriel says.

Chapter Twenty-four

THE SOUTHERNMOST wall on the Pooch Tunnel makes a noise like a soft clap, then almost immediately makes another, much louder. There's a blast of rock and concrete dust, the roar of the detonation all the more deafening in the enclosed space, and even with his hands clapped over them, it's enough to make Bell's ears ring, to make his head begin aching all over again. Debris sprays and falls, leaving a cloud of mist and dust.

Cardboard steps through the breach. He's geared, rig and harness over his blue jeans, top of an AC/DC T-shirt just visible above his vest, M4 in his hands, light from one of the fixtures kicking glare off his shaved head. Bonebreaker flows through right behind him, similarly heavy, his jeans black and his shirt the same color, moving like he's following the steps of a dance. Both men give Bell a nod, and he returns it, then pivots and begins leading them back north, quick-stepping, not quite running.

"Always picking the best vacation spots, Top," Bone says. He's as tall as Bell, thinner, and about as white-boy as they come, blond and blue-eyed.

"Yeah, I know how to treat my crew right. Where were you?"

"Orlando."

"You have eyes on?" Cardboard asks. Of the four, he's the smallest, a barrel top on lean legs that seem too long for his body. "No change?"

"Situation is dynamic," Bell says. "They're taking out the cameras where they can. We have two of their radios, but they've cut commo, no traffic."

"Moving the hostages?" Bone asks.

"What I'd do."

"What we'd all do," Cardboard says. "Need to move fast, then."

"Like our asses are on fire," Bell says.

They enter the command post, coming through the tunnel at the back of the Sheriff's Office, then up the stairs. Amy is standing by the door when they enter, and both Board and Bone greet her by name. Bonebreaker moves immediately to the Spartan, but Cardboard stops in front of her, offers an apologetic smile.

"Been a while," Cardboard says.

"You'll forgive me, Freddie," Amy says. "Not long enough."

"Roger that," Bonebreaker murmurs.

Bell puts a hand on his ex-wife's arm. "You stay in this room, you need to stay quiet."

"Don't waste time." She glares.

"I don't waste time." Bell turns to Nuri. "Where are we on the Spartan?"

"Just got it recalibrated." Nuri has stepped out of Bonebreaker's way, now bends past him, working the keyboard on the biochem monitor. "Sampling for radioactive material, but if it's a dirty bomb, if they shielded the payload when it was assembled, it's going to come back negative."

"Do it anyway."

"Gets worse," Chain says. "Tangos have wised up. We're losing our eyes fast."

It's not good news, but it was the news Bell expected. Whoever is calling the hostiles' shots in the park, he's not being stupid and he's not planning on making things easy.

Bonebreaker moves from the Spartan to where Chain is sitting. "Isaiah."

"Hey, Jorge."

"Shoshana Nuri, Angel," Bell says. "Sergeants Freddie Cooper and Jorge Velez, Cardboard and Bonebreaker, respectively. Now we're done with the pleasantries. Let's break this down."

Bell steps to one of the terminals beside the surveillance bank, taps the keyboard, brings up the park map on-screen. Slides his index finger from their position to the northwestern quadrant of the park, settling on Fort Royal.

"Group One consists of seven hostages and two Tangos. Isaiah, show them."

"Right here," Chain says, swiveling in his chair to bring up another monitor, a paused video. He clicks and the image springs into motion, two men armed with MP5Ks pacing around a cluster of seven men and women, none of them children, thankfully, all seated in a bunch at the heart of the open courtyard. "They're in sunlight, getting hot and tired and bored, from the look of it."

Cardboard nods, almost imperceptibly.

"Group Two," Bell says, moving his index finger

south and even further west, almost to the border of the park. "Flashman Ranch, six hostages, two Tangos. Almost an identical setup."

"You can see it here." Chain taps keys, the video changing to show the interior of the Flashman Corral. "The approach here is harder, but there's tunnel access, and before we lost the cameras it looked like they didn't even know it was there."

"Last group, Group Three." Bell indicates Hendar's Lair on the map. "Seven hostages, two Tangos. This one is mine."

Bonebreaker clears his throat. "Top—"

"This one is mine," Bell repeats. "We have identified eight hostiles at this time; we have three groups, and we have five shooters. There's no way this breaks into even numbers. One of us is flying solo, that'll be me."

"Wait," Nuri says. "Five shooters?"

Bell turns to her as the phone at the coms desk begins to ring. "You're coming to the party, Angel."

She shakes her head, grabs the phone.

"Jad," Cardboard says. "Athena's in Group Three, maybe you ought to let me and Chain take that one."

"You think I'm going to miss?"

"Never on purpose."

"Then state your objection, Sergeant."

"If it was my little girl—"

"You'd be on point, Freddie, don't bullshit me."

Cardboard shrugs, and Nuri says, "Warlock?"

"I'm not arguing this," Bell says to Cardboard, then turns to glare at Nuri. "If that's Brickyard, you tell him we're about to move."

"It's not Brickyard." Nuri is holding out the handset to him, one hand over the mouthpiece. "He won't identify himself. He's asking for you by name."

Bell stares at her.

"He says he knows where the bomb is," Nuri says.

"This is Bell."

The voice that answers is American, soft-spoken, male. Of the men he's seen on the monitors, Bell wonders which it could be, if any of them. "Hello, Mr. Bell."

"You know who I am."

"I was in your office. You don't really work for WilsonVille, do you?"

"No," Bell says.

"I didn't think so. Special Forces, maybe? Are you a SEAL, Mr. Bell? A Navy SEAL?"

"You know where the bomb is."

The man laughs, and it's bitter, and sparse. "I do."

"I'm not sure I believe there even *is* a bomb."

"That's a dangerous mistake, but if you want to make it, you go right ahead. How many people do you think will die if it goes off? I mean, beyond the immediate panic. The cancer cases. Fifty thousand? Twice that? Five times?"

"Maybe. Could be. You tell me where it is, could be no one."

"That would be nice, wouldn't it? No one else dying. Be nice if we could arrange that. Let WilsonVille live. That's the real damage, isn't it? If it detonates? It'll kill WilsonVille, maybe kill Wilson Entertainment. They'd have to turn this place into one big parking lot, wouldn't they? Could scrub and sandblast it for a year and a day, they'd never get people to come here again, bring their children here again. That's billions, maybe hundreds of billions of dollars. That's an economic crisis right there. And here we are, struggling out of a recession."

Here we are, Bell thinks. *You're American.* "Yes, it would," he says. "You think maybe we can arrange something?"

There is a long pause. "What I want," the man says, finally, "is out. Get on the line to someone with pull. FBI, whoever. You get them on the line, and you tell them this: I'll give you the hostages and the bomb, but we walk."

"You want them to just let you go."

"There are two employee lots north of the park, northwest and northeast. There's the main lot southwest of the gates. I want a van waiting in each of those lots, identical vans, and nobody in sight of them. Me and my people will walk the hostages out to the vehicles, we'll leave them there, and we'll go. Once I'm satisfied we're clear, I'll call and tell you where to find the bomb."

Now it's Bell's turn to be silent. Nuri, listening in on the coms headset, is watching him, frowning. He sees Amy at the back of the room, holding her elbow in one hand, looking like she's gnawing her fingers, and she's watching him, too.

"No can do," Bell says.

"Maybe you don't understand me," the man says. "I'm offering you an end to this, a walkaway."

"I understand. It won't work. What you're asking

for, it won't work, not like you're asking. I get on the line to FBI, whoever, you've got to know they'll never let you go clean. They'll say sure, whatever you like, they'll give you the vans, they'll stay clear. But they'll bug the vehicles, they'll follow you on the ground, put a bird in the air, but they'll never let you get away. You know that. And you know I'm not FBI. So between you and me, let's make this work."

"How?"

"My team is in the park," Bell says. "We're here and staged, you understand me? We are here and we are staged. Our vehicle is parked off-site; the rest of my unit made entry through the tunnels, via the sewer. The keys are still in the truck, passenger-side visor. That's our vehicle, you understand? You take it, no one will follow."

"I am not going into the tunnels. That's a kill zone."

"I'll give you a free run. You turn the hostages loose, we stay above ground."

Another pause as the man considers. "You keep your people clear?"

"In exchange for the hostages. You release the hostages, we'll move in to collect them, you'll have a free run."

"You have two of our radios."

"We do."

"Keep one with you. Thirty minutes."

The line goes dead.

Bell sets the handset down.

"We've got twenty-nine minutes to free the hostages and find that device," he says.

Chapter Twenty-five

Ruiz is still in the conference room, staring out the window. Directly below, the media circus is at a full three rings. There are clown cars with satellite antennae and competing ringmasters strutting and gesticulating in front of camera crews. It's blown wide, global news, and the political repercussions are already beginning to be felt. Multiple pundits all singing variations on a theme. Is this a state-sponsored act of terrorism, and if so, will the Global War on Terror be opening yet another front in another country? More boots on the ground in Yemen, perhaps? If this is Pakistani in origin, will this be the last straw? Or perhaps somewhere even more problematic—one of the CIS, perhaps, or Southeast Asia?

Speculation only, but not one of the options makes Ruiz happy, and if it's giving him dark thoughts, he can only imagine what's being said in the White House Situation Room or the Pentagon. The same White House Situation Room he just finished speaking with, listening as orders have been relayed, from Washington back across the country to California, to the FBI HRT, now staged at the southernmost of WilsonVille's parking lots and holding, down to the SWAT commander standing with his men less than a mile away. Everyone ready to move on WilsonVille; everyone all dressed up for a party nobody really wants to attend.

My people are in motion, Ruiz told the president. My people are moving to rescue the hostages, they will give the all clear to breach once they are secure.

Your people, can they do this? Your four operators and this fifth, this woman from the CIA?

They are the best in the world, Mr. President, Ruiz said, and he did not add that he believes this despite the fact that his team leader has been compromised. He has not said anything about Master Sergeant Bell's ex-wife or his daughter. He feels this is a fair exclusion, as no one has said anything about CIA operating domestically, or the military doing the same, for that matter. Everything has been authorized, but should the shit hit the fan, those authorizations won't matter for spit.

Ruiz hopes he will not regret this silence.

All stations will hold until your all clear, the Commander in Chief said. You have command, Colonel. We are holding on your word.

Yes, sir. Thank you, sir.

Out the window, there's local law enforcement and federal and there's a rumor that the governor is coming down from Sacramento, though Ruiz is sincerely hoping that someone back in D.C. has put a stop to that plan. The last thing this circus needs, he thinks, is one more elephant.

Some of those people in D.C., Ruiz suspects, are more than happy to give Ruiz this amount of rope. After all, if this goes wrong, lives will be lost. If lives will be lost, prospects will vanish and futures evaporate. If this goes wrong, far better to let four soldiers nobody has ever heard of and one CIA agent who shouldn't be operating domestically anyway take the hit. Let them, and their immediate superiors, fall on their swords in failure.

Ruiz raises his gaze, sees WilsonVille two miles away and still for the first time in more than thirty years, minus the one dark day when everything fell silent. The sun is beginning its descent toward the Pacific, but it's still high enough for the world to be blue and hot, not gold and graceful.

He thinks about the update he just got from Warlock. He thinks about the lies Bell told, and how every one of them was the right and proper one. He's thinking that, by his watch, things are twenty-five minutes, give or take, from getting bloody.

He thinks about the man Bell spoke to, the man who had been in Bell's office, who knew Jonathan Bell's name. The inside man, who he is, and what he is doing right now. No plan is static, and this man would be an extraordinary fool to believe that Warlock would simply sit tight for the half hour he requested. This inside man, who knows the park as well as Warlock or even better. Where that inside man might plant a bomb.

Who are you? Ruiz wonders.

The door opens, and Ruiz turns, hoping for Marcelin but instead finding Eric Porter. The man is no longer perspiring, but he seems no less agitated, and a moment later, Wallford is coming into the room after him.

"Listen," Porter says, and he's making the effort, Ruiz can tell, struggling to keep his voice reasonable, his tone calm. "Listen, you cannot let these people go,

Colonel. They clear the park, there is nothing to stop them from detonating that bomb. Nothing at all. And they will do it. They fucking well will do it."

Ruiz exchanges looks with Wallford, or tries to, but Wallford isn't having any. The man has shut the door, turning his back to Ruiz to do it, and now makes his way down the opposite side of the conference table, apparently more interested in the PowerPoint maps still displayed on the far wall than in what's being said.

Not for the first time, Ruiz wonders what Wallford's true agenda is. Angel is his agent, this much is clear, and certainly Wallford wants the park freed, wants the hostages released, the bomb discovered and disarmed. But there's more, and now Ruiz thinks more equals Eric Porter. That Angel's placement was one matter, but that Wallford's himself was another.

"I understand your concern," Ruiz says. "But rescuing the hostages is my team's first priority."

"These men are terrorists, they have committed a terrorist act," Porter counters. "You let them go and they'll be free to do it again."

"No one responsible is going to leave the park."

Porter studies him. "You just said—"

"You're concerned that Master Sergeant Bell guaranteed them free passage. I understand that. Master Sergeant Bell lied to them, Mr. Porter. He'd have told them he would give oral to a bulldog and let them film him while he did it if that was what they wanted and he thought saying so would give him an advantage."

"And what advantage has he gained?"

Wallford, from the far end of the room, head tilted back to look up at the park map being displayed, speaks.

"C'mon, Eric, you know the game. Whoever they are, they're cracking. Their plan is falling apart. So maybe the bomb is real, maybe it isn't, but now the shooters know these guys want out. And they've given them a route, maybe even a route they'll take."

Wallford turns, shoots a toothy grin at Porter.

"Maybe even get a live one. They do that, we can find out what this was all about. Who was pulling the strings. This isn't the kind of incident we've seen before, after all."

"We know what this is all about. This isn't a mystery!" Porter waves his hand, indicating everything around them. "It's about this! It's about hitting this, making a statement! Corrupt America! Evil Empire! Destroying the Satanist Culture we export and all that bullshit!"

"Looks that way, maybe." Wallford is still grinning. "Though I've never heard of a true believer willing to negotiate like this before. Have you?"

"Because they don't want to negotiate. Because as soon as they're clear, that bomb is going to go off."

"My men will not allow that to happen," Ruiz says.

Porter nods in approval at Ruiz. "I'm pleased to hear you say that. These men have to be stopped. Your shooters, they have to understand that. These men can't leave the park alive."

"My men will do what is required."

"This isn't about intelligence, Jerry," Porter says to Wallford. "That's past. This is about ending the crisis now. When it's over, when it's done, *that's* when we can worry about who was responsible."

Wallford shrugs, returns to studying the map projected on the wall. Porter stares at his back for a second, then nods to Ruiz once more and slips out of the room. The door closes softly after him.

Ruiz waits the better part of a minute before speaking. "How is he involved?"

"No idea."

"But he is?"

"Sure as hell looks that way, doesn't it?"

Ruiz considers, then moves down the length of the room, to stand beside Wallford. Wallford is still studying the map.

"If I was a dirty bomb, where would I be?" Wallford asks.

"Come clean, now."

"That's against Company policy, you know that."

Ruiz moves closer, forcing Wallford to turn and face him.

"CIA knew?"

"Same answer you gave Marcelin, Colonel. If we knew, we'd have shut it down. We're all one big happy intelligence community, remember?"

"Then what is this bullshit?"

"The device, if it's real, it's not a baby bomb, Colonel." Wallford's game face drops, the cheerful mask fading. "It's not something some clever grad student managed to put together with cesium 137 or strontium 90 or whatever they could scrounge. We're talking about a weapons-grade plutonium device. We're talking the real shit."

"You know this."

"What we know is that somebody paid somebody who paid somebody who paid somebody else a metric fuckton of money to get a couple of ounces of weapons-grade plutonium out of Iran. So maybe, yeah, maybe it's ended up in WilsonVille. If we can recover that device, we might be able to take a signature off the plutonium, determine its source."

"Iran isn't behind this."

"Maybe not, maybe so. They sponsor terror attacks globally, you know that. Could be they sponsored this."

"I'm slow on the science, but a plutonium dirty bomb, that's signing the letter. Cesium, strontium, those are more effective agents, more dangerous, more lethal. You pick plutonium for headlines."

"Maybe. Yes."

Ruiz shakes his head. "Doesn't wash. If this is a terror attack."

"You don't think it is?" Wallford's grin returns. "You're a suspicious bastard."

Ruiz looks pointedly toward the closed door, then back to Wallford.

"Yeah. I don't buy him being in bed with the Revolutionary Guard, either. Twenty-seven years with the Company, out with the change in administrations, he takes up with WilsonVille. Unless there's a bank account we haven't found, it doesn't track to me, either."

"So something else."

"So some*one* else, yes."

"Who?"

Wallford brightens. "That's the question. That's been the question all along."

"We're looking for an inside man," Ruiz says.

"We're looking for more than one."

"Know the man," Ruiz says. "Win the war."

"That so?" Wallford shakes his head, stares at the map once more, searching for the one place in a million where someone has hidden a dirty bomb. "Then, as of this moment, we're losing, Colonel."

Chapter Twenty-six

WHAT ATHENA is seeing scares her, because what Athena is seeing is men who are scared.

Most of the men, that is. The one who stayed with Vladimir when they took Mom and the family away, he's definitely scared. Athena thinks his name is Oscar, and she's been watching him get more and more tense, and he's jumpy, too. Whenever one of them moves, just tries to adjust how they're sitting on this cold floor against this not-real bed, he'll spin about. He does that, and he looks like he doesn't know what they are, like the idea of human beings outside himself is alien and strange. Then his expression hardens, like he's thinking mean thoughts. He stares most at the boys, Leon and Miguel and Joel.

Then there's the new one. Sonny, she thinks his name is, if she's reading what Vladimir said correctly. He got here just a little bit ago, came in and must have been calling out, because Vladimir and Oscar and Dana all looked in the same direction, and then here he was. Went straight to Vladimir, and they talked quickly, and she caught maybe less than half of that, but the gestures made it clear, and Vladimir left for a couple of minutes.

Vladimir and Oscar, they carry their guns sometimes like they forget they have them. Like, in one hand, and sometimes Vladimir just lets his hang from its strap, over his shoulder. But not Sonny. Sonny holds his in both hands, and he paces, back and forth, and each time he's caught Athena watching him, he shouts at her. This last time he pointed his gun at her and came toward her. He was calling her a deaf bitch, Athena could tell, and Dana wrapped her arms around her, could feel her shouting back at Sonny, and Dana's whole body was trembling.

But that wasn't just fear, that was anger, too.

Leon and Gail have both been crying. They're all scared.

Except Vladimir.

Athena doesn't know what to make of Vladimir.

When he came back, he went to Sonny, and he called Oscar over, and he spoke to them. He looked worried, furrowed his brow, and nodded a lot. They were on the other side of the room from where Athena and the rest of the class were seated, maybe fifteen feet away, but standing in the light, and she could make out his mouth. She really focused, too, tried to read everything from his lips and his body language, and he was being very calm, and she thought quiet, maybe, too, but she just couldn't understand a single word. She signed to Dana.

What saying?

Dana shook her head. *Different language Russian?*

That explained that.

Whatever he said to Sonny and Oscar, it seemed like it helped. They both nodded, and then Oscar went into the tunnel on one side, the place where the cars would enter this area on the track, and walked down it with his gun in both hands until he was out of sight. Sonny did the same thing, but in the other tunnel, where the ride would have exited. Vladimir watched them, and when both were gone, Athena thought he kinda smiled, just a little. He walked toward where they were all seated, and Athena felt her stomach ache and tighten, and Dana, still holding onto her, tightened her grip again.

But Vladimir didn't say anything to them or even look at them. He just looked down the tunnels in both directions, and then he moved back to the other side of the room, near where there was this open chest of fake gold coins and jewelry. Athena tried to watch him from the side, not looking at him directly, and he was pulling a phone from his pocket. The way he did it, the way he held the phone and turned away slightly, Athena could tell he didn't want the others to see him doing it, or maybe even to know he had it.

Vladimir looked at the phone for a second, maybe, pressed a couple of buttons, frowned. Raised his head, and Athena took that moment to rest her own cheek against Dana's knee, pretending to close her eyes. When she opened them again, Vladimir had the phone to his ear, was looking from one tunnel mouth to the other. He looked at her, and she looked back at him as blankly as she could, and he didn't seem to care. His mouth started to move.

It was hard, he was almost too far away, and she couldn't catch more than every eighth or ninth word as he spoke them. At first, she was sure he was speaking in another language again. Then she thought she saw "scared," and "fill," and "men," and she was *sure* she made out "move."

Then he said "bomb."

He wasn't on the phone for long, not long at all. It couldn't have been more than a minute. Looking at the tunnels the entire time, from one to the other, and then, when he was finished, quickly tucking the phone away again. His eyes found Athena, and her heart jumped, the fear of having been caught instant and overpowering. But he didn't do anything, maybe frowned just slightly, and she realized he wasn't looking at her at all; he was looking at Dana.

Ignoring Athena because she was deaf.

Then he opened his mouth and called out something, and Sonny and Oscar came back. There was another brief talk that Athena again couldn't follow— it was in the other language, what Dana thought might be Russian—and then Vladimir went up the tunnel one more time, and disappeared.

Athena twisted, pretending to adjust her position, turning her head to look up at Dana. Moved her hands, signing.

Phone did you hear him?

Dana shook her head, barely.

He said bomb, Athena signed.

Dana bowed her head, and pulled Athena in closer, and held her, and both of them tried not to be scared.

Now Dana shifts, and Athena lifts her head, and she sees what Dana is looking at. Vladimir has returned, he's talking to Sonny and Oscar, and again, it's not taking him long. Finished, he turns and walks over to them, all of them, and his lips are easy to read this time.

Get up.

The other men have followed Vladimir, spreading out slightly, holding their guns. Looking at them, and maybe they're still a little scared, but now they look mean, too. Athena feels Dana speak, and suddenly Vladimir is leaning forward, grabbing her with one hand by the arm and yanking her up so fast that Athena is nearly knocked on her side. Along the line, Joel starts to move, reaching to help Athena, and the one called Sonny steps forward and kicks him in the belly, and then he does it again, and again.

Athena makes a noise, feels it escaping her throat, and on her hands and knees goes to Joel. Miguel is trying to help him, and Athena finds Joel's eyes, sees the pain and the tears in them as he lies on his side, holding his arms around his middle. She helps him sit up, sees Miguel gesture, understands that something is happening behind her. Before she can react, before she can turn, there's a hot pain across the back of her head, the tearing of hairs as someone tries to pull her to her feet. She cries out, trying to rise, but he pulls so hard she's falling back, hits the concrete. The pain, if anything, gets worse, makes fresh tears fill her eyes, and she's being dragged, now, shouting and struggling and maybe screaming, too.

It stops as suddenly as it started, the pain still echoing as she lies on her back, gasping. Blinking through blurred vision, seeing Sonny standing over her, and Vladimir, and he's got a fist in Dana's hair. She sees their guns, not pointed at her but not pointed away. She sees their expressions, and she understands they do not care about her, about Joel, about Dana, about any of them at all. It's not hatred; that would require feeling something.

They look down at her like she's a piece of driftwood. Like she's gum on the pavement. They look down on her.

Vladimir shakes Dana slightly, speaking to her, and Dana starts signing. He points his gun at Athena, then at Dana.

Dana signs, *Everyone stand up.*

Athena starts to do as she's told, but she's not fast enough for Sonny. He grabs for her again, but she sees it and jerks away. Shouts at him, maybe saying "No," maybe saying "Don't," but she knows it's loud, feels it ripping out of her, all the frustration and pain and shame, and the noise makes him balk, eyes widening. Athena gets to her feet, angrily clears the tears from her cheeks, the snot from her nose.

"Fuck you!" Athena shouts. "Goatfucking cocksuckers!"

The one called Sonny jerks his head back, and she reads his shock, his confusion. Then it turns to rage, and even in the light of Hendar's Lair, Athena sees the color flooding up into his cheeks. He steps forward, dropping his gun to one hand and raising his other, and she knows he's going to hit her, and she doesn't even care, so filled with her own fury that she's shaking.

Sees Dana, shouting, *Stop!*

Sonny is over her now, and Athena won't look away from him, hating him, and that fist is going to fall, she knows it. But he doesn't hit her, he doesn't move, frozen, and from the corner of her eye, past him, she can see that Vladimir is speaking, and he looks as angry as she feels. Sonny lowers his hand, grabs her shoulder with it, forces her to turn, and Athena finds herself in line with the others. Joel, ahead of her, still has one arm around his stomach, his jaw flexing, and she thinks he might really be hurt a lot.

Vladimir pulls Dana with him to the front of the line, turns her to face all of them. She's wincing as he twists her hair, speaks to her, and he's making his words deliberate now; Athena can read them even before Dana begins to sign.

Follow and don't do anything else or he will kill you.

Then Dana adds, *Just do what he says it will be okay.*

Athena has to wonder if she really believes that at all.

When they come out of the tunnel, the sunlight blinds Athena. She blinks rapidly, trying to restore her vision, and the first thing she can make out is Pooch, his giant head and his puffy costume, except he's standing on his hind legs, like a person. It's vaguely disturbing, not to mention unexpected, but what makes it all the worse is that his hands are hands, not paws, and he's holding one of the same guns Vladimir and Sonny and Oscar have been carrying.

The second thing she sees are the costumes, spread out on the ground in front of all of them. There are pieces of Gordo and Betsy and another Pooch, and two of the space suits with helmets from the Star System Alliance, and one of the S.E.E.K.E.R. Robot suits, and Smooch, and Valiant Flashman, and Kurkur the Unending, too. More than enough costumes for all of them, Athena realizes, and she looks from the piles to see that Vladimir has pulled Dana close to him, is speaking in her ear. She's trying to pull away, and then he shoves her, and when he does that, she sees Pooch with a Gun take a step forward, like he wants to catch her.

Dana doesn't fall. She moves so that all of them can see her, begins signing. *Put on costumes we have to put them on.*

One by one, the line breaks apart. One by one, Athena and all the others disappear inside bodies too big for them. Then Sonny and Oscar and Vladimir do it, too, one after the other, until all of them, every single one, is dressed like a WilsonVille character.

She's not surprised that Vladimir chooses Kurkur the Unending. Athena doesn't know anything really about the Flashman stuff, but she knows who Kurkur is; he's the worst of the worst, the only villain to have ever killed any of the Flashmans, and now he hunts down every incarnation of them throughout time and space. He wears a helmet that has horns coming out of the mouth, like an insect's, and large red eyes, and a big black cloak, and his is the only costume that, once it's on, looks like it should be holding a gun.

Pooch with the Gun points Dana toward Betsy.

Athena picks Agent Rose.

They're putting on the costumes, and Dana has half of Betsy on, the lower part, and she moves to help Lynne with the Smooch body. She's signing when she can, checking with them, *Okay?* and of course they're not, how can they be, but everyone nods. When she reaches Joel, she signs *Stomach?*

Hurts.

Dana tries to smile at him, helps him with the Dread Flashman coat. Athena thinks Joel is looking a little pale.

Then Dana is in front of her, holding the comedy-tragedy mask, and she hands it to Athena, then signs.

Hold on they'll let us go.

Athena gives her the look that says, *Bullshit tell me another one*.

Those were bad words you said. Dana tries to smile at her. *Where did you learn to swear like that?*

Athena grins. Uncle Jorge taught her to swear like that, helped her out, would do it whenever Mom and Dad weren't looking or listening. Teach her to swear like a soldier, deaf or not, he'd said.

Dad and friends.

Dana grins, helps her put on the mask, then settles Agent Rose's fedora atop Athena's head. Athena doesn't move. She can see just fine through the mask, but her breath bounces back against her face, makes it hot and damp.

Dad coming, Athena signs quickly.

Dana raises an eyebrow.

He will kill them.

Dana throws a quick glance over her shoulder, to where Pooch with a Gun and Kurkur the Unending and now Gordo with a Gun are watching them. She looks back to Athena, pretends to adjust Agent Rose's trench coat, and signs.

Good.

Chapter Twenty-seven

EIGHTEEN MINUTES left, and Bell tells Amy, "I need you to stay here, stay with Michael and his family. Don't let them leave, nobody leaves until someone comes for you."

Amy says, "Freddie is right, Jad."

It knocks Bell out of his stride for a moment. "You're going to give me operational advice, Amy? Really?"

She simply stares up at him, what she thinks and what she feels all too apparent to Jad Bell. Then she turns away, down the hall, back to the conference room. She doesn't look back and she doesn't wish him luck, and that's no different from any other time he's gone on mission. Personal and professional kept separate, a distracted soldier is a dead soldier, keep your head in the game, all the clichés and watchwords run through his head.

He moves back through the command post, where everyone is gearing up. Ideal deployment would be a squad of four targeting each hostage group, primary shooters with secondary to sweep and clear. That is impossible here and now, and Bell's original intention was to pair Bone and Board, Chain and Angel, and take the group holding Athena by himself. The admonition echoes, makes him doubt, and that is enough, because if there is doubt, there is no doubt.

Much as he wishes it could be so, he cannot ride to his daughter's rescue alone. In point of fact, he shouldn't ride to his daughter's rescue at all.

"Freddie, Isaiah, you two take Group Three," he says. "Nuri and I will take Group One, Jorge takes Group Two."

Freddie Cooper, Cardboard, looks Bell in the eye and nods once. "Right call, Jad."

"We'll bring her home," Chain says.

Nuri says nothing, any objection she has to being paired with Bell not one she wishes to share with the room. Instead, she finishes checking the MP5K that Bell brought back with him from Wild World along with his wounds, then throws a glance to the surveillance bank, to the increasing number of charcoal-blank screens. She checks the Spartan again.

"Anything?"

"Dick-all," she says, and Bonebreaker laughs.

Bell finishes his check, surveys the team, reads their commitment. Even Nuri has brought her game face, and Bell once again wonders what she's capable of. The CIA lies, it's their job, and they're good at it. She killed an armed man who had taken her by surprise in his office with her bare hands, he reminds himself. She can put the bullets where they belong.

"Time to go to work," Bell says.

Without the need to avoid surveillance there's no reason to use the tunnels. The confusion of WilsonVille:

at this time, on a normal day, going underground would be the only way to cross the park quickly, efficiently. Today, with the landscape barren and hostile, Bell and Nuri cover the distance from the Sheriff's Office to the border between Wild Horse Valley and Pirate Bay in just over four minutes. With crowds, it would have taken four times as long, easily.

Bonebreaker runs along with them, keeping pace. The two target locations are relatively close together, and even though Jorge has studied the map, Bell wants to guide him to target as best he can. At the bridge west of Nova's Tower, Bell puts up his fist, and they all slow to a stop.

"That way," Bell tells Bonebreaker, pointing south, past the Race for Justice. "There's a bridge, crosses from Terra Space north into the valley."

Bonebreaker nods. "And if I get lost, there are signs."

"Don't get lost. Call it in when you're good to go."

"Roger that."

Bonebreaker takes off, weapon in hand, and Bell begins moving again, feeling the weight of his own pistol in his grip. Bone and Board brought a resupply, and with knowledge of the map, with determined points of entry, this is a by-the-numbers operation. They do what they do, and it should come off without a hitch.

That nagging doubt again, and Bell knows it isn't going to be that easy.

"You did the right thing," Nuri says.

They're skirting the Old WilsonVille Railroad, where the original steam engine that used to run on the track circumscribing the park was decommissioned.

Now it's an attraction of a different sort—a restaurant, a shop, and a play area. Heading north, toward Fort Royal, and Bell can feel the humidity in the air, rising from the man-made Pirate Bay.

"The right thing is doing this, now," Bell says. "There isn't anything else."

Bell pulls into cover behind the ticket booth at Royal Hunt. They're in the shade from Mount Royal, the sun now having descended far enough to be blocked by the imitation Everest. Nuri stacks close to him, almost touching, and he feels her turning, covering their back.

"It was a hard call, that's all I'm saying," she says softly. "I can't imagine having to make that choice."

"What choice?"

"Between your job and the people you love."

Bell looks at her, suspicious, unsure if he's being mocked and truly not in the mood for it. Instead, he finds that she's watching him, her expression somber. There's sympathy, and something else, and for the first time in almost two months of knowing this woman, Bell can see something aside from the professional demeanor, the park mask.

"My whole life has been that choice," he says.

He leans back against the kiosk, peers out, checking his lines, seeing nothing. Ahead of them, to the north, is Fort Royal, built to resemble a seventeenth-century Caribbean fortress on one side and an early pioneer trading post on the other. This side, facing south and the Wild Horse Valley, is the more rustic. He starts to turn to Nuri once more, to give her the run, direct her where she should go, when he sees movement. One hand goes to her, pulls her back with him, presses her into cover at his side.

The service door on the southeast side of the fort swings open. As Bell watches from cover, two figures emerge, immediately followed by two more. Then three, and another two, and by his count that's everyone who was in Fort Royal, now all outside. They move in a cluster, staying close, and almost as one begin walking, heading in their direction.

Bell doesn't move.

Nuri slips his arm, looks past, says what Bell is thinking.

"Shit," she murmurs.

"Move," he answers, and they retreat from the kiosk, back toward the wall bordering the Royal Hunt. She goes over it first, Bell after, dropping into the fake foliage, landing between an animatronic gorilla and its mate. Each listening, and each hearing nothing. Nuri begins picking her way carefully through the overgrowth, following the wall, stops after a dozen yards or so, dropping to one knee. Bell leans over her, can see the walkway through a gap in the wall.

Bell brings his left hand to his ear, is about to activate the earbud, but Chain beats him to the punch.

"We have a problem," Chain says. "They're mobile, and they're concealed. Repeat, we cannot identify the Tangos."

"Same," Bell murmurs.

"Same," Bonebreaker says.

"Hold."

The group is beginning to pass them now. Walking close together, almost touching one another, and all of them, every single one of them, is in some costume or another. They're not perfect fits: a Gordo whose cuffs drag on the ground, a S.E.E.K.E.R. Robot with one hand out on the back of a fully armored Valiant Flashman. A Pooch; a Rascal with his tail wrapped around his middle like a belt; a Clip Flashman in full encounter suit, including visored helmet; two dressed as Betsy, one in the soccer player costume and the other in traditional cutoffs and a plaid shirt; and finally a Lola, the oversized toucan, wings dragging alongside.

With only a couple of exceptions, Bell can't see their hands. Sleeves hang empty at the sides of costumes, sway disturbingly with each step. No way to tell who's armed, who is pointing a weapon, and who has their hands perhaps bound inside the confines of their outfits.

No easy way to tell the good guys from the bad, despite what each costume may say.

The procession passes them by, and not one head turns, not one costume looks their way.

The dead Tango's radio on Bell's hip crackles to life.

"Mr. Bell." It's the same soft-spoken man, the same voice. "Let's talk about how this is going to work."

Chapter Twenty-eight

GABRIEL WAS so worried about Dana recognizing him in the Pooch outfit that he almost missed the obvious.

The pretty, strawberry-blond deaf girl, in the shorts and the Hollyoakes T-shirt. From inside the headpiece, looking past the black grille that serves to hide his eyes inside Pooch's nose, Gabriel stared and wondered where he'd seen her before.

Then they were all getting into the costumes, and Dana was interpreting, moving along the line of kids, and she got to that girl and handed her the mask. The girl signed something, and that was what did it, maybe, the intuitive leap.

An overtime authorization on Jonathan Bell's desk for Dana Kincaid.

A photograph, framed, on the corner of the desk.

Jonathan Bell, his wife, his daughter.

Strawberry blondes, both.

Jesus Christ, Gabriel thought. *Oh Jesus Christ, it's his daughter.*

He thought, then, that he had damn well better be sure nothing happened to her.

Then a part of him he didn't like, a very old part of him, that once lived in Odessa, wondered how he might use this knowledge to his best advantage.

* * *

From the top of Gordo's Flying Ball, Gabriel Fuller has a pretty good view. It's not the highest point in the park by far, but below, he can see Vladimir as Kurkur and the others, Sonny and the other one and Dana in the Betsy costume, all of them in a group, waiting at the edge of Yesteryear Ballpark. He can see the approach, the wide walkway from Town Square heading this direction.

He can see them, and he can see the two men who have now stopped just between the Wilson Restaurant and the Sweets Emporium at the northwest corner of Wilson Town. Inside the giant baseball, Gabriel can see them, but they can't see him.

He keys the radio in his hand. "First thing you're going to do is tell your men to lay down their weapons and fall back."

"Why am I going to do that?"

"Because I'm looking at them right now, Mr. Bell, and they're looking at a bunch of people in costumes. Unless they are very clever and very quick, they don't know which of them are hostages and which of them aren't. I'm sure you've figured this out already. Tell them to fall back."

There's a pause, dead air on the radio. Gabriel adjusts his position, staying low in the ball. The ride is a simple one: guests climb a set of stairs, or, if they're handicapped, take a gantry-style elevator up to the giant hollow baseball where he's now crouched. They buckle up, hold their breath, and the whole thing drops in a free fall, only to bounce up and down, swaying back and forth. This, Gabriel understands, is supposed to be fun.

The two men set their weapons on the ground, two M4s and their pistols, then raise their hands and begin to back away.

"Done."

"Thank you. Call them back. Call all your people back, wherever they are, tell them they need to form on you."

"Form on me."

"That's what I said."

"You're military."

"What I am doesn't matter, Mr. Bell. What I can do, what I want *you* to do, that's what matters. You see where we're going with this? Do I need to spell it out?"

"Why don't you do that? I'd hate for there to be a misunderstanding."

Gabriel can't keep himself from laughing, but there's no mirth in it. "God, no, we wouldn't fucking want that, would we? Not at this point, no, we wouldn't want that."

"I'm listening. Talk."

Gabriel shifts. The Pooch costume is hot as ever, bulky in the confined space of the giant baseball. With the headpiece and gloves off, there's some relief, but not much. Not nearly enough.

"You can't tell us apart, you understand that, Mr. Bell? Everyone is in a mask, everyone is in a costume. Some of the men are dressed as women, some of the women as men, you understand me? Even the deaf kids, it's mix and match. You don't want to take a shot you can't take back, that's what I'm saying. Some-one starts shooting, hostages are going to end up dead. That's not a threat, now, that's just a fact."

"I understand," says Bell.

"You ever gone on the Terra Space ride, Mr. Bell?"

"Haven't had the opportunity."

"No, I imagine you've been busy. Once you have your people with you, you're going to head to the Terra Space ride. You'll take it up to the Lunar Platform, and you'll wait there. Once you're up top, we'll line up at the bottom. I'll start sending people up, two at a time. You won't know who's a hostage and who isn't until we're done, understand? You won't know if I'm sending my people up along with our prisoners or not. And if you move, if any of you comes off that platform before we're finished, you know what I'll have to do."

"Yeah," Bell says, and Gabriel swears the man actually sounds bored, if not annoyed. "I get it."

"One more thing, Mr. Bell. I see that your men here, they had long guns with them. I see any of you with a long gun, I don't care who's on the platform and who isn't, I'm going to start shooting. You have fifteen minutes to be there, or I start killing my hostages."

"Did you kill Vesques?" Bell asks.

The question takes Gabriel by surprise, so much that he loses his next words.

"You did, didn't you? Had to be you."

"We're not talking about me, this is not a confession. You want to listen to me. Get your people up on the Lunar Platform. You have fourteen minutes."

"No," Bell says.

"You don't want to fuck around."

"You've got to give me something here. A good faith gesture, something."

"I'm going to give you the bomb."

"Not enough. I let all of you walk, that's me having a very bad day, here. You're asking me to fail. You've got to give me something."

"What I have is your daughter," Gabriel says. "And that's what I'll give you if you do what I say."

He shuts off his radio before he can hear the response, stuffs it back inside the front of his Pooch costume, hooking it onto his belt. Carefully, he climbs out the open door at the side of the giant baseball, makes his way down the steps, feeling naked and exposed, his eyes on Dana in the Betsy costume the whole time. Her back is to the attraction, to him, and he wills her not to turn, not to see him. He's almost at the bottom when the giant head begins to swivel, and there is a horrible moment when Gabriel thinks it's all lost, it's all for nothing.

Then her head tilts, dips, and even in the costume, Gabriel can see her fatigue and her fear, and that is almost worse.

Almost.

He drops off the stairs, recovers his headpiece and the gloves. Vladimir as Kurkur looks his way, and Gabriel gives him a nod. Vladimir, and Sonny in a Gordo costume and Oscar in an original Clip Flashman outfit, nudge the rest of the group forward, and together, they begin making their way toward Wilson Town.

Gabriel pulls his headpiece back on, tucks the gloves into his costume, falls into line at the back. He's behind Bell's daughter, dressed up as Agent Rose. She's walking beside the Dread Flashman with the bandanna over his face. Gabriel can feel his subma-

chine gun pressed against his side, where it's hanging
from its strap over his shoulder, feel it digging into his
hip, trapped by Pooch's ample padding. Dread Flashman is walking a little slowly, and Jonathan Bell's deaf
daughter now puts a hand out to help him, and Gabriel
opens his mouth to tell her not to do that, to keep
her hands hidden, but stops himself. She's deaf, she
wouldn't hear him anyway.

But Dana can. Dana could.

He moves up between them, forcing them apart.
His ungloved left hand settles on Bell's daughter, her
shoulder, and she looks at him from behind her own
mask and beneath her fedora. He can see her eyes, and
the hatred in them, and he doesn't care. Uses his other
hand to push Dread Flashman along, forcing both kids
to keep pace.

If everything works right, if everything works the
way he has envisioned it, then Bell and his people will
be forty feet off the ground and almost three hundred
feet from where Gabriel and the others will line up.
Three hundred feet and no long guns, anybody takes a
shot, they'll have to be damn sure and damn lucky. Bell
and his others will be out of play. He'll send Dana up
in the first group, to keep her safe, then the rest of the
hostages, leave Bell's daughter for last. Then it will be
just his people, Vladimir and all the rest.

Then Gabriel will shut down the ride, trapping Bell
and the hostages up top for as long as it takes them to
make their way down the ladders. By the time they've
done that, Gabriel will have his own people out of
there, into the tunnels. He'll do a head check, tell them
to get out of the costumes. When they're all doing that,

he'll take the submachine gun digging into his side, and he'll shoot each and every one of them dead.

He'll ditch the Pooch costume with the bodies, leave it behind for the last time, and head north. Even if Bell is telling the truth about his team and how they entered and their vehicle and all of it, Gabriel isn't interested. Too risky, too easy to be tricked, and Bell lied, anyway, Gabriel is sure of it. So Gabriel will head north, and come out near Lion's Safari, and he'll wait until it's clear, and then he'll just walk out of the park much the same way the others walked in. Exit to the northeast employee lot, and get as far away as fast as he can.

That's his plan, and he believes in it. Despite everything, he believes in it.

He still believes in his dream.

Chapter Twenty-nine

"CAN YOU take them?" Ruiz is asking.

"Not once we're on that platform," Bell says.

"Shit," Wallford mutters. "They made all of you?"

"Not sure. He knows we're at least three, maybe four. Don't think he knows about our Angel."

Wallford raises his head to look across the conference table to Ruiz, over the speakerphone between them. "Cue HRT? Try to flank them?"

"Same problem." Ruiz is leaning, hands on the table. "Warlock? Nothing about the device?"

"Presumably he's holding that back."

"How do you want to proceed?"

"We go up there, they can do whatever they want," Bell says. "They can kill the hostages, anything, and we won't be able to stop them."

"They see you're not there, they'll do it anyway," Wallford says.

"Know your targets, Warlock," Ruiz says.

"Sniper one-oh-one." Bell's voice drops, almost muttering, perhaps only to himself now. "Costumes. Costumes, costumes, the key is the costumes...."

The conference room door opens, a harried and excited Matthew Marcelin entering. From the looks of him, he's been dancing for the media again, but now he's loosening his tie with one hand, holding a sheet of paper up for them to see in the other. He opens his mouth to speak and then closes it without a word as Ruiz looks a warning to him.

"Warlock?" he asks.

Bell doesn't respond, and Ruiz realizes the line has gone dead. Whatever witchcraft Warlock is planning, he's already casting the spell. Wallford reaches out, closes the call.

"You know who takes the hit on this if the hostages die, right?" he asks.

Ruiz nods. He takes the hit. Takes it hard and straight, and goes down from it, too.

"No different from any other day at the office," Ruiz says. "Mr. Marcelin?"

"Personnel finished their list."

Wallford checks his watch, purses his lips, impressed. "Fast. Thought it would take until tomorrow, at least."

"They were motivated." Marcelin lays the sheet on the table, starts reading off the names. "There are five park employees unaccounted for. One of them, Sarah Koos, was assigned to play Xi-Xi today. We think she was the woman who was murdered. There are two more who were in costume: Gabriel Fuller was playing Pooch, and Steven De Rosario was playing Hendar. Cassie Zurrer was on concessions at the Tropical Treats stand at Wacky Wharf. Last one is Dana Kincaid, she was called in late, to act as an ASL interpreter for a special-needs group."

"Only two men," Wallford says.

"Do you have personnel files on Fuller and De Rosario?" Ruiz asks.

"I can bring them up." Marcelin moves down the table to its head, sits, and opens the laptop sitting there. Ruiz looks to Wallford, who nods, takes out his phone.

"Wallford," he says. "Word of the day is 'buzzsaw.' Run the following, do it fast. Fuller, Gabriel, and De Rosario—two words—Steven. Call me back."

Ruiz is watching as Marcelin seems to assault the laptop's keyboard with his fingers. The stress of the day is taking its toll, and he hunches as he works, shoves his glasses back up his nose with an angry thumb, typing again, faster, clumsily. Swears, retypes.

"Here they are," Marcelin finally says. "Fuller has been with us since the beginning of summer, hired on near the end of May. Qualified for Pooch, passed his security screening, student at UCLA. Prior job experience, U.S. Army.

"De Rosario, he's been with us for four and a half years. High school education, previous experience is all acting. Did a couple of commercials, and worked at a theater up in Portland, Oregon."

"Want to take a wild guess?" Wallford asks as his phone starts to ring again.

"I don't have to," Ruiz says.

In three minutes, they learn the following.

They learn that Gabriel Fuller has no criminal record.

They learn that Gabriel Fuller served a 4YO with the United States Army, and went to Afghanistan for two tours.

They learn that he left the army as a sergeant.

They learn that he was born in Culver City, California, on the seventeenth of March, and that he's twenty-four years old.

They learn that he has seventeen thousand three hundred and twenty-seven dollars plus some change in his account at Bank of America.

They learn that he lives in Westwood, but that he's rented an apartment here, in Irvine.

They learn that he signed the rental agreement with Dana Kincaid.

They learn that, prior to eight years ago, Gabriel Fuller doesn't seem to have existed.

"Long-term sleeper," Wallford says.

"For who?" Ruiz wonders.

"Iran?" Wallford grins, and Marcelin, still seated, looks alarmed. "Joke."

Marcelin doesn't seem to think now is the time for jokes.

"Dana Kincaid," Ruiz says.

"Think she's in on it with him?" Wallford asks. "Dana Kincaid?"

Ruiz considers. Thinks about what Marcelin said, about the woman being brought in as an ASL interpreter. Knows exactly why, and knows, too, who it was who brought her to the park. He shakes his head.

"Then she's in for one hell of a surprise," Wallford says.

Chapter Thirty

BELL LOWERS the radio, and Nuri, who heard it all, says nothing. Nuri, who has heard the soft-spoken man say that he has Bell's daughter, that he has Athena, says nothing at all.

What she does, she takes the radio from him, sets her fingertips on his cheek, only for a moment. She doesn't smile. She doesn't offer platitudes. She just touches him, like that, and Bell knows she is with him.

Then Bonebreaker is coming up on their position, followed by Chaindragger and Cardboard, and Bell takes a breath, lets himself feel it, then lets it go, and tries to let the emotion he is feeling go with it. Watches as Nuri hands over the MP5K she's been carrying to Board, who nods his thanks, and then all eyes are on him. Bell pulls his phone, makes the call, and tells Brickyard the news.

When the call is done, Bell says, "Costumes. We have ten minutes. Costumes. Target selection, target identification. Costumes don't mean a thing, the way their hazmat and Tyvek didn't mean a thing. They're coming from the east, heading toward the Terra Space ride, we know that, we know which way they're coming, which way all of them are converging. Watch them walk, hear them talk. They'll have to put at least one guard at the front of each group, the other will be in the middle or at the back."

"Ambush," Board says.

"You better fucking believe it." Bell looks at Nuri. "You have five minutes, most, to get into costume."

She blinks. "And do what?"

"Infiltrate. The group we were going to take, they're coming down from Fort Royal. There's tunnel access north of the Terra Pad."

"One of the dressing rooms," Chain says, nodding.

"Fall in the back, find out who is who, kill the ones who don't belong."

Nuri hesitates. "I'm not trained for this, Warlock."

"You are, you are trained for this. This is intelligence gathering. Shoot the ones you're sure are wrong in the head. Any doubts, drill them in the leg. They try to return fire, you know they're hostile."

She needs a half moment to accept this, and then she's gone, sprinting for the nearest tunnel entrance.

"Angel of Death," Bonebreaker says.

"Who has optics?"

Bonebreaker pulls a monocular from his pocket. Bell indicates Chain with his head, watches the handoff.

"Find a high hide, take overwatch," Bell tells him. "Don't let them see you. Pick out the targets."

"Nova's Tower." Chaindragger turns the monocular in his hand, makes it disappear into a pocket of his wrinkled coveralls. Then he's sprinting away as well, north, the opposite direction that Angel took.

"What I said to Angel." Bell looks at Cardboard, at Bonebreaker. "Any doubt, take the leg. No doubt, two to the head."

"Done deal," Cardboard says.

They move.

Bell is ducking beneath one of the on-ramps at Race for Justice, moving fast and low, making for the faux garage, when Brickyard calls him up on coms.

"We have an ID on your inside man," Ruiz says. "Fuller, Gabriel. U.S. Army, Tenth Mountain, Third Brigade. Was on Operation Mountain Viper, left after his second tour as a sergeant. Prior to that, a model citizen, and before that, he doesn't exist."

"Sleeper."

"That's the read. No idea who placed him."

"Understood."

"The woman you brought into the park today, the ASL interpreter. Dana Kincaid."

"What about her?"

"Any reason you picked her?"

"ASL-certified and at the top of the call list. Why?"

"Her name's on a rental agreement with Fuller. We don't know their relationship."

For a moment, Bell flashes back to all his paranoia, the Hollyoakes visit and his inability to keep it from coming to pass. A trip planned almost a year in advance of today. A trip planned before Jad and Amy had divorced, and ages before Bell himself knew he would be asked to live his lie in WilsonVille. Rotten fucking luck.

He's really hoping he's seen the last of it.

"She can't be in on it," he says. "There's no way whoever put this in play knew I'd need an ASL interpreter today. She wasn't ever scheduled to work today."

"Unless this goes deeper and darker than we think."

"One conspiracy at a time," Bell says.

"Agreed. Out."

In the Race for Justice garage there's a miniature Formula 1 car with WilsonVille characters painted all over it, and a similarly sized NASCAR racer on the lift. There are also fake tools, fake engine parts, and a collection of fifty-gallon oil drums, scaled down to perhaps hold twenty-five, stacked in a pyramid by the entrance. Bell takes his position there, clear lines of sight in almost every direction, including toward Terra Space.

Chaindragger's voice comes into his ear. "I have eyes on three groups, repeat, all three groups. Converging, ETA two minutes. White, nine. Red, eight. Green, eleven."

"Bone, Board, take Green," Bell says. "Four Tangos, the rest are friendlies. Remember, they're deaf, they won't respond to verbal."

Board comes back, says, "Understood."

"Angel, I have eyes on you. Hold." Chain pauses. "Red is crossing the bridge at Wild Horse Valley. Hold."

"I'm going to throw up," Angel whispers.

"You will not," Bell tells her.

"Hold on Red. Warlock, White, Soccer Betsy is a Tango, repeat, is a Tango."

"Soccer Betsy is a Tango."

"Angel, Red, Lola is possible Tango. Cannot confirm."

In his ear, Bell hears Angel whisper something about shooting a giant toucan in the leg.

"Angel, Red, they are off the bridge, turning to Green. Recommend you join when they pass the restrooms opposite Warlock's position."

"Jesus," Angel says. "This is not going to work. This is not going to work, they'll spot me."

"And do what?" Bell says. "Their whole plan relies on them not revealing themselves. They spot you, they won't be sure you're not one of them."

"You believe that?"

"Yes."

"Liar."

"Never to my friends."

Chain cuts in. "Cardboard, Bonebreaker, I have no positives on Green, repeat, no positives on Green. Angle is bad. Warlock, two more possibles, White, Pooch and a Flashman."

"Which Flashman?" Bell asks.

"It's the armored one."

"Valiant Flashman," Cardboard says.

There is a pause.

"I used to collect the comics," Cardboard says.

"Contact imminent," says Chaindragger.

"We have no targets." Bell can hear the anxiety in Bonebreaker's voice. "We have no possibles."

"We have no time," Bell says. "Do it."

And God help us if we miss, he thinks.

Chapter Thirty-one

THERE'S SOMETHING really wrong with Joel.

He's having trouble walking, and where Athena can see his eyes above the bandanna mask they're making him wear, there are tears, and sweat is running down his face. She tries to hold his hand again, but the man walking between them, the one in the Pooch costume, he won't let her. He keeps separating them. Athena tries signing to him, but Joel doesn't even acknowledge her.

They're about halfway through Wilson Town when Athena suddenly pushes forward, past Lynne in the Smooch costume, trying to get to Dana. She reaches out and catches Dana/Betsy's arm, and then feels that hand again, grabbing the back of her trench coat, yanking her back. She's still holding on to Dana's costumed arm, and Athena won't let go, pulls her around as she's jerked back herself, and suddenly Pooch's grip on her is gone, and the whole group comes to a stop.

Help him! Athena signs rapidly to Dana/Betsy, then points to Joel. *Needs help!*

Hands concealed within Betsy's, Dana can't answer. Her head inside Betsy's, Dana can't even look directly at Athena. Vladimir/Kurkur pushes Dana with his left hand, his right beneath his cloak and holding his gun,

Athena is sure. Dana/Betsy turns around slowly, and Pooch pulls Athena back again, and she tries to shake off his grip, but he just tightens it around her arm.

They resume their march, coming out of the square, and Athena is watching everything, her eyes moving from Joel to the others and beyond them, flicking quickly. Using her vision to supply what her ears cannot. There's a kiddie ride on their right, Rascal's Tailspin; it's like a teacup ride except instead of cups there're bowls. The lights are flashing, even though nothing is moving, and Athena can feel a thrum coming from it, too, what she suspects is music. On her left, there's Smooch's FunHouse, which is like three different things all at once—a bounce house, and a ball pit, and something else she doesn't even know what it is. It looks like it has something to do with skydiving, maybe, or blowing air, but she's not sure.

The Terra Space ride is ahead of them, still a ways off, but the giant Clip Flashman Rocket is easy to spot, and she can see the little mock rocket sleds that run up on rails at one side of the ride, to Lunar Space, and then descend on the other, back to the Terra Pad. They were going to have lunch there, she remembers, down at the bottom, then ride up and maybe buy souvenirs. Thinking about it, she realizes how hungry she is, how thirsty.

She keeps looking for her dad, but she doesn't see him anywhere. He's coming, Athena knows he is, he has to come, because these are Bad Guys. He fights Bad Guys. All those nights and he wasn't home, all those days he was gone, it was because he fights people like this. He has to come.

Almost directly ahead of them, there's a group of people approaching. They're in costumes, too, just like her own group. Eight or nine of them, she isn't sure, they're still too far away, but she can see one is a Flashman in shining armor, and maybe at the back there's another one, a Clip Flashman in his space suit and helmet, the same costume that Oscar in their group is hiding inside. She glances to her right, still ahead, past the Race for Justice, and another group is coming from that direction, too. More costumes; she counts eight total, including two Gordos, a Soccer Betsy, and another Smooch like the one Lynne is wearing.

First group getting closer. Eight of them, she now sees, the two Flashmans and the first Lola that Athena's seen all day. Second group, nine, and Athena wonders how many of them are Bad Guys, too. She can't tell.

Vladimir/Kurkur is looking around, and so is Sonny/Gordo and Oscar/Clip Flashman. They stop, abruptly, and Athena thinks someone must have said something. Dana/Betsy turns in place, trying to look back at them, maybe to check on Joel, and Athena does the same. He's looking down at the ground, both hands at his middle, like he's going to throw up. Something past him moves, and Athena thinks it was one of the bowls on Rascal's Tailspin, turning slightly like it's been disturbed.

She glances behind her. Pooch is standing very still now, and one of his ungloved hands is at his middle, like he's thinking about pulling his suit open. Athena looks at Dana/Betsy, sees she's turned around again, back to her. Beyond, Athena sees that first group, still coming closer, all nine of them. Her eyes skip to the other ones approaching, and then, just as quickly, she's looking back, past Dana again.

Nine getting closer?

There were eight. Athena knows there were eight of them, she is certain there were eight. Now there are nine, and she is trying to see what is different, what has changed. The Lola and the one Flashman in his shining armor and the other one at the back, the original one, wearing his space suit, his helmet on and his mirrored visor down, just like the one that Oscar in their own group is wearing.

There's a Penny Starr, too. She's almost next to Flashman, Athena thinks, just hanging back a little bit. Athena can see the shiny almost-purple black jumpsuit, the glint of the late afternoon sun bouncing just off the top of her silver space helmet.

Penny Starr wasn't there before.

The horrible, angry, gnawing that feels like it's been eating at her insides since they took Mom away starts to fade. She still can't see her dad, but Athena knows now, she's certain that he is nearby, and relief, apprehension, fear, joy, all of them mix, make her breathing catch. She glances quickly around once more, and nobody is watching her. For the first time, maybe, nobody is watching her. Whatever Pooch and Vladimir/Kurkur and Oscar/Flashman and Sonny/Gordo thought would happen, whatever they expected to see, Athena realizes that they're not seeing it.

Their tension is sudden, palpable in the way they move, in the way they don't, in their new stillness, despite their costumes.

Athena edges closer to Joel, and nobody grabs her, and nobody tries to stop her. She reaches out for him, like she wants to see how he's doing, and they let her. She wonders if they're talking to each other, if they've even noticed, but it doesn't matter. Turned like this, Athena is facing Rascal's Tailspin, where one of the bowls moved when it shouldn't have. Keeping her hands close to her body, she signs as quickly as she can, spelling the names.

K-U-R-K-U-R G-O-R-D-O C-L-I-P P-O-O-C-H K-U-R-K-U-R G-O-R—

Movement, the corner of her eye. She starts to turn her head, but not before she sees the bowl that she thought was moving spin around, the door in its side open, and there's Uncle Jorge sort of half inside, half out. He's got his gun in both hands, coming forward already, and she sees the gun rocking, feels the vibration of the gunshots.

Athena twists, sees the first group across from them, sees Penny Starr with a gun all her own, and she sees her put it against the helmet of Clip Flashman and pull the trigger, just like that. The people on the bridge start to scatter, and Lola tries to turn around, to face Penny Starr, an arm rising beneath the floppy wing, one of the guns like Vladimir and Sonny and Oscar are carrying, but it never gets to come up. Penny Starr shoots the giant toucan, and Lola falls down, wings flopping.

Movement erupts all around her, the vibration in the air and her body, shots and more shots. Pooch shoves her aside, rushing forward, and Kurkur/Vladimir is sweeping his cloak back and bringing up his gun. Athena shouts, throws herself into Joel, knocking them both to the pavement. She sees Oscar/Clip is on his knees, hands moving to his helmet, like he wants to take it off, and then the helmet shatters and he falls sideways. Gail, Lynne, Miguel, Leon, all of them in their costumes, they're still standing, and Athena pushes herself to her feet, launches herself at Lynne from behind. They tumble to the ground together, landing absorbed by the Smooch costume.

Sonny is turning toward them, yanking his big gun free from where he's been hiding it inside Gordo's baseball glove. Big, happy Gordo eyes seem to find her, and Athena sees a shower of color behind him, plastic spheres suddenly erupting from the ball pit, bouncing every which way. Uncle Freddie is there now, and he's shooting, too. Gordo's eyes stay big and happy, but he twists, falls to his side like someone let the air out of him.

Athena rolls off Lynne, sees the second group, to the side. There's a S.E.E.K.E.R. Robot down on the ground, clutching at his leg, and there's a Pooch face-down, not moving.

She sees her dad, watches as he fires the gun in his hand. Soccer Betsy jerks like she's been punched in the face, and he shoots her again, and she falls. He steps over her like she's not even there, that pistol in both hands, swinging it around. The look on his face is one she's never seen before. It's not a scary face, but it's not a happy face, either. For that instant, she thinks her father is feeling nothing at all.

"Dad!" Athena shouts, shouts as loud as she can, not even certain what that is. Using all her air, making the words, "Dad! Dad! Dad!"

His head snaps in her direction, but his eyes don't find her, skip past her. Athena remembers the stupid Agent Rose mask on her face, yanks it off, knocking the hat away at the same time.

"Dad!" She's screaming it, now, feels her throat tearing, wonders if she has ever been this loud before, wonders if it matters. "Daddy! Daddy!"

He finds her, and the blank face isn't blank any longer, and he's shouting something, starting toward her, gesturing with one hand while the other still holds the pistol high. Swiping, telling her to get down, and Athena thinks that all of this, it's almost over, it's going to be all right.

Her dad is here, and it's going to be all right.

She's wrong.

Chapter Thirty-two

GABRIEL DOESN'T know why they've stopped at first, only that they have, and Vladimir half turns, calls back to him, voice muffled behind the Kurkur mask.

"I don't see them," Vladimir says, using English. "Something's wrong."

He thinks that means Vladimir just can't see the two other groups, Charlie One and Charlie Two, and Gabriel takes another few steps forward then. He is aware of Bell's daughter in front of him, looking at her friend in the Flashman costume, but beyond the front of their group, where Dana is positioned beside Oscar, Betsy and Clip Flashman side by side, his vision is impaired. It's hard to see extreme distance through the Pooch headpiece, and Gabriel wants to remove it, the same way he wants to answer Vladimir. Again, he keeps his silence, afraid of what his voice might mean to Dana.

"They're not here." Sonny, dressed as Gordo, anxious, nervous. Oscar starts to turn back his way. Just at the edge of Gabriel's vision, fuzzy through the grille, he can see Charlie One coming in from the north. He moves his hand, thinking to reach into his suit and pull his radio, to ask Jonathan Bell just what he thinks he's doing, if he really wants to do this, to play games with the lives of so many, with the life of his daughter.

Then it all goes to screaming hell.

"Contact!" This in Russian, Vladimir shouting, and Gabriel can't tell where the shots are coming from, only that Oscar is going down, Clip Flashman helmet bursting into shards as a round finds his face. The reports echo across pavement and bounce from buildings, the rides, from the heavens, it seems, all of them muffled, confused, inside Pooch's head.

The girl, Bell's daughter, has fallen, or maybe she's diving, knocking down the Flashman boy, and Vladimir is turning, freeing his submachine gun, but the others are only now beginning to respond. In the back of Gabriel's mind he understands, intuitively, how this is happening, how Bell and his team are picking their targets, at least in part, at least in front of him. How can they tell who is a hostage and who isn't? The last ones to move, those are the hostages. The last ones to move, because they are the last to understand, because they are deaf. They cannot hear the shots.

Sonny is falling, and just in the edge of his vision, Gabriel sees Vladimir with his weapon out, laying down fire. Gabriel starts forward, wanting to reach Dana, to protect her, but stops himself, instead steps back. Tears at the front of the Pooch costume, reaching for his own submachine gun, still trapped against his side.

Then the weapon is in his hands, and he swings it right, fires off a burst toward the spinning bowl ride, shooting blindly. Bell's daughter is on her knees, screaming for her father, and he can see that Dana in the Betsy costume is trying to protect the kids, trying to pull them close to her with oversized arms, to pull them down.

"The girl!" Gabriel points at Bell's daughter. "Vladimir! The girl, get the girl!"

He looses another burst, same direction as before. The fucking Pooch head has killed his peripheral vision, and what he can see as he moves comes stuttered, like broken film. He tries to back up, almost trips over his own paws, sees a man amid the bowls coming forward, pistol in his hands, firing at him. Something punches through his mask, creases pain along his scalp, and he lays on the MP5K again, watches the man jerk backward, fall out of his line of sight.

Bell's daughter is still on her knees, the girl in the Smooch costume flat on the ground in front of her, and Gabriel can hear her still screaming for her father, screaming bloody murder. Vladimir cuts into his vision, reaches down for her, pulls her up and against his costume armor. Gabriel raises the MP5K, puts another burst downrange, the direction of Charlie One, begins backing away again.

"Tunnel!" His voice is too loud in the mask, makes his ears throb, but he's shouting anyway. "Back! Toward the theater!"

Vladimir adjusts his grip on the girl, lifting her under one arm, goes on his trigger with the other, firing in the direction of the ball pit. Then he's pivoting, the girl shrieking incoherently, kicking and clawing, and Gabriel sees Vladimir bash the barrel of the SMG along the side of her head, and the girl stops struggling.

Gabriel fires again, almost randomly, lets Vladimir

get behind him with Bell's daughter, checks over his shoulder to see they're making their retreat. Turns back and then he sees him, sees Bell, or at least he thinks he does, distorted through the mask, a hundred feet or so away. Starting to run toward them, and Gabriel brings the gun up again, lays a burst at him starting up the sloped path in their direction. The man cuts right just as Gabriel fires, throws himself into cover against the curving wall along the pathway. Gabriel lays down a second burst, close after the first, still backing away.

Retreat is the only thing that matters now, salvaging this is the only thing that matters right now. That, and Dana, and Gabriel sees she's huddled on her knees, big Betsy arms around two of the costumed kids. Head bowed, and he doesn't think she's been hit, can't see if she was, prays that she wasn't. Prays that Bell and his people take better care of her than he's managed to.

Gabriel runs, chasing after Vladimir. Yanking the Pooch head off with one hand, feels a new shock of pain along his scalp. Whoever shot him must've hit high on the mask, just skimming his skull. He lets the mask drop, feels blood running through his hair and down his neck.

"This way!" he shouts, leading, running as fast as the Pooch costume will let him to the FRIENDS ONLY door alongside the Dawg Days Theatre. Hits it with his shoulder, costume cushioning the impact, knocking it wide and then covering their backs as Vladimir, still half carrying, half dragging Bell's daughter, crashes through past him. Gabriel takes a last look, sees nothing, nobody chasing, and steps fully into the little courtyard, allowing the door to fall closed.

Vladimir has dropped the girl, is yanking at the Kurkur costume, and Bell's daughter is still for a moment, holding her head in her hands where she was clubbed with the gun. Then she's on her feet with a burst of speed, and Vladimir, his arms caught in his costume, tries to reach for her, misses. She's coming straight at Gabriel, trying to get past him, and he catches her with his arm across her chest, sends her bouncing back. She tries again.

Gabriel brings the MP5K up, both hands, barrel straight at this teenage girl's face. She stops herself, mouth in a scowl, eyes full of the same hate, stares at him, and for a flicker of a moment, Gabriel actually thinks she's daring him to do it, to shoot her, and he wonders if it's courage or rage or both that's fueling her.

Then Vladimir's out of Kurkur and his hands are free, and he's grabbing the girl from behind, spinning her around. Before Gabriel can speak, before the girl can react, Vladimir is punching her, swearing in Russian as he does it, once, twice in the stomach, then in the face, and the girl collapses, broken, and Gabriel is shouting.

"Stop it! Stop it, we need her! We need her!"

Vladimir rounds on him with a snarl, catches himself, catches his breath. There is a silence, broken only by the sound of Bell's daughter, a soft, keening noise that she's making. She's fallen from her knees to her side, one hand guarding her stomach, the other to her mouth. When she looks up, Gabriel sees blood coming between her fingers.

He moves closer to Vladimir, into his face, hissing in Russian. "We want her alive."

"You care too much about them. They're meat, to be used." Vladimir spits off to the side, then turns away, retrieving his own submachine gun. Without looking at Gabriel, he asks, "Now what?"

Gabriel reaches down, offers Bell's daughter his hand, and she recoils. He reaches again, and she tries to hit his hand, and he has to reach a third time before he can catch her arm. He pulls her to her feet, points at the flight of stairs leading down into the Gordo Tunnel. Vladimir grunts, starts down the flight of stairs, and Gabriel follows, hand still on the girl. She comes docilely now, more slowly, head down. Blood is running from her mouth, her lip already beginning to swell.

At the bottom, a view of the tunnel stretching north, bright and vacant. Vladimir, not more than ten feet ahead of him, turns to look at him.

"Which way are we going?" Vladimir asks.

"Straight to the junction, then right," Gabriel says. He's pulling at his own costume now, trying to shrug out of it.

"To do what, Matias?"

"To get the fuck out of here."

"What about the device?"

"Fuck the device!" His raised voice echoes, bounces off the finished concrete surfaces all around them. "Do you want to do that Uzbek fuck's bidding or do you want to live?"

Vladimir turns without a word, shaking his head slightly, begins walking down the tunnel. Gabriel kicks the Pooch leggings free, then gives Bell's daughter a shove, and she offers no fight, stumbling along, and they are moving slowly, steadily, ten paces, twenty. Vladimir looks over his shoulder once, shakes his head again.

He has to do it now, Gabriel realizes. Now or it'll be too late. Kill Vladimir and Bell's daughter both, and then run for it, just run and run until he is out and free and clear. Dana is safe now, there's that, at least, and with her safe, he still has hope.

Then he hears Dana's voice, and hope, along with what remains of Gabriel Fuller's dream, dies.

Chapter Thirty-three

BELL PUTS two rounds into Pooch, and another two rounds into Soccer Betsy, because he's certain; he puts one round into the S.E.E.K.E.R. Robot's leg because he isn't, and there's always time for apologies later. Chain chattering in his ear the whole time, traffic overlapping, Bonebreaker repeating the message from Athena, relayed via sign.

"Kurkur, Gordo, Clip, and Pooch."

Bell swings his weapon left, up and away from Soccer Betsy, tracking. Identifies White, Angel is moving forward, firing at the Tango in the Lola costume.

"Tango down." Her voice is hoarse.

Tango down, Angel advancing.

Continues tracking, swinging about, eyes on Green, furthest away, over a hundred feet, bad range for a pistol shot, he has no shot. Hearing the gunfire as he starts to advance.

"Tango down," Cardboard saying.

Rip of gunfire, still advancing, Bonebreaker echoing Cardboard. New cascade of shots and then his daughter's voice, calling for him, and he feels a new rush of adrenaline, is sprinting up the path, climbing the lazy slope. Sees Pooch, sees the weapon, hears Athena screaming for him, hears Chain in his ear, urgent, all of it at the same time.

"Bonebreaker, Bonebreaker," Chain says. "Bonebreaker, respond."

Training trumps passion. Bell shifts, throws himself to his left, against the retaining wall along the side of the path. Can smell the flowers planted there, feels his pulse thrum, the .45 in his hand. Bonebreaker isn't responding.

"Cardboard!" Bell says.

"I'm pinned, Bone is down," Cardboard comes back immediately. "No shot, no shot."

Bell moves to break cover, hears another burst of shots, hears rounds whine past as they skip high off the ground.

"Bonebreaker is down," Chain says. "Bonebreaker is down. Angel, do you have the shot?"

"No shot, I have no shot. Two Tangos moving back, they have a hostage, they have—"

She cuts off, another fusillade, the echo off the wall beside Bell disorienting, making it seem as if the shooters are somehow behind and above him. Chain swears in his ear.

"Warlock, move, move, move," Chain says. "I have eyes on Tangos, go, go, go."

Bell pushes away from the wall, sprinting forward, pounding his way upslope, pistol low and ready in both hands. More shots, the rattle from the MP5Ks, and Cardboard curses. Bell crests the rise, finds eight figures lying on the ground, and back toward Wilson Town, he sees Kurkur the Unending disappearing around the side of a building, Pooch chasing after him.

Eight figures on the ground, blood pools, soaks a Gordo, saturating his costume. Clip Flashman lies dead, his helmet in fragments around his head. Smooch face down, his trunk trapped beneath his body, and Bell hears a girl sobbing from within the costume. A Betsy is struggling to get out of her own outfit, her hands already free, a Hollyoakes student on either side of her, and she's using ASL. He sees Dread Flashman, the same boy whom Athena was flirting with hours before, lying with his arms around his belly. Cardboard is coming up on Bell's right, Angel behind him, already out of her helmet.

He doesn't see Athena, he doesn't see his daughter, and he knows what that means.

"Chain," Bell says. "Track them."

"On it, looks like they're going for the tunnel at Dawg Days."

Cardboard is moving past, toward the bowls of Rascal's Tailspin. "Bonebreaker!"

The woman in the Betsy costume is moving now, pulling masks from more of the students, pausing in between to struggle out of her costume. Frightened faces blink up at them, some recoil, some try to hide, and Bell scans them all, and still, he cannot see his daughter.

"Got him!" Cardboard calls.

"He okay?"

"He's a lucky motherfucker."

Bell spares a look, sees Cardboard is helping the larger man make his way out of the ride. Three distinct tufts of Kevlar curl from Bonebreaker's chest, the material white and willowy against the black fabric covering it. The vest held.

"Ribs," Jorge manages to say. "Fucking ribs."

Bell nods, pops the magazine from his pistol, replaces it fresh, readies the weapon. Looking over the students, his eyes finally settling on the woman now out of the Betsy costume.

"Angel," Bell says. "Take the tunnels, swing around to Gordo from the north."

Angel is kneeling by Dread Flashman, and she looks up at him. All around them, the Hollyoakes class minus his daughter is signing in a flurry, too fast for Bell to hope to understand, the shorthand the deaf use among themselves. Tears and relief and fear.

"This kid's hurt," Nuri says. "He's in shock, I don't know what's wrong."

"Tunnels," Bell repeats. "Go."

She nods, getting to her feet. Bell looks down at the boy, the boy his daughter was walking with. His skin has taken an ashen cast, his lips touched with gray, pinpoints of perspiration on his forehead, his cheeks, his upper lip.

"Top," Cardboard says.

Bell ignores him, turns to the woman who isn't Betsy. "Dana Kincaid? You are Dana Kincaid?"

She's signing to three of the kids at once, stops abruptly, looks at him in alarm. "I am. I'm...you're Mr. Bell, aren't you? You're Athena's father."

"I am." He extends one hand to her. "I need you to come with me. Now."

"What?" She looks confused, on the verge of despair. "I don't understand. I need to stay with the kids, they need an interpreter—"

"You know Gabriel Fuller?"

"Gabe? Yes, I know Gabe, he's—"

"Your boyfriend has my daughter hostage," Bell says. "You're coming with me, now."

He doesn't wait for her agreement, steps in, puts his hand on her back, turns her with him.

"Top," Cardboard says.

"Help the others."

Bell and Dana Kincaid move into Wilson Town, together.

Dana Kincaid tries to keep pace with him as Bell jogs along. She opens her mouth to speak, but Bell raises his hand to silence her, listening to Cardboard in his ear.

"One of these kids is hurt," Cardboard says. "He's decompensating. We need a medic."

"On it," Chain responds. "HRT is at the front gate, waiting confirmation to breach."

"Tell them to fucking move it."

"I'm coming down," Chain says.

Cardboard says, "Top, Brickyard wants status."

"Keep HRT out of Town Square," Bell says. "Going to try to talk a surrender."

"Good luck with that," Chain says.

"Surrender?" Dana Kincaid asks. "I don't understand! I don't understand, what's going on? Why do you want to know about Gabe?"

"Gabriel Fuller has my daughter." Bell keeps one hand on the woman's back, the pressure as light as he can manage, guiding her.

"No. No, that's not right. Stop that!" She twists, turns out of his touch, stopping in front of him. Confusion on her face, masked with defiance. "No, you're wrong."

"Then you'll prove me wrong. Do you love him?"

She stares at him, taken aback by the question.

"Do you love him?" he asks again.

"I—yes! What...he isn't, he..." She falters, trails off, and there's a new look in her eyes, and Bell sees the realization. "He plays Pooch. He plays Pooch, there was a Pooch, he never said anything...."

"Gabriel Fuller is involved in this, in what has happened today. He is involved, Dana, and he now is holding my daughter. And I will kill him to get her back, I will do that, do you understand?"

Dana Kincaid opens her mouth, but cannot find words. She nods, just barely, then nods again.

"If you love him, if you do not want that to happen, you will talk him down." Bell is staring into her eyes, forcing the eye contact, giving her nowhere to look and no way to escape. "Do you understand me?"

"Yes." She swallows, nods again. "Yes, I understand you."

"Good." Bell starts moving again, and she stays close by his side now, and he can see she's processing what he's said, still grappling with it, but she knows it is true, and he can see that as well.

They reach the double doors at the entrance to the Dawg Days Theatre. Bell stops, looks to her.

"Does he love you?"

She doesn't pause, and answers with confidence. "Yes, he does."

"Don't let him forget that," Bell says. "Stay close to me, move when I tell you. Don't speak until I tell you."

Bell goes through the doors, weapon up and ready, into dim light and air-conditioning that has made the empty theater too cold. The sound effects of a cartoon playing on a loop, the squeak of a mouse, Pooch's unmistakable bark. He drops one hand from his weapon, reaches back for Dana Kincaid, finds her hand. She returns the grip, and he leads them into the seating area, advancing as quickly as he dares, up to the lip of the stage. He hears a voice, loses its words behind the sound track.

Up, Dana Kincaid's hand still in his, and Bell scans the arc of the stage, gun leading, then pushes through the curtains. Seeing nothing. Another voice, another man's, and he advances toward it, deeper into the backstage and toward the door at the rear of the theater, the one that leads into the little square courtyard that leads, in turn, to the mouth of the Gordo Tunnel. The door is ajar, left open during the evacuation.

Bell takes the wall, releasing Dana Kincaid's hand, breathing through his nose. Trying to steady himself. If he has the shot, he will take it, but when he ducks his head forward to peer through the gap, he sees nothing, just the empty courtyard, the discarded pieces of Kurkur and Pooch, the top of the flight of stairs that leads down to the tunnel.

He looks to Dana Kincaid. "Call for him."

She nods, takes a deep breath, raises her head.

"Gabriel?"

There is no response, but Bell didn't immediately expect one. He pushes the door farther open, thinks he hears the echo of movement from the stairs, the entrance to the Gordo Tunnel.

"Gabriel, it's Dana. I'm here with Mr. Bell. I'm here with Mr. Bell, he says you took his daughter. He says you're involved in this, in everything that happened today. I don't want to believe it. I don't want to believe him."

Still no answer, nothing, and Bell pushes the door farther open, then slips back, pausing, before moving again, stepping through and out. Gun high, quick scan, and the courtyard is clear. He holds back, not wanting to expose the top of his head to the bottom of the stairs, freezes in place, listening. The park is still silent, but he can hear a distant helicopter, wonders how much longer the no-fly zone is going to last.

Dana steps through the doorway, and Bell moves a hand to catch her, to hold her back. She presses against him, not trying to get past, he thinks, but rather using him as her excuse to not move.

"God, please, Gabe," Dana Kincaid calls. "Answer me, please! Are you there, baby? Please, this isn't you, this was never you. They made you do it, your friends, those people you were meeting. I knew something was wrong, I knew it. Why didn't you tell me?"

There is no answer, no noise at all. Just the distant sound of the helicopter coming closer.

Then, from the tunnel, he hears his daughter scream.

He hears shots.

He runs.

Chapter Thirty-four

ATHENA IS tasting her own blood, salty and warm and wrong. It's running from her lip, and she wipes at her mouth with the back of her hand, sees it bright red on her skin.

They've stopped, and she's not sure why, just stopped all of a sudden in the middle of this tunnel. The one who hit her, Vladimir, he's standing to her right, keeps looking from the direction they were heading in to the direction they came from, looking at the man who was dressed as Pooch. That one, the one who made Vladimir stop hitting her, he's a little closer to her left, looking back the same way as well. The stairs they came down, maybe fifty feet away, and Athena can't see anyone there. But the man who was dressed as Pooch, his chin is raised slightly, and the gun in his hands is pointing down a little bit, and she knows he's listening to something.

The look on his face makes her think he's going to cry.

Vladimir keeps looking back at them. Keeps looking back at him, really, only ever barely looks at her, and when he does, she can tell he doesn't think she's worth the trouble at all. She can tell he wants to kill her, that he's thinking about doing it. Her chest hurts, and her head, and it's not just from being hit.

She saw Uncle Freddie and Uncle Jorge and she saw Dad, and none of them came to get her.

She understands that she is going to die, maybe die right here, and the terror of it makes it hard to stand. It takes the strength from Athena's legs, and makes her sink against the cool concrete wall of the tunnel. Opposite her, there's a painting of Gordo, grinning and happy, pointing in both directions, the way they came and the way Vladimir is supposed to be looking when he's not looking back at the other man.

Gordo looks so happy, Athena thinks, and it's so a lie. All of it is a lie, everything WilsonVille is a lie. Friends and fun and sun and rides, and Mr. Howe died right in front of her, she saw his brains. Joel on his side, shaking and crying, maybe dying, too, and all the other people, the bodies. Her mom, they took her mom away, and she can feel the tears trying to get out again, and she hates that, she's fighting that. She doesn't want to cry. But they took her mom, and for the first time, Athena thinks that means she's dead.

And now Athena is going to die, too.

And she is so scared.

She knows she was angry before, wonders when that left. Was it when Vladimir hit her, and hit her again, and then hit her again, and wanted to keep doing it? Was it when he picked her up and made her come with them? Was it when Uncle Jorge fell down, and she was sure he had been shot?

Or was it when she saw her dad, and he didn't save her?

The man who was dressed as Pooch moves, takes a half step in the direction of the stairs. She wishes she knew what he's hearing, what Vladimir is hearing. Now Vladimir is looking back at him again, then to her, just for a second, then down the tunnel once more. His shoulders shift, rise slightly, then fall.

Suddenly, Athena understands the phone call she saw Vladimir make back in Hendar's Lair. She understands the words she read on his lips, and understands that she was wrong about them. Maybe whoever he was talking to, maybe he was telling Vladimir to kill her and Dana and the others. But it is more than that, and she can see what Vladimir is about to do before he does it, the start of the movement.

She doesn't want to die.

Athena screams, uses the last of the strength in her legs to throw herself at the big man, throws herself off the wall and into him, trying to hit and bite and everything at once. He's bringing his gun up, starting to turn, and she's not large enough and she's not strong enough to move him more than a step or two back, but it's enough. She feels the vibration of the world, the feeling of gunfire, and Athena is clawing at him, clinging to him, hanging on that arm with the gun. He hits at her, and a flare of light and heat crosses her vision, blinds her, and she feels him hit her again, and she's losing her grip. Then she's falling back, flailing. Her back collides with someone, the man who wore the Pooch suit, she thinks, and she knows it's over, that Vladimir is raising his gun and will kill them both.

She feels the air shake with gunshots, and her vision resolves, and Vladimir is standing in front of her, only a half dozen steps away. Pointing his gun at them, just as she knew he would be.

The top of his head is missing.

Vladimir falls down, and Penny Starr is standing there with a gun in her hands. The man who was Pooch pulls Athena against him, and she sees his gun come up, and Penny Starr is shouting. Athena feels something hot and hard hitting her cheek, spitting from the side of the man's gun, feels the vibration in the air one more time.

Penny Starr falls to her knees. Her mouth is open, but she's not making words that Athena can read.

Then the man who was Pooch is shoving Athena away from him, and he's running, running away, down the long tunnel, and Athena's legs finally abandon the last of their strength, and she falls to her knees, too. Penny Starr is trying to get up again, but she can't do it, leans against the wall instead. Athena pulls herself to her, sees that the woman's eyes look flat, like they're cooling.

Penny Starr opens her mouth, and bright red blood runs out of it. She's trying to tell her something, but Athena can't read it. Shakes her head at the woman. Penny Starr tries again, then points past Athena's shoulder.

Athena looks, sees what Penny Starr wants her to see. Understands the word she was saying.

Dad.

Chapter Thirty-five

SHOSHANA NURI, call sign Angel, is dying when Bell reaches her.

Slumped against the side of the Gordo Tunnel, blood slicking her form-fitting flight suit, the last trickle escaping her mouth, her eyes are open, fixed on his approach. Athena sits before her, still and silent, and Bell stops another ten feet past them, in time to see Gabriel Fuller rounding the corner onto the Flashman Tunnel, heading east and out of sight.

He doubles back, and Dana Kincaid is coming down the stairs, rushing toward them. Bell takes a knee beside his daughter, reaches out for Angel, but the woman shakes her head weakly, blinks with what appears to be a supreme effort. Her mouth works.

"Hold on," Bell says. "Hold on."

Cherry-red blood froths over her lips. She's saying something, the same thing, over and over again, weaker and weaker as she stares into Bell's eyes.

"Didn't," she says.

She says it four more times, until it is her last word.

Bell reaches out and closes her eyes. He looks at his daughter, and Athena answers with an expression that breaks his heart, that will haunt him for the rest of his life. It is the look he has seen on children all around the world, on boys and girls, young men and women, who have seen too much and felt too much and suffered too much. The light and joy that was his daughter is gone.

He puts a hand to his daughter's cheek, puts his lips gently to her forehead. Meets her eyes again.

"I am so sorry," he says, because in this moment, his duty will not allow him to release the gun in his other hand. In this moment, he cannot sign. He says it again, and he says, "Mom is safe. I love you."

He gets to his feet, hoping that she understands why he cannot stay with her. Hoping that she will not think him the monster her mother does. Hoping that somehow, someday, she will forgive him.

"Get her out of here," Bell tells Dana Kincaid.

He heads down the tunnel, after Gabriel Fuller.

Chapter Thirty-six

AT FIRST, he's just running, he doesn't even know where he's going. Painted park characters flash past him on the walls, and his legs keep pumping, and he turns, turns again, until he realizes he's coming up on Agent Rose's Safe House, the entrance to the Speakeasy. He pushes through the door, stumbling, knocks over one of the tables, nearly trips himself against first one chair, then another. Makes it to the stairs and stops, leaning against the rail fixed to the wall. The MP5K is still in his hand, and he pops the magazine reflexively, replaces it with the last of his fresh ones.

He should have just surrendered then and there, Gabriel thinks. He should have just given up when Penny Starr saved his life, just as he should have given up when he heard what Dana was saying to him.

Everything he had, he realizes, is now gone.

His phone is ringing.

His hand shaking, he pulls it from his pocket, puts it to his ear.

"Arm the bomb," the Uzbek says.

Gabriel's pulse is beating so hard he feels his temples throb.

"Vladimir told me everything, Matias. It was his job

to tell me everything. I can get you out. You need to arm the bomb."

"You can get me out?"

"We put you in," the Uzbek says. "Of course we can get you out. Out of the park and out of the country and out of this pretend life you've been living. But you must do your part, and you must do it quickly. I am watching the news, and they have heard the gunshots, they are coming. You are almost out of time."

"How?" Gabriel swallows. "How will you get me out?"

"Helicopter."

He closes his eyes. A helicopter.

"Put the device in position, arm it, and we will lift you out. It will be..." the Uzbek pauses, then continues. "Eight minutes. You have exactly eight minutes. Can you do it?"

Gabriel looks back down the stairs, to the bar, the open door leading back into the tunnel. To where Vladimir, who would have killed him, is lying without his brains. To where he repaid Penny Starr's rescue with murder. To where Dana has been abandoned, and with her, this life he has deluded himself into believing is his own.

To where Jonathan Bell is surely coming for him.

"I can do it," he says to the Uzbek. "Eight minutes."

"I will see you soon, then. Good luck."

Gabriel closes the phone, then tosses it away in a fury. He pushes open the door, steps out into the early evening of the park. He knows—he *knows*—the Uzbek is lying to him. There is no helicopter, there is no escape, there is no return to the old life.

But he doesn't care.

His life has ended here in WilsonVille, and his only hope for a new one is in choosing to believe the lies. In choosing to believe that somehow, some way, if he does as ordered, the helicopter will come.

If he does that, he can believe he will live.

If that means killing WilsonVille, so be it.

Chapter Thirty-seven

BELL RACES down Flashman East, hearing broken bursts of static in his ear, the transmissions all but murdered by the layers of concrete and steel that make up the tunnels.

At first, he thought that Fuller was trying to escape, to get out of the park, but that would've required sticking to Gordo or at least looping back around to it at the first opportunity. Cutting beneath the river, perhaps, hoping to come out on the north side of the park, the employee lots. He's at the juncture of Flashman and Pooch when he hears something clattering, plastic meeting wood, and he zeroes in on it, advancing up Nova, finds himself at the entrance to the Speakeasy once again. A cell phone on the floor, abandoned, and he picks it up, pockets it before climbing the stairs and stepping cautiously outside.

Fuller is nowhere to be seen, but immediately, he can hear Chain in his ear once again.

"—lock respond, Warlock, please respond."

"Go for Warlock."

"You get him?"

"Negative. Nobody's seen him?"

"Nobody has eyes. Could be he's out."

"Could be."

Bell turns in place, scanning, thinking. Gabriel Fuller, alone. Gabriel Fuller, who promised him his daughter's life, who promised him the dirty bomb, if only they would let him go.

"He's going for the device," Bell says.

"We have no eyes, no contacts," Chain says. "Bone has been evacuated, I've got Board with me. Where do you want us?"

"It's a DB. Where do you place a DB to do the most damage?"

"Highest point, best wind dispersal of the fallout. You're damaging property, people are incidental."

"Highest points in the park." Bell turns in place, looking at the WilsonVille skyline he's been living within for almost two months. "Cardboard, take Mount Royal, west side of the park. There's a ride goes up to the summit, you should be able to reach it via service ladders."

"Roger that."

"Chain?"

"Terra Space," Chain says. "Would make sense, that's where he wanted us to stage, the top of the Clip Flashman Rocket is almost as high as Mount Royal."

"Go."

Bell stops, staring at the big wooden roller coaster smack in the heart of WilsonVille. Pooch Pursuit, the fastest, tallest wooden roller coaster in the world.

There's a single train of cars parked at the apex, at the very top of the ride.

Bell looks to the east, toward Soaring Thyme, sees none of the chairs on the line, all of them presumably parked. He looks west, and sees the same is true at

Nova's Tower, and as he does so he remembers that all the rocket sleds at Terra Space were likewise grounded. His eyes go back to Pooch Pursuit, and the single train, motionless, at the top.

He's been stupid, he realizes.

He starts running for the fastest, tallest wooden roller coaster in the world.

Chapter Thirty-eight

IT TAKES Gabriel two minutes and forty-three seconds by his watch to reach the control room at Pooch Pursuit. The same idiotproof console still on power, registering Train One locked at the top of the lift hill, at the summit of the first peak. He looks out the Plexiglas window of the booth, and, yes, the cars are there—224 feet above the ground.

It's going to be a long climb.

He raises the MP5K, fires a burst into the console, killing the controls. Glass shatters and metal tears, sparks spit and fly. He lowers the weapon, moves to exit, crossing the platform and jumping over the parked cars, one to the other, until he can drop down onto the wooden track. It's a gradual slope at first, wooden coasters not as radical or tolerant of extremes as their metal counterparts, and the first forty feet or so are an easy ascent, enough for Gabriel to remain upright.

He's at sixty feet, and the going is becoming rougher, when he glances down and sees Jonathan Bell on the platform, coming after him. Gabriel swings the MP5K off his shoulder, into his hand, drawing the strap taut, trying to sight him. He fires a burst, and the man jumps down between the parked cars. Gabriel takes the opportunity to climb again, fast as he can, and the slope is now more cruel, more than forty degrees, and he has to let the submachine gun dangle from its strap, needing both his hands.

"Gabriel!" Bell shouts at him. "Gabriel Fuller! Stop!"

He keeps climbing, swings out to the edge of the track, reaches around to pull himself into the snarl of support scaffolding. He can see Bell starting to climb the track after him, but now Gabriel has cover, and he leans out, freeing a hand and firing once again. The man drops prone on the track, and for a moment, Gabriel believes he may have hit him, but then Bell is up, coming after him still.

Gabriel pulls himself back into the scaffolding, reaches up, uses his arms, then his legs. It's a faster ascent this way, but more perilous, like climbing a ladder. His lungs are beginning to burn with the effort, sweat starting to spill down his back. He swipes his hands on his shirt one at a time, keeps climbing. When he looks, Bell is still on the track, now scaling hand over hand, perhaps no more than eighty feet below him and off to the side. The wooden slats provide cover, but that works both ways, and neither man has a clear shot.

Gabriel climbs. He climbs, and he wants to laugh.

Because this is madness, and to participate in it, he must be mad. And he knows he is, he knows he was. To ever have imagined a happy ending to this day, to ever have imagined that the Uzbek would let him go, that the Shadow Man would release him. To ever imagine that the boy from Odessa who murdered Old Grigori with a tire iron could ever keep and hold Dana, and make a life that didn't need death to pay for it.

Sweat stings his eyes, blisters form on his palms, and still, Gabriel climbs.

And Jonathan Bell, damn him, is climbing with him.

Gabriel reaches, and suddenly there is nothing more for him to grab. He's at the top of the lift peak, his arms aching, his legs trembling from the effort, and he pulls himself the final inches, grabbing hold of the side of the parked car, and heaves himself inside. Gasping for air, and the duffel and the device are exactly where he left them, and he pulls the device from where it has been waiting on the floor, moves it onto the seat beside him.

He looks for Bell, can't see him because of the angle. Frees the MP5K from his shoulder, leans out and forward, trying to locate the other man.

From beneath, Bell's arm shoots out, up, grabs hold of the weapon, twists, pulls. Gabriel feels the gun tear from his grip, almost taking his index finger with it, as the weapon is yanked free. Then he's lost it, and Bell has tossed it away, straining to reach the side of the car, to pull himself the rest of the way up.

Gabriel leans back, kicks at Bell's fingers, a bandaged hand, once, twice, a third time, and the man's grip slips away, vanishes, leaving a bloody smear on the side of the car. He hears something clatter beneath them, leans over to see Bell hanging on to the scaffolding fifteen feet below.

His attention goes back to the duffel bag. He runs the zipper open, shifts the device into his lap. Slides his hands along it, searching for the wires he has to connect to the battery. Finds the first, wraps it to its post, securing it, then the second, repeating the procedure, and the timer face suddenly lights up, blinking at him. Gabriel is surprised to see that it's set for one hour, a full sixty minutes. More time than he imagined the Uzbek would have given him, and even as he thinks that, he knows that what the clock is telling him may well be a lie.

He hears a helicopter, looks up, and is shocked to see one circling the park, coming in lower.

The thought occurs to him that he might live through this.

He's turning his attention back to the device and Bell is there, coming up over the front of the car all at once, one hand pulling him up, the other bringing his gun into line. Gabriel lashes out blindly, the duffel falling back into the footwell as he tries to get hold of the weapon, manages to just knock it askew as it goes off. The round sears his shoulder, cutting a furrow in his skin, and Gabriel roars with a new fury, smashes Bell's wrist against the edge of the car again and again until the gun is gone from his hand.

But he's still coming, still pulling himself up, and Gabriel punches at him, hits him across the nose, feels it give. Blood splatters, and still Bell won't let go. Gabriel punches at him again, and again, and again, and then Bell has caught his fist, yanks, twisting, and Gabriel has to push himself back with his legs to keep from toppling out of the car.

He falls backward, into the next set of seats, struggles to right himself, to get his feet beneath him again. The helicopter above swings in closer, lower, the roar from the rotors deafening, buffeting Gabriel with downdraft. Bell is in the front car now, bloody nose, and shouting at him, something that's lost in the engine whine. Gabriel scrabbles backward into the next car, nearly loses his balance, nearly falls again, manages to swing himself around.

Bell doesn't pursue, reaching for the device.

Gabriel goes for his pocket, finds his knife, the same knife he used when he was Pooch and had to kill that man. Draws it, flicks it out, and Bell is still hands-deep in the duffel, and Gabriel lunges, cutting at him. The other man sees it at the last moment, jerks back, catches the blade across his forearm, and Gabriel feels it dig deep.

Then Bell's grabbed his wrist, forcing the blade free from his arm, and both their hands go for it, and Gabriel screams, rage and fury and desperation, throwing all his weight forward. Bell topples backward, doesn't let go, pulling Gabriel down with him. Hits the front of the car, and Gabriel is on him, literally, trying to shove the knife in and up, and Bell is holding him back. Gabriel can feel it, gravity, so much gravity, and it's on his side, and he can feel the older man's strength giving way a fraction at a time, knows it will take just a moment more before it breaks, and steel will slide home between flesh and bone.

Then Bell kicks, rolls, and Gabriel feels gravity betray him, sees a dusk-lit sky and the helicopter swinging around. Feels himself sliding free of the car, losing the knife, bouncing off the edge of the track, wooden slats digging into his back.

He sees the helicopter, and now he can see someone

leaning out the side. Someone leaning out the side, with a television camera at his shoulder.

The Uzbek lied.

Gabriel Fuller closes his eyes.

Gabriel Fuller falls.

Chapter Thirty-nine

THE MAN who received half a billion dollars to plan and execute the events at WilsonVille, the man whom no one will or can name, stares at the Uzbek's image on his monitor, and considers all things. What the news has reported around the world, and more, what it has not. What the Uzbek has told him and what, he suspects, the Uzbek has not. As objectively as he can, the man no one can name considers the events of the last day, and views them in an ever-expanding context.

Mistakes were made. The Uzbek has acknowledged as much. The basic, fundamental miscalculation in regard to Gabriel Fuller, that he had been allowed to go native, though the man who refuses to be named wonders if that could have been prevented. It is the risk with all long-term sleepers, that they will become who they pretend to be so thoroughly that, when the time comes for them to awaken, they will do so without their full measure. This is not a new problem, but it is one to which he feels closer attention should have been given.

So much time, so much patience, so much effort, all to waste.

The sleepers will have to be monitored much more closely, the man decides. Wherever they are, they will now be subjected to closer surveillance, and perhaps occasional in-person meetings with their handlers. So they do not forget whom they work for. So they do not forget their purpose. So they do not forget who owns them.

In that, then, the operation was a failure. Gabriel Fuller and all that he was—and, more, what he would have been—are lost.

The man no one can name types:

Can he damage us?

On the monitor, the Uzbek shakes his head. "There should be no means of connecting him with me or with any of our other assets. Any investigation into his life will reach a dead end. We are secure."

The man sits back in his chair, reaches for a glass of very hot, very sweet, very strong tea, and sips at it. He likes how the glass burns against his palm, grips it tighter while thinking past the pain, now considering the success they have achieved.

They are half a billion dollars richer. They have made a mark, and shown exactly the extent of their reach, their power, their cunning. There are those who will notice. There are those who will seek them, and seek their services.

He sets the glass down again, carefully and slowly, forces his fingers open. He types again.

Confirm contact with client remains sterile.

The Uzbek gives this due consideration before saying, "Yes. He is arrogant, and spoke with arrogance, but we knew this about him from the start, his bluster. He is an ideologue, with an ideologue's ego. But I was never anything less than absolutely cautious, and even, in the worst-case scenario, if he should somehow find his way back to me, it is impossible that he would then find his way back to you."

The man types immediately, quickly.

Nothing is impossible.

He pauses, then adds:

Vosil.

Watches as the Uzbek reacts to the use of his name. Watches as the Uzbek shakes his head.

"I would die first."

Yes. You would.

The Uzbek shifts, repositioning himself in his chair perhaps. He opens his mouth to speak, then stops. Removes his glasses, and sets them carefully aside, out of the view of the monitor, the camera. He looks directly at the man no one can name.

"What would you have me do?"

This is a very good question, and the man in front of the keyboard has given it much thought already. He has thought about eliminating Mr. Money, though that seems like an excessive gesture at this time, for two reasons. The first is that doing so would not guarantee their security, and, in fact, could quite possibly compromise it further. There is no way to know what Mr. Money has on them. Killing him will silence the man, but there is no telling what traces or trails he may have left behind. The man no one can name must trust that the fear they have engendered will preserve silence.

So that is the first reason. The second is more pragmatic. Just as the Uzbek represented the man who sits at the keyboard now, he knows that Mr. Money represented others. Men of like mind, and like money, and like power. They have seen what was accomplished, and the man no one can name is certain they will be back, asking for more, and willing to pay.

Your work is finished for now. Return home. New orders await you there.

The Uzbek leans forward slightly, reading the words on his monitor, squinting slightly without the aid of his glasses.

"You may rely on me," the Uzbek says.

I have, the man at the keyboard thinks. *I have, and you have succeeded, and yet you have failed. You are not a pawn, but you are not the king, or even the queen.*

The man at the keyboard kills their connection, takes up his too hot, too strong, too sweet tea once again. There was one thing he and the Uzbek did not discuss. One thing that the man now sipping his tea has been considering among all other matters.

This man who was in the park.

He sips at his tea, and wonders how best to make an example of Jad Bell.

Chapter Forty

YOU CAN get an awful lot of intelligence from a cell phone.

The following day, WilsonVille opened at its regular time. Almost all rides resumed operation, with the notable exception of Pooch Pursuit, now closed for maintenance. Attendance was, as expected, poor, with just under three thousand day passes sold.

"It's three thousand more than I thought we'd sell," Marcelin tells Ruiz. "It'll come back. People have short attention spans, and technically, Bell was working for us."

"So when you tell the media that WilsonVille security played a crucial role in retaking the park and rescuing the hostages, you're telling the truth."

"My understanding is that your people don't want me to tell the truth."

"That is correct."

Marcelin nods slowly. "Bell."

"What about him?"

"I'd like to thank him. Him and the rest of your men."

"I'm afraid that's not possible," Ruiz tells him.

"He's on a new assignment. But I'll be sure to pass it along."

When Wallford offers to shake Bell's hand, Bell grins and holds up his right, showing the bandaged palm.

"Ready for this?" Wallford asks.

Bell nods, the grin fading. He aches—his back, his face, his arm, his hand, all of him. When he fell, he's certain he tore muscles in his shoulder and arm catching himself. Physical pain, and it rides a dull shotgun with the emotional pain, with the way Athena looks at him now and the way Amy won't. With Dana Kincaid's broken heart and broken life, and with Angel, which everyone tells him wasn't his fault, none of whom he believes.

Wallford pushes open the door to Eric Porter's office, where the man is seated at his desk, staring vacantly out the window. He turns in his chair, registers surprise as he sees Bell entering behind Wallford. Starts to rise.

"Jerry," Porter says. "I was about to call you. Mr. Bell."

Bell says nothing, fixing Porter with a stare.

"You were about to call me?" Wallford says. "That is remarkably ironic, Eric. Let me show you why."

From his pocket, Wallford produces a cell phone, and sets it on Porter's desk.

"Know what that is?" he asks.

Porter looks from one man to the other, bemused if not puzzled. "There's a lot to do today, Jerry. Playing games isn't one of them."

"That is the cell phone that Master Sergeant Bell here

recovered from Gabriel Fuller," Wallford says. "Mr.
Fuller discarded the phone after killing Shoshana Nuri,
but before moving to arm and detonate the device."

Porter says nothing.

"We got the prelim back on the device, as far as that
goes." Wallford flops into one of the two chairs facing Porter's desk, throws his feet up on the edge. He's
wearing a suit and a tie, but the shoes, Bell notes, are
Adidas. "Couple interesting things about that device.
Want to hear them?"

"I'm sure you'll share them even if I don't." Porter's
response is dry, or starts that way, but he looks at Bell
halfway through it, and the sarcasm fades.

Bell just stares back.

"Had a timer, set to read sixty minutes from arming.
But the timer was bullshit, it was to detonate immediately. Would've killed whoever set it off, blown them
to pieces even before the radiation did its number. But
the radioactive material? That's very interesting. That
radioactive material came out of Iran, the facility at
Chalus, we think."

Porter tears himself away from Bell's stare. "Iran?
Jesus Christ. That's...that's huge, Jerry, that's a fucking act of war."

"Sure looks that way." Wallford moves his right
foot, nudges the phone. "Gabriel Fuller didn't have a
lot of calls on this thing. Received one or two from a
location within the park, one of his compatriots. Received a couple from a dead-end disposable, some guy
in Los Angeles. That one was interesting, that took
heavy lifting, but we were able to zero the location of
origin on those calls, the L.A. calls."

"You know who made them, then?"

"We do not." Wallford looks at Porter, gives it a moment, then adds, "But there were other calls from that location, and those calls were to a man in Texas. A man in Texas who called *you*, Eric. A man in Texas who, it turns out, you've been talking with at least once a week for the last three months, and who you talked to three times yesterday. You want to tell us what you and he talked about?

"I—"

"I would think very carefully about how you answer this," Wallford says. He leans back in the chair, craning his head to look pointedly at Bell, then to Porter.

"Jerry—"

Bell says, "We have a code. One of ours dies, someone answers."

"One of yours? None of yours died."

Bell takes three steps forward and grabs Eric Porter by his silk necktie, wraps it once around his fist, and yanks. Porter falls forward onto his desk, a strangled cry, and Bell puts his other hand to the back of the man's head, pushing down, hard, so that Porter's neck is caught at the edge.

"Angel was one of mine," Bell says. "And I think you're responsible for her death. Tell me how I'm wrong."

Porter gags.

Then Porter talks.

The planning is completed quickly, in the passenger compartment of a chartered Learjet, with Chaindragger assigned to back Bell on the ground, Cardboard on overwatch. Bonebreaker is still out on medical, two broken ribs needing time to heal, though he was adamant that he wanted to Charlie Mike.

"You are continuing mission," Bell told him. "You're just doing it on medical leave."

"Fuck you, Top."

"Not with a stolen dick."

"When you deliver, make sure a stamp comes from me," Jorge said.

"To be paid in full," Bell agreed.

Doctrine varies on the best time to make a night raid, but when Bell has the luxury of making the call himself, he prefers to roll between three and four in the morning. This time, Ruiz has given him the reins, and it's 0340 when he and Chain begin the breach of the big house overlooking the lake outside Austin, Texas. Their target is a very, very rich man, who can pay for very, very good security, but what he cannot pay for is absolute privacy, and with the right floor plans and the right tools, nothing is impossible.

With the right plans and the right tools, sometimes it's even easy.

By 0344, Bell and Chain are inside the big house, with the security guards outside still believing everything their cameras are telling them, and the alarm system on the house still believing it works properly. Floor plan memorized, it's seventy seconds later before Bell is silently pushing open the door to the master bedroom. Chain follows him inside.

Night vision gives them two figures in the bed, one old man and one young woman, and Chain moves to the latter while Bell moves to the former. Bell waits while Chain puts the woman under, gets the nod, and then brings his gloved left hand to the mouth of Lee Jamieson. With his right, he puts the silencer on his pistol against the man's forehead.

Eyes snap open in sudden terror.

"Eric Porter gave you up," Bell says. "Eric Porter says you bought the hit on WilsonVille. What Eric Porter doesn't know is who you bought the hit from. Give me a name."

Bell lifts his hand from the old man's mouth, moves the silencer a fraction away from the old man's forehead. Lee Jamieson coughs softly, looks to his side, sees the woman asleep, and Chaindragger, a black silhouette that mirrors Bell's, standing silently by. He looks up at Bell.

"You're a soldier," Jamieson says. "You should applaud what I tried to do."

"I don't care. I want a name."

"But you should care. Everyone should care. We're at war, you know that. What are you? SEAL? Delta? A soldier, a warrior; you know the stakes."

"Name."

Jamieson chuckles, sitting up more fully, adjusting the pillows at his back, and Bell has to admit he recovers himself quickly. "Now, let's be reasonable. I know many people, and I have more money than you can imagine."

"You have five hundred million less than you should," Bell says. "Which seems to me a bit steep for faking a terrorist incident, but I don't normally buy such things, so I may not be equipped to judge."

"They fucked me, you understand that, don't you?" Jamieson squints up at him. "Nobody was ever supposed to die. The device was never supposed to be operational, it was just there to lay the blame at the feet of the Revolutionary Guard. To push us, to speed us along."

Bell stares at the man, thinks it must be appalling arrogance rather than incredible naïveté that allows him to imagine that no lives would be lost. In a park filled with fifty thousand people, the fact that so few died was a miracle, one achieved only by the presence of himself, Chain, and Angel at the start.

He cannot help but wonder if his presence in the park was coincidence, or something more. If those whispers that put him into play didn't start from this man here, or others connected to him. Or if those whispers were started from the inside, by this man's associates, by others who share his agenda.

He doesn't like thinking that. It would mean a betrayal of trust at the highest levels. It would mean that what this man before him put in motion was done with someone's tacit consent.

"Name," Bell says again. "You are running out of time."

"These are the end times, son." Jamieson leans forward. "This is the end of an ideological war. We're fighting savages, they know nothing of civilized society, of the rule of law, of peace, they have no faith in God. We've got a president who gets down on his hands and knees in front of these people, their religion, we've got a populace who thinks that's appropriate. They're 'war-weary,' but they don't even know where we're fighting, let alone what we're fighting for. You know this! You know they've forgotten. They make movies about the day the towers fell, in the name of Christ!

"We have to send a wake-up call!" Jamieson is warming to his words, more confident, defiant before Bell. "We have to bring this country back together, we have to reunite, focus ourselves on our common foe! This is the *end,* you've got to see it! They're fighting a holy war? *We're* fighting a holy war! You think I could do this alone? There are others like me, others who know what happens if we do not recover our will to fight. Others who share with me the understanding that we cannot falter. If that means showing America what these people are capable of, then I'm proud to have done it."

Bell nods. Then he puts his hand over the old man's mouth, and shoots him in the knee. The scream is muffled, dies against his glove, and Bell keeps his hand there for almost thirty seconds longer, watching as Jamieson's eyes go from wide to half lidded before releasing his hold.

"Give me the name of the man you paid," Bell says. "Or I shoot you in the other leg."

"You fucking son of a whore," the old man gasps.

Bell raises the pistol, sighting the other leg.

Jamieson's hands fly out, tears of pain shining in the night of the room. "He tried to keep it from me, he tried to keep it all anonymous! But I was careful, I was...I was careful, I did a lot of checking before we moved the money. I don't know if it's a real name, I don't, but it's the name I found. He's some Uzbek bastard, lives in Tashkent."

"Name."

"Tohir! Vosil Tohir!"

Bell moves a hand to his ear. "Get that?"

"Got it," Ruiz says. "Finish and go home."

"You go after him," Jamieson says. "You go after him, you let him know it's from me. Son of a bitch double-crossed me, tried to take me for a billion dollars. You go after him, you tell him you came from me."

"I don't work for you," Bell says, and shoots the man twice in the head.

He and Chain leave as silently as they arrived.

By the time they're wheels-down and have their gear stowed, Ruiz is ready to brief them for Tashkent.

Acknowledgments

The list is long, the gratitude not nearly enough. All the names here represent contributions, large and small, to the creation of this fiction. I have done my best to remember those who asked to be commended. For those omissions, I plead negligence rather than malice.

First and foremost, Gerard V. Hennelly, the warrior-poet who, once again, answered the most absurd questions at the most inopportune times, and did so with the precision and skill he brings to all aspects of his life.

Sterling Hershey, who agreed to make a map, not knowing exactly what he was getting into. WilsonVille came alive under his guidance, became real as a result of his work. A professional, a gentleman, and a man in whose debt I shall remain.

Gratitude to Eric Trautmann, who contributed in ways too numerous to mention; John Kozempel, who taught me about LD50 and other terrifying things; Christopher Schmitt, who took the implausible and injected reality into it, and who also taught me about terrifying things; Corinna Bechko, who told me that gazelles are stupid, and that you never want to work with a tired cat. No animals were harmed in the making of this novel. Special thanks to Dann Fuller and Alexander Hammond.

An enormous thank-you to Danny Perkins and Heather McCormack-Perkins. Athena belongs to you, and my debt to you both for your support, your eagerness to assist, and your time is quite literally incalculable. Truly and sincerely, I cannot thank you enough for all you did.

Thanks also to my editor, John Schoenfelder, who showed me a new way to write a novel, and had my back at every step. Where John had my back, David Hale Smith, my agent and my friend, took point. Both of you guided me through a very dark wilderness. I thank you for seeing me out the other side.

Finally, always, to the Raccoon. I love you.

About the Author

Greg Rucka is the *New York Times* bestselling author of more than a dozen novels, including the Atticus Kodiak and *Queen and Country* series, and has won multiple Eisner Awards for his work in comics and graphic novels. He lives in Portland, Oregon, with his wife and children.

You've turned the last page.

But it doesn't have to end there . . .

If you're looking for more first-class, action-packed, nail-biting suspense, join us at **Facebook.com/ MulhollandUncovered** for news, competitions, and behind-the-scenes access to Mulholland Books.

For regular updates about our books and authors as well as what's going on in the world of crime and thrillers, follow us on **Twitter@MulhollandUK**.

There are many more twists to come.